D0458216

ALSO BY WHITNEY OTTO

How to Make an American Quilt

Now You See Her

Now You See Her

Whitney Otto

Villard Books • New York • 1994

Copyright © 1994 by Whitney Otto

All rights reserved under International and Pan-American
Copyright Conventions. Published in the United States by
Villard Books, a division of Random House, Inc., New York,
and simultaneously in Canada by Random House
of Canada Limited, Toronto. Villard Books is a registered trademark
of Random House, Inc.

Library of Congress Cataloging-in-Publication Data
Otto, Whitney.
Now you see her / Whitney Otto.
p. cm.
ISBN 0-679-41583-1
1. Women—Fiction. 2. Aging—Fiction. I. Title.
PS3565.T795N68 1994
813'.54—dc20 93-6321
Manufactured in the United States on acid-free paper
9 8 7 6 5 4 3 2
First Edition

For my parents, Bill and Connie

Acknowledgments

Thank you to Bram Dykstra for his wonderful book *Idols of Perversity*. And to Alice Prin for *Education of a French Model*.

Thank you, Simone Seydoux and Jan Novotny, for things too numerous to mention here; Carol Riley and Bob Tavetian for concrete solutions to abstract problems.

Since it is not possible to thank my editor, Diane Reverand, and my agent, Joy Harris, enough, I will simply say that they are living proof this writer is twice blessed.

And, finally, thanks to John and Sam, sweet distractions both, and without whom I'd be a little less distracted but not nearly as happy.

Categories

Now You See Her

Now You See Her

In the weeks preceding her fortieth birthday Kiki Shaw made the uncomfortable discovery that she was disappearing. That is one fact of her life.

Another is that she spends her days as a fact researcher for a popular TV game show filmed in Los Angeles. It is her job to invent categories and answers; three categories daily with six answers awaiting six questions, though only five will actually be used.

A third fact of her life, as she reviews her life, is that it seems to consist primarily of Other Lives; that is to say when she recalls her childhood, for example, she remembers the people who lived on her street:

Richard Carter was a pathologist married to Clarisse Carter, a woman chronically "broken down." The Carter children could not have friends over to the house because Mrs. Carter was "resting." Or, if she appeared from the sanctuary of her bedroom, she often had a distant look in her eyes. Possibly chemically induced or the result of too much drink.

Dr. Czarcek was foreign born and his very pretty wife was also foreign born. Their four children were unruly to the point that most of the neighborhood kids avoided them.

LuAnn Soames drove a blue Dodge and gave out candy to the children.

Mr. Huntington never landscaped his yard and the rumor spread that he was a bachelor who spent his time chasing women and that was the reason for his untended garden and closed shutters.

Mr. Parker did not prefer women at all despite the fact of his marriage and two children. His wife, a husky-voiced European woman, traveled each summer to France, where, it was said, she conducted a string of affairs.

The Newmans had money, owned race horses and gave terrific parties that everyone gladly attended.

Al and Jean Bennett were originally from Indiana. Al worked at one of the studios in the Valley and Jean stayed home, happy, with her brood.

Julie Abbott lived alone and taught school in "town," as Los Angeles was called by these residents of Pasadena. Her parents gave her the money to buy the house, which was as lovingly cared for as Mr. Huntington's was neglected.

The Dorys, an elderly couple, inhabited the smallest house on the street and frequently vacationed in places with names difficult to pronounce.

And the Shaws, Kiki's parents, seemed a classic case of opposites attracting.

Similarly, Kiki can note the people who currently make up her life; a natural listmaker she takes a break at work, beginning with herself, writes:

What I have:

1. Gainful employment.
2. Three close friends: Nora, Collier and Henry.
3. Two living parents.
4. A small house.
5. Good health.
6. Education.

This last item certainly has not stood up well in the ensuing years. Her education seems to have slipped a bit here and there, although Kiki's job gives her the illusion of recalling something she once knew, as well as attaching a scholarly aspect to her research of some new fact or patch of trivia.

What I want:

Here she decides not to include things like world peace or an end to hunger because Kiki figures that things like cures, peace or satiation are givens. As wishes go.

1. Love.
2. More money.
3. More beauty.
4. Travel.

Since Kiki is bored at work and curious about the desires of other people she knows, she calls up her friend Collier, asks for her list of wants:

1. Love.
2. And, as a subset of Love, to quit the man she is seeing because he is not good for her.
3. More money.
4. More beauty.
5. A new apartment.
6. A new career.

Kiki calls Nora:

1. Love.
2. A dependable car.
3. More money.
4. Travel.
5. Adventure.

Kiki calls her mother, Gen, now a widow:

1. A man.
   ("Could I say 'love'?" Kiki asked her mother, who only answered, "Call it whatever you want.")
2. Everything.

Kiki, who slides the lists beneath the paperwork on her desk as her boss passes by her door, only pulling them back out when he has gone, cross-references and finds that all want more or less the same things: money, looks, travel—but the top of each list is love. Kiki relates this discovery to Nora, who says, "Are we awful? I mean, is it some sort of weakness that desires love more than satisfying personal ambition or educating yourself or taking off down the road alone?"

"No," says Kiki, "nothing is more important than love. Nothing."

As with her childhood memories that are essentially about the neighbors on her block, Kiki is incapable of making a list of her own possessions and desires without including those of the people in her life. Instead of lists she could have just as easily typed this:

Collier Grey at forty is a woman who catches the eye, despite her wish for "looks," which appeared on her

list. She makes a good living from her own independent video production company, despite her wish for more money. And she sees a man named Gordon who is not good for her.

Nora Barrie was one of those girls in college who were well liked and always seemed to be everywhere at once. She was the one who looked as though she enjoyed wherever she was: a party, a class, the dining hall, the library. She seemed to know everyone—"A speaking acquaintance," she would say—yet somehow remained basically unknown. It could be said she used her warm manner as a wall.

Henry plays cards with Kiki. They have known each other for years and occasionally experience long periods of silence.

Gen is a woman who was certain her life would turn out differently.

Gordon is a man who cannot be true and

Les is the woman he frequently betrays.

The Moon

At work, Kiki is fashioning a category about the moon.

How funny, she thinks, that I should be employed by this particular television show. As a child, she watched it as often as she could—usually during vacations, holidays, or the infrequent day spent home from school ill. She recalls being frustrated and surprised by what she did and did not know; occasionally, arriving at a correct question to an answer made her stop and wonder, *How did I know that?* And it was still later in her life, when the girl and the woman comprising Kiki intersected, merged, that she began to understand that answer to her question, *How did I know that.*

Growing up it was not unusual for Kiki to attempt to read books slightly sophisticated for her reading skills and child's mind; nor was she a passive listener, particularly when around adults. She had only to hear someone use an unfamiliar word, name an unknown location, mention a disease, a historical figure, an artist, a theory, an animal, a tool, a war and so on to send her immediately to her dictionary or encyclopedia. This behavior continued into her teen years, with lazy hours after school spent with girlfriends, at Collier Grey's house, talking, eating, smoking, and Kiki only half listening, magnifying glass in hand, as she "read" Collier's *Oxford Dictionary*. Which was one of the reasons she liked these aimless afternoons at Collier's. Kiki marginally participating in conversations about boys, books, school and clothes; Kiki absorbing definition after definition of words.

When she arrived at college, she felt shy in regard to her education. It did not seem as thorough as that of the other freshmen. Maybe she had not paid attention in high school, since she had a tendency to follow her interests, ignoring the directives of her teachers. A number of her teachers were aware of Kiki's solitary pursuit, finally allowing her generous leeway, which, at the time, Kiki thought was a good idea, but now in college was not so sure. Her lack of attention and participation may have hurt her academically. She might have willingly stayed behind.

No one else at college had read the *Oxford Dictionary* for pleasure. No other college students could say they covered the entire *Encyclopaedia Britannica,* front to back, including the yearly updated books that came in the mail. What this did for her—besides separating her from the other students—was give her a general understanding of the world and universe. These pieces of truth and detail did not add up to a great and deep education, no, they could only provide her with a vast, far-reaching yet shallow knowledge of things. So, in some ways, Kiki knew more than the other kids, without knowing anything well.

She could not determine if this constituted any sort of education, or knowledge, at all.

During these years it was easy for her to fall into her old patterns of learning; that is, chasing down her own interests while letting the class lose her. She would read a book and some name or concept or place would catch her attention, compelling her to the library, where she began her exploration of that person, place or idea. Years later, she would say of college, "The library was wonderful. It had everything anyone needed," by way of explaining the caliber of her university.

Ultimately, her grades were terrible, though she did excel at research. Her professors would call her into their offices, shake their heads, say, "I don't understand. You seem bright. You strike me as interested." Then would bestow upon her a passing grade that would allow her to barely get by.

Toward the end of college, Kiki would ask herself, "What does one do if one is a fount of useless information?" Though trivia, she conceded, was not altogether useless but it was, well, *trivial.* Certainly a fragment of the truth is still truth but sort of an abridged version for those without the time or inclination to grasp and wrestle with the whole.

These habits of childhood, high school, college persisted into her adult years and, almost fatefully, she got the job with the TV show, paying her for what she was prone to do in any case, and causing her to muse during her daily freeway commute that this was an argument for the notion of a fated universe.

Odd little facts filled her days, caught her attention when she was at parties or on the bus or browsing in a bookstore, museum, historical landmark, garden. She was constantly looking up the small and minor details that connect a culture.

Last week at lunch she was seated near a woman who wore an intricate heart-shaped silver brooch.

"Excuse me," said Kiki, "I don't mean to bother you, but what is that you are wearing?" She lightly touched the heart. The woman, startled by Kiki's touch, did not smile. Kiki noted her very serious suit, upper management probably, the barrier of her magazine and her concentration on eating her lunch, reading an article and making it back to work on time. Kiki understood that this woman's lunch hour belonged entirely to her and that she had made herself entirely unapproachable but Kiki, drawn by the unusual brooch, decided to talk to her anyway. I should not have reached out, she thought, knows it was an impulse and it was now too late; the only thing she could do was to ignore it.

The woman stared at Kiki for a minute, then said, "It is called a *luckenbooth.*" She turned again toward her magazine.

"How is that spelled?" asked Kiki.

"Excuse me?" said the woman.

"I'm sorry. Would you please spell it for me?"

The woman's eyes glanced up toward the ceiling. Slowly, haltingly, she went through each letter, finished by saying, "I think that's it." She smiled. Resumed reading her magazine by holding it upright, as if to block Kiki.

Kiki was silent, then, "Excuse me."

The woman put down her magazine, sighed and unpinned the luckenbooth from her blouse. As she placed it in Kiki's palm she said, "It is a replica of brooches that were sold in Edinburgh during the early 1700s. Usually heart-shaped, often incorporating an *M* for Mary. The man gave it to his betrothed who saved it for the firstborn. It was then pinned to the infant's clothing to ward off evil spirits. I'm eating my lunch now, okay?" She held out her hand for the brooch.

"Thank you," said Kiki. Kiki rubbed her thumb along the surface, as if memorizing it with a caress, then returned it.

Kiki learned that a *portafiori* is a tiny bud vase one wears as jewelry; this at someone's dinner party.

Thumbing through a clothing catalog she saw two models, father and daughter, sitting on strangely constructed tricycles drawn by plastic horses, and looking closely at the credits for the photograph saw that these contraptions were called *Victorian velocipedes.*

Somewhere, in the middle of all these loose bits of fact came the desire toward order, and out of order came lists. Thankfully, Kiki is not a compulsive listmaker, rarely using them for the mundane tasks of her daily life. That is, she usually does not jot market lists, or "lists of things to do today." No Christmas lists. No stacking of New Year's resolutions. She marks down items, one by one, if a problem presents itself and she feels it can only be puzzled out by breaking it down into its tiniest, most manageable pieces; as if by prying it apart she can understand the inner mechanism. Kiki will sometimes dream lists of fantasies: The *If I had a million dollars* variety.

And because Kiki is an observer, a listener, it is with great ease and small awareness that she frequently includes her friends in her lists. As if she has wandered back to Collier's house in high school, hearing the desires and days of her friends.

And because she is paid to work in the framework of categories, trivia, lists, groupings of ideas, it is only by natural extension that these tendencies permeate her personal life. This smashing down big truths and large mysteries to littleness.

Having to form categories out of the information she has amassed is a minor challenge; it is not always easy to include facts that are fairly "known" without including the ones that are too common or too esoteric. As her boss says, "A balance must be struck." So there she is at her desk, trying to assemble facts and assess the public's knowledge of these facts at the same time. Once Kiki wrote a category called *Remains,* which dealt with the physical remains of people. It went like this:

Answer: Jeremy Bentham.

Question: Whose fully dressed skeleton used to attend meetings at University College in London?

Answer: Dorothy Parker.

Question: Whose ashes can be found in a file cabinet of a New York law firm?

And so on. While this run of answers and questions had its admirers, it was not accepted. Too odd was the verdict. And now she is enmeshed in the moon. She begins by making notes:

A blue moon is the second full moon in a single month.

There is a place called *Lacus Somniorum* (Lake of Dreamers) and another called *Mare Nubium* (Sea of Clouds).

Footprints can remain undisturbed and indefinitely on the moon.

A Lagrangian Point is the place where two large celestial bodies orbit each other and their gravitational and centrifugal force cancel each other out, leaving a fairly stable area behind.

Diabole is slandering your enemy to the moon.

Native Americans had many names for the moon, depending on the month: A January moon could be called a Hunger Moon, or a March moon an Earth Cracks Moon. December could hold an Ashes Fire Moon, and April, a Do Nothing Moon.

Kiki does not want to be forty; she does not feel ready and finds it funny that one could be unprepared to be a certain age, as if growing old were voluntary. Inside, she certainly doesn't *feel* forty (not that she would know first-hand what forty "feels like"), so why should she have to be such a foreign age? Not old, not young, definitely not young, regardless of how you are inside. Everything reminds you that this birthday is something to be "gotten through," not a day for celebration. She can only hope that no one will throw her one of those mock wakes, everyone wearing black and the living room festooned in black crepe paper. Silly cake fashioned in a skeleton design.

Recently, she saw an ad in *The New York Times Magazine* for an expensive line of women's cosmetics. It said: *Because it doesn't matter how old you are. It matters how old you look.*

It is surprising how many people tell her, "Oh, honey, forty isn't old," all the while ticking off a list of women past forty, remarking on "how well they look." Actresses and celebrities, mostly, and, no, they do not look their age. But see, Kiki wants to say, that is my point: What if they *do* look forty, I mean, that *is* what forty looks like; or, Do you realize that you bring them up because they do not look forty? And if they do not look forty, then what is the meaning of a statement like "Forty isn't old, just look at ______"? Fill in the blank.

It just seemed to Kiki the only comfort you can find in turning forty is being told that you do not look or act forty and that you can still have a baby and that, Kiki thinks, is scant comfort. It makes her feel as though she has been pitched into a race or competition in which the winner is the woman who does not look, or "act," her age. The prospect renders her breathless.

On top of which, Kiki has noticed this new trick of the

eye or, as Dylan Thomas called it, "fib of the eye." This disappearing thing. She thought she tripped over her cat only to discover that she did not truly stumble because her foot passed, undisturbed, through the fat body of her furry pet. And the cat registered no reaction at all; no yowl, no sudden darting from the impact of her mistress's foot; no backward look of accusation as if the kick had been deliberate. Kiki stopped in astonishment and disbelief, stamped her foot once, then twice on the carpet to assure herself of her solidity. Her foot complied and did not fade through the floorboards.

It was like a heat mirage, like phantom water on blacktop. The difference being that one only thinks the water is there when it is not, unlike Kiki's foot, which *was* there, then reappeared when she ceased movement.

She pressed her palm to her forehead, only to notice her hand fading away with the motion, from fingertips to forearm, coming back in time to strike her resoundingly on the head.

Was it her eyes?

As her mother, Gen, had said often enough, "I had perfect vision until I was forty, then, boom, overnight I needed glasses. So I bought those little Ben Franklin things at Woolworth's. Nice magnification. I recommend them highly."

A prank of the mind? Was it something to do with growing older? She did not know. This aging, it happens so suddenly and so gradually, and gently, with only the occasional fit or start, as with her early teens or right around the time she turned thirty, an age she thought of as unpredictable as adolescence. These were the foreign periods that she had passed through, emerging perfect and rested and ready to continue with her life, even though these cornerstones never seemed to match her image of that age. Her "life affect" she used to call it.

So, maybe this evanescence had been happening all along and she was only lately aware of it, because she was weeks away from another milestone birthday: this leaving the world without leaving it. Kiki thought she was quietly losing her colors like a bright painting or vivid woven rug left out a little too long in the sun.

Now Kiki and her friend Collier always laughed and said the worst thing about growing old was having to do it in America; a young country that simply lacked a tolerance for history, age or decay, graceful or otherwise. It loved youth and money and pretty things and success, lots of success, but mostly it revered youth. Youthful accomplishments. Youthful looks, at least where women were concerned.

"So?" asked Collier.

"So," answered Kiki, "we'll move to Europe. They like old things there ["old" being a relative term since Collier and Kiki would not be considered old, not really, just middle-aged]." And, naturally, they had heard the same stories about young men and older women and even aging European actresses who never seem to fix themselves up much and still seemed to remain visible.

A co-worker, a man named Bill, came into her office as she was working through her *Moon* category. When Kiki looked up at him, said "Yes?" he ignored her. Instead, Bill glanced around the room, chewed a bit of his cuticle and left, muttering something that Kiki could not make out. He closed the door quietly behind him.

Kiki was dumbfounded, puzzled. As she rose to follow him, he suddenly reentered her office, reached for her pen and, before scribbling something on a piece of paper, he paused to read some of her work on the screen. As he turned to go, she laughed, said, "Bill, what do you think you are doing?" Causing him to turn around, startled.

"Oh, there you are," he said.

"But—" she began.

"I just wanted to say, well, never mind, I wrote it down for you so you can read it yourself." He picked up the note he had left to hand to her, stopped, examined her closely, then, "God, you've got beautiful skin. It's almost—I don't know—translucent."

Kiki smiled and looked away. She did have nice skin, as she had been told more than once but never so often as lately. Still, this compliment was especially sweet coming in the midst of this age anxiety she was experiencing. Most well received.

Then he was gone before she had a chance to ask him about his strange behavior.

It turned out that this was not to be an isolated incident. Someone, often Bill, would come searching for Kiki for one reason or another; sometimes she was "found" and sometimes she was not, yet she was always present.

Another day while in the stacks of the show's research library, book propped open in front of her, transcribing information on a pad, Kiki felt someone come up behind her, lean into the length of her body as the other figure stretched and reached above her head for a book on the shelf. Kiki knew it was a woman pressing her into the volumes from the softness of the form at her back, the breasts and small belly.

"Uh, excuse me," said Kiki, twisting around to see Ellen's shocked face.

"Oh my!" said Ellen. "Oh, oh, I don't know—sorry." She stepped back quickly. "I didn't see—I mean, I *saw* you there—of course, I saw you, but I didn't—" she smiled at Kiki and finished by saying, ambiguously, "well, *you know.*"

You know? thought Kiki, *I know what*? Ellen, twenty-two and newly graduated from college, worked two doors down from Kiki and up until this moment they had only shared the minimal contact of acknowledging each other as they passed in the hallway.

The hand that held the book Ellen had taken from the shelf was slightly bobbing up and down as if measuring the weight of the volume. "So," said Ellen, "I better get going. I'm working on *Strange Sounds.*"

"The Moon," answered Kiki, conversant in the language of categories.

She attributed these incidents to Bill's and Ellen's absentmindedness. Her career was "different," surrounded by trivia and miniature truths. Details that sometimes obscured the larger view. Her co-workers were a mismatched bunch, almost as outside the norm as the contestants who had weird hobbies ("I collect redundancies") or highly personalized ambitions ("I would like to be the first person to walk from California to Hawaii"). The majority were collectors, amassing everything from Wild West lunch boxes circa the fifties and sixties to comic books with Eastern European superheroes; from mechanical bears, doll-size evening wear, labels, trucks, trains, streetcars to door mats found west of the Rockies. They loved arcane language and tried to pull it into the present century, or mazes, or any sort of excavation, foreign or domestic.

Kiki frequently wondered about their daily lives; wondered if they were empty. Or did all these little dreams fill them and scare off loneliness? She could not decide: Does one look to fill one's life because of loneliness or does the unusual obsession create a full life, indicate a happy solitude? Which left her wondering about her own life.

Sometimes she could hear herself saying, *My mother only sang what she called "sweet songs" around the house. Those soulful, gentle songs like "Chances Are" or songs about dreaming a million dreams that can never come true if "there will never be another you."* But it would be a lie; Gen, when she sang, belted out Broadway tunes, then said, "Some people thought I should have been a singer." Her voice was neither pleasant nor pure; it was loud and moderately tuneful, as if volume would suffice in place of harmony. Still later, when Kiki listened to her parents argue, it was her mother's voice she would always recall, her father seemed to drop his tone as he became more and more angry. As if it was written somewhere that he who shouts the loudest wins.

Kiki taps her pencil as she runs her finger down the pages of the two moon books open on her desk. Maybe she can finish this before the end of the workday.

***Mare Frigoris* (Sea of Cold).**

The limb of the moon is the visible outer disk.

Librations are inconsistencies due to the orbits of earth and moon. A libration can expose a small area of the moon's other side. A different sort of libration can create irregularities (a wobble, for example) in the moon's orbit.

The moon always has a hidden dark side.

Waxing moon has light on the left; waning moon has light on the right.

The phases of the moon can be broken down into eight categories: young crescent, first quarter, waxing gibbous, full moon, waning gibbous, last quarter, old crescent and new moon.

Bill wanders into Kiki's office and back out again. She no longer looks up when he does this. She thinks about turning forty and disappearing and her life and wonders if it would be possible to dismantle each thing, break it down into uncomplicated categories in an effort to make sense of it all. Instead she types:

Occultation means the moon seems to swallow a star.

Kiki: An Introduction

Kiki Shaw may be able to examine her nature—that is, the distillation of information to comprise myriad categories, as well as the lesser impulse to dismantle and tame a troubling thing through the order provided by lists—but she cannot fathom her own disappearance.

The backward glance at one's own life is a start, she thinks. So, she asks herself, how would I define my life? Categorize it? Catalog its contents? She tried that earlier and, before she was aware of doing it, had taken an inventory of everyone else's life, her own list now placed underneath the others, out of sight. Their dreams languishing upon hers.

She laces her fingers in her hair. She is softly fading and does not know why and although she is unaccustomed to the idea she thinks she ought to begin at the beginning, turn the fragments of the hours of her life over in her palm. If she knows the lives of her friends like the back of her hand, then surely her life must reside on the other side. Her life. Her life. Her palm.

. . .

Kiki Shaw had a mother who was shaped like an acoustic bass. Because of her body silhouette, it was natural that she should be enamored of Kiki de Montparnasse. Man Ray's Kiki. When Gen was pregnant, mourning the loss of her figure, she grew attached to the image. So fond was she of *Le Violon d'Ingres* that when her daughter was born—an easy delivery, she told dinner guests sometime later—"I decided her name would be Kiki."

Liz Beth, Gen's best friend, asked, "What about when she is grown? Hardly a name for an adult."

"It is French," explained Gen. "She'll tell people *it is a romantic name.*"

Now, for many people the name Kiki does conjure up dreams of mistresses and Paris and cafés and men in colorful scarves; all art and jazz. But not for everyone. And that is the naked reality of it: Kiki will be hampered by this name for the rest of her life—explaining, laughing, joking about her mother's choice, as if she had been consulted prior to her own birth, which, given Gen's devotion to metaphysical turns of thought, could appear probable. (Gen believes that children "choose" their own parents.) Kiki wondered where her father, Walt, fit into this grand scheme of a name. Did her father remain mute and, if so, why? Perhaps he fought the name that sounded as if it belonged to a spoiled pet. Or an infantile utterance. *Kiki* almost resembles pure noise; not really a word at all. "Like something caught in the throat" were the exact words of Walt Shaw.

"Do you think I care? Do you think it matters to me?" asked Gen, so bored by the fifties and her existence in this dull little California suburb, routinely longing for a life that was bright and richly hued. "Our daughter will have an unpredictable life and it starts right here, with her different name."

What would make a father surrender this point? And,

no, Gen would not consider modifying the name to read Katherine, giving their daughter some sort of choice. Was he humoring a pregnant woman? Or was there something else in their lives, something that happened during the pregnancy (which was not his wife's first) and after Kiki was born, something larger than this small matter of a name, that resulted in a sorrow, a thing so powerful and all pervasive that they were rendered exhausted by trying to live through each day?

Kiki Shaw daydreams in her office. She is arranging and rearranging Colorforms on a slick blackboard. When she was growing up every kid she knew had a Colorform set very similar to the one she has now spread across her desk. She builds a road from shiny yellow lines; floats a green boat on blue water; constructs blue skyscrapers. Kiki is supposed to be constructing a column for the show; the Colorforms remind her of the fifties and sixties. She lays out circles and sticks and imagines them as people. Next to the people she places boxes with triangle hats. She begins a category called *Postwar America,* opens a history book on the United States in the twentieth century, begins making notes on her computer regarding the sameness of suburban houses (reaching over to arrange the Colorform boxes and triangles); the proliferation of highways (the yellow lines on a black surface); the enormous increase of money in advertising, greater than the amount spent toward higher education (a green boat sailed in blue water); lessening of privacy (circles and sticks); increased church membership (crossed sticks, no circles).

Kiki glances over what she has written and is dissatisfied. Too vague and too specific at the same time. Her boss would never allow it. As her fingers move the Colorforms, now restored back into circles, squares, triangles and lines, her mind wanders to her childhood; to Gen and Walt. She considers Gen, narrows her category to *Women in Postwar America.* Returning to the research library, she looks up her topic, locates two books and walks back to her office, passing no one in the halls, which causes her to wonder if they are turning invisible as well and, if so, then perhaps this is a work-related problem, something in either the ventilation system or in the water, or a hazard like that wrist thing visited upon data-entry workers. Then she sees Bill, which forces her to admit that, no, she is alone in this phenomenon.

At her desk, Kiki types notes on her narrowed subject:

1. **Wife & mother were the highest vocations. By 1950 nearly 60 percent of all women ages 18 to 24 were married as opposed to only 42 percent in 1940.**
2. **Larger families.**
3. **A 1946 poll revealed that 25 percent of women would prefer to be men while 3.3 percent of men wanted to be women.**
4. **Even though more women showed up in the workplace they had low positions, were underpaid, rarely promoted, did not compete for male jobs. Many were from the middle class.**
5. **Consumption of tranquilizers rose from 462,000 pounds in 1958 to 1.15 million pounds in 1959.**

Kiki tucks her pencil behind her ear. This tic is a holdover from her precomputer days. Sometimes she chews on the center, stripping off the paint to the wood. She rubs her eyes, wonders if she needs glasses (her eyes have been a little unreliable lately) and thinks she is really off the mark today. She cannot force these facts to comprise an acceptable column for the game board. Although she liked the tranquilizer item very much. Which makes her think of Gen, which makes her think of Walt.

Walt Shaw, just turned twenty-nine, posed in front of a bed of wild unruly flowers with his arm around his small wife. Gen wore a coat of pale yellow and black cotton gloves, crushed at the wrists. In one hand she held a sleek Cadillac clutch made from alligator. Her belly carried seven enormous months of baby—her first, not Kiki—and the pale-yellow coat did nothing to hide her condition. She kept a diary in which she wrote: *I most accurately resemble a big, fat, lazy cat. One of those nasty spinster-owned things. Something with stripes,* and flinched at her own description. She continued, *I have always maintained that I am too short to be pregnant and I find that I am right.* This was noted under the heading Things for Which I Am Too Short.

Her heavy dark hair was held back by a velvet cord and she wore far too much black eyeliner and cake mascara (rather immodestly, thought her new in-laws). The red of the flowers was matched by the deep red of her full painted mouth, arranged in an awkward semismile; not quite demure, not quite reserved. One black-pumped foot was placed before the other as she had been taught in the self-improvement class she took before moving to Los Angeles from New York City.

Gen and Walt faced his parents, reserved people from the Midwest, who really did not understand this woman, this Gen, with her faint smile and whorishly made-up eyes. Maybe it was Walt's father who could not fathom the attraction, for Walt's mother seemed to like Gen just fine. But Walt's mother, remaining true to the implied conditions of her marriage, believed by her to be a successful one, more or less followed her husband's lead.

Much simpler that way. Walt watched as his mother stood by his father's side as he focused the camera; Walt and Gen with frozen smiles.

When the shutter snapped, Walt and Gen relaxed their faces and stepped away from each other, not noticing how naturally this separation came to them, and moved toward the older couple. Gen needed to locate a bathroom; she wrote: *During pregnancy, day and night, from beginning morning sickness to bladder-crushing end, it is one long bathroom quest.*

Then they all repaired to the nearby overpriced diner for lunch.

Gen wrote in her diary: *Cocktail party at Al & Jean's. The usual. Ken tried to make a pass at Jean and Jean pretended not to notice. Al had some dirty movies that a guy at the studio loaned him. Something with nurses in it, I think, or WACs—women in uniform, at any rate. I was having a nice time but Walt was bored so we left early.* She wrote this after having come home from her neighbors' house, Al and Jean Bennett, where only a few hours before Walt, now turned thirty-one, was absentmindedly strolling around Al's moonlit backyard. In this Pasadena neighborhood of modest homes, although a step up from a "starter" home (affordable, cozy, Loads of Charm, the sort of place one could buy on a young man's salary, VA loan, postwar; hardwood floors, solid baseboards, bathroom down the hall). Walt's house has two stories and wall-to-wall carpeting.

Now Walt has his back to the large picture window, which frames the soft home-movie glow of the light from within Al's house. When Walt looks in the window he can catch a glimpse of the occasionally rapt, sometimes tired faces of the party guests staring at the screen. He is puzzled by their interest in the film; sees Liz Beth lean over to Gen and whisper something that makes his wife laugh; the Newmans have consumed numerous highballs and still no visible signs of drunkenness. Walt often observes the Newmans, who can put away tumblers of liquor and never seem to lose their composure, at any party, at any time and just once he wants to see them transformed by drink and so this is his own private party game. He smiles to himself.

In Walt's hand is a martini from which he extracts the olive and pours the remainder into a gravel-filled planter. Still clutching the empty glass and wondering why Julie Abbott has never married and doesn't she find these parties tedious? Being the only single woman in the place. Walt wanders over to a pine tree, oddly placed in the corner of Al's backyard. His fingers reach up to take hold of the branches, only to release and watch them sway and shiver. It is Walt and Gen's old Christmas tree from two years back. (Gen wrote: *I sent Walt out for a Christmas tree and he brings back this pine in a bucket. He said our first holiday together should be celebrated with a live tree instead of the traditional dead one.)*

And its dusky bright smell delivers tears to his eyes; not the sort that roll down the cheek, he does not cry, just catches his breath and puts his hand to his mouth.

Now Al, the evening's host, is standing beside him.

"Hey Al," says Walt.

"Walt," replies Al.

Silence. Then, "Nice yard," says Walt for lack of anything he wants to say. "I'm thinking about growing dichondra next year. No mowing. Too much like shaving."

"The kids'll kill it," says Al. "Oh, you have to baby it. It's not like sod, you know."

Walt shrugs his shoulders, notices Al has four fingers of Scotch in his glass, which Al, tilting his head back, downs, finger by finger. "Excuse me," he says, walking over to his other neighbor's wall (not Walt's; as if it mattered, as if it weren't Al's side in any case), relieves himself. "Better." Al smiles as Walt turns away, uncomfortable, settles himself into a redwood lawn chair, asks, "How come you aren't inside watching the movie?"

Not interested, thinks Walt, but says nothing.

Al stretches his long legs and plants his elbows on the wide arms of the chair. "Elliot is screwing that little secretary of his. Jean told me that Katie knows all about it. Katie says the secretary is a whore and it is going to take more than a whore for him to get a divorce. So what, huh, buddy? Big deal." Al looks away drunkenly.

"So they'll fire her."

"That is the way of it," mutters Al. "I guess." He looks up at the full moon, centered in a sky that resembles the tight black-out cloth full of pinpricks used by the movies to simulate a star-scattered night sky. "What the hell, maybe they won't this time. Fire her, I mean. Ah, maybe they will. Things change and they don't." Al pauses. "So, the secretary finds another job and Katie divorces Elliot anyway and the guy gets stuck, one way or another." Al laughs a strange little laugh (full of Scotch, thinks Walt); such a sad small sound. "And where do you suppose does that leave love?"

Walt wants, of course, to return to the house awash in blue light and cut this conversation; does not want to listen to drunken Al because he has heard rumors, from Gen, because women talk and know so much more than anyone ever understands. Even though Al has fallen silent, Walt cannot, does not move. Al's eyes are shiny, unfocused, moonlit and as Walt clears his throat, Al asks, "Does Gen get bored with you?"

Probably, thinks Walt. "I'm not sure," he says.

"Jean is bored with me." Al begins to cry, looks surprised and moves his hand across his chin and back down to his lap. "I notice her walking around the house—restless, aimless—like some tiny animal looking for an open door. She thinks I don't see. What does she know?" Al took a deep breath as Walt whispers, *Stop,* only he cannot be heard.

"Ten years we're married," continues Al, his voice increasing in volume the way a drinker's voice does because he is without any sort of gauge of normalcy. He is beyond all that, inebriated. He drinks to get beyond all that. "Of course, there are the kids, the house, the job, and she says to me the other night as I'm getting out of the shower, 'Honey, I can't live this life.' Just like that, Walt. *'Honey, I can't live this life.'* Well. You know how women get sometimes and I'm thinking, oh, this is one of *those* times." He shifts in his lawn chair, looks to his house, confused, dreamy-eyed and seemingly intimate with regret. Walt, wishing to be anywhere but here. Still, he cannot walk away. Goddamn Al. Goddamn Elliot and his secretary and Katie. And, to Walt's surprise, the next name to follow the others into damnation is Gen's. Her fault, he thinks. Odd to think that.

"Jesus, I was tired, it had been a rough day and I was about to ask Jean if we could discuss it another time when she starts telling me that there is no other time and how much she really *likes* me and what a terrific friend I am and that she has no complaints about me as a father to the kids. I'm a 'terrific friend,' " and there is wonder in Al's voice. "Then she says we never talk about anything, just the kids and the neighbors, and how lost she feels during the day and how the weekends look a lot like weekdays to her and, well, you know the bit. I don't have to tell you. But the capper is when she informs me that she feels this way about sex, too. Then she tells me how truly sorry she is.

"So, I'm standing there, drip-drying, feeling like a jerk

and angry. I mean, what more can I do for her? I'm the kind of mad where"—his words turn to whispers—"I almost want to hit her. I don't know what to say—it isn't like she's asking me for a divorce—so I tell her that I am having an affair with Elliot's secretary. You hear me, Jean! A goddamn affair!"

"But," begins Walt.

"I know, I know. Like how can everyone be sleeping with that one woman and I'm not even sure Jean's buying it but it doesn't seem to matter because she is sobbing into her hands and I feel like crap, as if I started it all and I'm not even sure what we are arguing about at this point."

Al leans his chin into his rough palms. "Jean started it all. Christ, she was something to see when I first met her and now I don't know what she wants—she used to want me—I can't give her what I don't know and I'm thinking I'm going to get stuck, one way or another, and I can't seem to save myself."

Al stands, stretches, tells Walt to forget about the dichondra. He says, "Walt, forget the whole thing. Kids are murder."

This dawn of the 1950s in a California suburb, in the garden with Walt and his discomfort and disquieting thoughts as he unwillingly listens to Al's troubles. His mind wanders over his own domestic life with Gen and her minimal interest in home and hearth and he thinks to himself: There are a million things to desire and a million ways to be told no.

For Walt, it must be said, never wanted more from life than to be a family man. He had a good education, which led to a good profession, shows up each day on time, has responsibilities, decent salary, is doing quite well for his age. But this other, this family life; romantic love figured into it all so slightly—either because it did not seem required of his dream or because it was so unattainable, so distant—he could not honestly say which was the true statement. Eminently practical Walt Shaw and his restless wife, Gen.

How terrible to realize that the track of your life is tracing a mistake and twice as awful that you do not consciously "know" this, only feel it, like a low-grade virus that lives in your otherwise healthy body, can't seem to shake the damn thing, until you grow accustomed to its presence in your system. The lassitude, the languor of the thing. Something so wrong yet you cannot name it.

There was a rosiness about Gen during her first pregnancy (the one she was experiencing when her in-laws took the picture of Walt and her in front of the bed thick with those wonderful red flowers that echoed the color of Gen's lipstick). She gained weight with abandon, ate everything with a pleasure and voluptuousness previously unknown. Food tasted better than it ever had, which only served to increase the nausea of the other pregnant women in the neighborhood in the midst of all manner of morning sickness. They would moan, *My God, how can you eat that?* Or: *How can you eat at all?*

But Gen could and did and felt wonderful.

Gen and Walt traveled to Las Vegas to see Louis Armstrong. A final trip, they said, before their family expanded. When they returned home, happy and safe (they would never feel this happy and safe again), Walt played an Armstrong record to her each morning for the next two weeks as she lay in bed. Gen, for her part, felt a genuine clean affection for this young husband of hers, even though it occasionally struck her that they really did not know each other very well; which sometimes seemed to her as strange a notion as these suburban surroundings; Gen who grew up in an apartment in New York City.

There was a photograph of Gen, pregnant with their first child, in Walt's possession. She was seven months along, pale and naked, leaning against the rose-and-green tile of their bathroom counter. Earlier she had wrapped herself in a large towel bearing the logo of the engineering firm Walt had worked for in Saudi Arabia, but now it lay down around her feet.

Her thick dark hair is loose about her shoulders but her face is still heavily made up; smiles at the camera; this "good girl" who does not look away, with her slim-boned hands and brightly polished nails. The light catches on the gold anklet of the two joined hearts, engraved: Gen & Walt 2/14/52. A gift.

The snapshot was small and perfectly square and bathed in a flattering yellow light and was kept in a box atop the dresser with Walt's cuff links and tie bars and Masonic pin and loose change. Middle Eastern coins of no value in the USA; a three-thousand-year-old clay bead that Walt unearthed in an excavation and an inexpensive ring that once belonged to his father, a railroad man.

Walt seldom looks at the picture.

When Gen was carrying Kiki she was drawn, exhausted. She lost weight and seemed to gain only grudgingly. Food made her slightly ill and had become a nuisance in her life. She worried about this unborn child but only in passing since she was caught up with concern for her firstborn, a boy, now quite sick with an illness progressing at an alarming rate. Gen knew her figure appeared even skinnier in contrast to her belly but mostly what worried her was the fact that all her love was being poured into her son with so little left for the other child not quite here yet.

Walt said: When my boy is gone people will drive by my house and will know that a tragedy has been visited upon it. They will be sympathetic and well meaning and after a while they will gently suggest that our lives continue. These people who have not lost a three-year-old boy. This is what they will say, *Your lives are long and you have other things to think about.* They will point out that Kiki needs to be attended to.

And, when time has past, it will come clear that what they were saying was that *their* lives must go on and they do not wish to continue to grieve for the neighbor boy who passed on too early for anyone's comfort. They do not want to be reminded that life is unpredictable and a puzzle and occasionally unjust and that whatever happened next door or across the street or down the road somehow skipped their house and that is what they do not want to think about. Their house was passed over without understanding *why* one is saved from sorrow; and without understanding why, one cannot guard against such events.

My little marked house and my little identified family, thought Walt. We are less like friends in the neighborhood and more like a warning not to take anything for granted. But, christ, there is so much effort in living a life not taken for granted.

It wears the body right out.

. . .

Gen believed, falsely, that marriage was everything. It was what a woman most wanted (recall the facts on Kiki's desk that during the fifties *wife* and *mother* were the highest vocations) and, therefore, she carried an unshakable faith in its goodness. She had left New York with a spoken promise of return but a deliberate lack of intention. Her best girlfriend, the only other single girl in the group besides herself, was getting married and Gen, in the grip of some sort of self-preservation, chose to cross a continent rather than witness the ceremony. Clearly, she forgot that it was an institution, a legal construct, a contract, a public agreement, as well as a joining of the spirit. Unable to see it for what it often is, Gen only wanted to lose herself in the dream of what it could be (unlike Walt, who saw the pragmatics of marriage). This notion included the dream of perfect children as well.

So Gen found herself in this passable, mildly disappointing life where she looked a bit like a foreigner in this California suburb with her eyes ringed in black liner and her nails sometimes polished green. She toted a small piece of luggage instead of a purse—"The only way I can carry what I need," she said—smoked a tiny rhinestone pipe and told herself she was "fitting in nicely." Gen still thinks she is part of it when the other women on the street happen by and sit in her den, painted red and black. And there are the parties she throws where she plays a xylophone, is very loud and Walt seems to fade.

Always dressed to the nines, even when she is pregnant ("I guess that is how they do it in New York," comments one of the neighbors, an unpleasant woman named Willie. "Who does she think she is?"). Gen's closest friend on the block is Liz Beth Vale, the only other Italian on the street, the one Gen laughs with and who makes her long for home during those endless California afternoons. Sometimes, Liz Beth asks her why Al Bennett insists on referring to Liz Beth and Gen as wops to their faces, as if it were a very funny joke. Perhaps, said Gen, he thinks it is a term of endearment. Gen sets him straight, prompting him to complain to his wife, Jean, "Christ, Gen is so sensitive."

Gen learned to drive, like a native, and in short order wrecked the car.

She listened patiently to the Jehovah's Witnesses who came to her door with their offers of salvation and truth.

When a man came down the street with a camera and a pony, Gen dressed up her son, her firstborn, like a cowboy and had his picture taken.

She went to the market, cleaned the house, made supper with her shinynew kitchen gadgets. After everything was wiped up and put in its proper place, Gen ate over the kitchen sink so as not to disturb her tidy house with spilled crumbs.

She took her son out in his stroller.

She wore large gold hoop earrings in her pierced ears and white short shorts.

She sewed a couple of shirts for Walt. Ugly, but homemade.

She tried new recipes from women's magazines. She talked with the other women in the midmorning hours. Kaffeeklatsching, it was called.

She tended to her boy and became pregnant with her second child, Kiki, only to be told that her son was very ill and, in all likelihood, would not become better.

She wept the most bitter tears of her life; saw this as a sentence, as some sort of punishment, and screamed in the night at Walt; because he bore his grief in silence. What happens when one can only express sadness with great noise, unable to keep it contained in as small a space as the human heart, while the other cannot locate an opening large enough in his own heart to let it all out?

Gen wrote in her journal: *We had a boy and a girl and a boy. The first boy we lost. Oh, you can retrace your footsteps in an effort to understand how you arrived at this place. For what it is worth. Most days I just feel like this bad mother who released the small hand of her child in a very crowded place, only for a moment, and he disappeared. Of course, I know that it is no one's fault; Walt could not have prevented it; I could not have altered things. But that does not make any difference; my interest in blame is decidedly limited.*

So missing him is the worst of it. At first, you think the illness is as bad as it gets; then you come to understand that the passing is much worse. You are wrong, though, because now you have hours and days and years to get through. You feel his absence most strongly, touched with longing, confusion and bartering with God until one day, when you are deep into the years of your own life, all you will think about when you look back is that little boy. You will ask yourself, Where did he go?

So. This was the household into which Kiki was born. Kiki with her middle name Serafina and her last name Shaw. And the three facts of her life:

1. That her profession consists of uncovering and noting small truths.
2. That her Own Story seems not to be her story at all but a recitation of Other Lives.
3. And, most crucial, that she is approaching forty rapidly and, just as quickly, disappearing.

Museums

One of the most popular museums, in Kiki's informal survey of friends and family, is the Jeu de Paume. People seem routinely to adore the French Impressionists. Most of the pictures that once hung there can now be found in the Musée d'Orsay, a converted Paris train station.

Another much admired museum is the Museum of Modern Art in New York City. Both of the aforementioned museums are housed in cities "friendly" to art. Or, perhaps, it is the other way around; that the artists themselves arrived first and the museums later.

It is a fact that a city atmosphere obliterates the stars. They cannot be seen because of the reflection of the lights against the sky, yet they are still sparkling above us. People seem to value other things more than the pure beauty and indifference of the midnight sky. This describes our relationship with the natural world in general. Do humans prefer the artificial? Gen Shaw has often said, "I don't really thrill to nature. Going to the ocean, taking long walks in a field, do not inspire me. I am unmoved by a mountain range or national park."

When asked why she would reply:

"Because nature is a product of God and since God is all-powerful, all-knowing and the Creator of Life, then this is nothing to Him. I mean, making this world, this universe—now that's his job, isn't it?

"Take the Empire State Building or a city like Paris and I am riveted, amazed. Because buildings, bridges, airplanes, rockets and railroad cars—those are manmade and altogether more remarkable."

Gen does not mention art. Because, as she writes in her diary, Art is a fusion of man and God and altogether something apart.

When the children were small and Gen had a particularly difficult day, she would pile everyone into the car (amid protests and whining and bartering for sweets) and take them down to the local museum, which was known for its little permanent collection of Man Rays. Just a few pieces, but enough. If there was a family fight: to the museum. If Gen had an important decision to make: to the museum. If she was angry or anxious: to the museum. And when she was preparing herself to leave Walt: to the museum.

The Moon and the Eighteenth Century

In mythology the sun is always a man: a brother, a husband, a stranger who stole a woman by force. It is said that the sun and moon, moon and sun chase each other across the heavens and that their union, which cannot truly occur, is sexual and imbued with a strong power. Apollo is the sun and Diana is the moon. Diana is also called Artemis and she represents the young and waxing moon. A full moon is named Selene. Hecate is waning and dark.

The Moon

The moon recalls the goddess and the strength of women, the Divine Feminine, and when aligned with the Father Divine the world will stand in a place of peace. The irony is that as the moon is the underpinning of all that is powerful and female so is it the embodiment of a woman's weakness, her inconstancy, her ability to reflect only the light of the masculine sun without shining any of her own. Her passivity, her round fullness, her monthly cycle, her influence on the tides and undula-

tions of water, her distance, her changing, unpredictable emotional life. Her waxing and her waning. Her mercy at the heat and hot light of the sun.

THE EIGHTEENTH CENTURY

Eighteenth-century Englishwomen wore their hair in elaborate styles, fixed with a lard that enticed rodents and insects to feast upon it. The entire business was then powdered white. Men, on the other hand, shaved their heads and covered their bare skulls with wigs, unlike the women who lived with their hairstyles for weeks on end until they had to be taken down and redone.

A woman's flesh was extremely pale, lunar, to match the white of her hair. And the powder she used contained lead and was applied from hairline to bosom in a solid field that left an absence of color. It could only be removed with a solution of mercury. As the moon is the source of lunacy in the spirit, so is mercury a cause of madness in the body.

Kiki stops typing, places her fingertips to her temples and massages. The unkind heat of this Los Angeles day is taking its toll; she imagines she looks weary and resigned. She wishes they would increase the air-conditioning in her office but energy measures only allow for a certain degree of comfort, not true comfort. Southern California "seasons" are a joke, but even in February there used to be some sort of relief. Perhaps a little rain. Not this year or last year, or the year before that. All this talk about a general warming of the earth unnerves her. It simply used to be that the heat did her in; now she experiences a nagging worry of global extinction on top of it. She laughs a little to herself when she wonders why so few people seem to care about this earth only to recall that the world, like the moon, is feminine, a mother who receives and gives back. And the sun, this intrusive warmth, is masculine. When Persephone was kidnapped by Hades, god of the underworld, her mother, Demeter, goddess of the earth, was forbidden to retrieve her own child; instead, she had to beg for mercy from Zeus in heaven. That is the eternal feminine, thinks Kiki, always having to ask.

In the bathroom, Kiki splashes cold water on her face, careful not to leave the water running, in this city of heat and drought. She examines herself in the mirror and sees that if she remains very still, the wall behind her begins to merge with the image of her face. This is not the first time she has noticed this doubling in the glass. Nor is it the first time it has alarmed her, set her heart pounding, made her palms moist and clammy. So far, she has kept these happenings, as she has come to call them, to herself, afraid to make them real by speaking out loud; does not want to think that she is losing her mind.

"Okay," she says to no one, "think of something else." This is her new trick, forcing her mind away from her physical state. Who, as she watches herself in the mirror (like so many people), sees and does not "see" herself. As long as her hair is relatively neat, the toothpaste wiped from her mouth, the sleep out of her eyes, her lipstick on straight, it is enough attention paid to her face. But every once in a while, she truly looks at her face, almost losing herself in the mirror, caught in the place between who she is and who she thinks she is.

Today, with the room merging with her face, she thinks she may as well be a vampire; some undead thing who only appears with the light of the moon, casting no reflection at all. "Well," she says to herself, "if I were a vampire, at least I could fly. I would be powerful and immortal." She hesitates. "I would be scary. I gather I would be quite thin." Then she imagines being thin, immortal, beautiful, pale and sexy, yet without a reflection. What is that supposed to be? Possessing all those attributes and unable to see them for yourself? How would you know they were you? Because other people told you so? Would you have to rely on them *all the time,* reassuring you that you are this amazing supernatural being? Oh, god, thinks Kiki, the worst sort of peer approval.

So. Would she be who everyone else thought she was, as if she had no valuable opinion on the matter? And if she protested, said, No, I am really like this, would people simply humor her? She recalls dinner last month with her friend Henry. He was complaining about a recent family get-together.

"The trouble with my family is that any random thing you had or did as a kid determines the adult you. Drives me crazy."

"So, who are you?" asked Kiki.

"Me? Oh, I'm Mr. Moody. My aunt wanders up to me and asks me if I would like a piece of cake. I say, No, thank you, I'm not in the mood for cake. And she says, Well, Henry, that is you. You were always the Moody One."

"Because of a piece of cake?" asks Kiki.

"Because when I was eight or something I was at her house and refused to play with the other kids. I was, obviously, in a nasty mood. I never would have shown it had I known that it was going to be my Ultimate Personality Trait, discussed at every family dinner."

"If you are Mr. Moody, who are the rest of the kids?"

"My cousin Jane had a bout of asthma at five, so, today at thirty, she is still the Sickly One. Lucy briefly rebelled at age fourteen—oh, she is rather conservative and successful today but still So Militant. In a three-piece suit."

Kiki laughed.

Henry laughed, too.

"What about your brother?"

"You'll like this. The guy has been depressed for three years—three years!—but because he told jokes from one of those *1001 Jokes for All Occasions* books when he was ten, Len is still the Funny One. He can say something like, 'I can hardly get out of bed in the morning,' and my father just cracks up, says, 'Oh, that Len, still the Funny One!' "

Kiki wonders what Henry's large family would make of her now. Would they talk about her, thinking she had left the room when maybe she had only turned momentarily invisible? What would they say? "She was always such a quiet girl. Sometimes you forget she's there."

It is almost as though the world were rife with artists waiting to commit your image forever to canvas until the line blurs between subject and depiction, truth and lie.

When Kiki returns to her office, she sees a woman in her chair, turned three quarters to the window. *Now* what, thinks Kiki. Did I forget to take my image with me to the bathroom? Is this some spontaneous astral projection?

The woman in the chair spins toward Kiki. "Where have you been?" asks Nora.

"Oh, thank god," sighs Kiki, relieved. "Nora. I am so glad to see you."

"You forgot, didn't you? About the Scotland thing today? I mean, you asked me."

"No, no, we have time."

Nora opens her large leather purse, shows the contents to Kiki. "Lunch," she says, "because I, the Perfect Secretary, think of everything."

. . .

Kiki and Nora pull up to a small auditorium at the edge of the Museum of Modern Art. From time to time, the museum runs a seminar and film on different countries. It is supposed to be a "total travel experience" with the presenters dressed in native costume, peppering their lectures with anecdotes from their travels, a few artifacts, showing what amounts to an extended home movie with only slightly better "production values," an expression Kiki picked up from Collier Grey. Kiki's company pays for her to go, with an escort, for research purposes. "I personally think they ought to send me to the country itself," she says, but that suggestion is not considered.

Today, Nora joins Kiki only because she had to drive her boss to the airport and he gave her the rest of the day off. She is saying to Kiki, "So, I had to go into the terminal and I am waiting to talk to a baggage person and this woman, sort of nondescript, is standing near me. We smile at each other, you know, because we are both waiting, and finally she says that she has had this terrible day and it isn't even ten-thirty. It is her job to transfer mentally disturbed patients to other cities by plane."

"You mean, they get on the plane, like regular passengers?"

"Apparently. Only her car broke down before she got to the airport and through some incredible coincidence on the freeway a co-worker was driving by and picked her up. Then, when she got here, her guy ran away. 'Ran away?' I asked her. 'Yeah,' she said. 'He headed out toward long-term parking.' And she was so calm."

"I can't believe they let unstable people on planes." Kiki is rarely happy to fly and tries hard never to think of her fellow fliers, particularly the one she is sure has little to live for and wants to take everyone with him. Another friend of hers has a similar fear in the air, which is that a crazy person opens the door. This makes Kiki scoff, Oh, as if *that's* a possibility.

The person on the stage is explaining the tartan of her kilt, and about clans and broken men. The film begins and after the first twenty minutes Kiki makes a mental note that there are an awful lot of sheep in Scotland. And quite a bit of knitting going on as well. Now some people are eating haggis in a very picturesque restaurant. Kiki and Nora are eating sandwiches, Kiki happy to be someplace cooler than her office. "Why is everyone here so old?" whispers Nora. And Kiki looks around and she, too, notices that they are in an audience made up almost entirely of what look to be retirees and/or elderly women.

"I guess everyone else is working," says Kiki.

"You mean, if this was a Saturday afternoon we wouldn't be the youngest people here?"

"So what?" says Kiki, her voice unexpectedly tight. "So what if they are old? Can't you leave them alone? Can't they just enjoy themselves?"

Nora says nothing. Even in the darkened auditorium, Kiki can see that the tip of her elbow, which is resting on the arm of her seat, has faded away.

Cards

Kiki is not good at games. They distress her in a profound sort of way; she always wants to win or, at least, perform with a certain gracefulness, and she is amazed and disconcerted by the intensity of her desire to triumph. It puts her off, this wanting to win, so she responds by shying away from competition; by believing that she is *not* competitive, does not enjoy being forced into the fray; that she does not care and cannot be made to care; that win or lose is indistinguishable in her world. Kiki takes to the proclamation of the moralist who says rather loudly, "It is how you play the game," and pontificates on matters of fairness, justice, honor and ethics. All the things that she holds dear but is using to her advantage, in this case.

To put it another way: If Kiki is holding something of value in her hand and someone else happens along and says—not in so many words—"I am going to take this from you," she will loosen her grip, imperceptibly relax and open her small palm. Later, she can tell herself: I did not lose it. I gave it away. I let go of it.

In this way, no one can ever take anything from her.

. . .

In England, solitaire is known as patience; it is the same game or games, though a patience deck is traditionally comprised of small-scale playing cards that are easier to reach and can be played with most anywhere. After all, only one player needs to see them. Arranging the tableaux for the games was soothing to Kiki; during times of anxiety she would find herself ordering the cards in a variety of foundations: clock solitaire (unchallenging since the game is predetermined); Canfield (a betting game); King's Corners (a game of ordered suits); quilt (played with two decks, everything doubled); and so on.

Does the moralist who desperately wants to win cheat when playing alone? And, if so, how would a fixed game soothe her troubled nerves? Is it the playing or the winning that motivates her?

When Kiki cannot abide her aloneness she calls up her friend Henry. She asks, How about a game of gin? Sometimes, he brings her chocolate or baskets of strawberries. They once tried to play hearts only to discover that more than two people are needed to make it interesting.

Henry and Kiki met in college, introduced by Nora Barrie, who is two years older than Kiki. Nora always seemed to know everyone. Henry was a business major whose dream was to open what he called The Paradisiacal Grocery Store. The shelves stocked with imported dry goods, jars of sauces and condiments, sweets, a variety of cheeses, meats, fish and poultry. Foreign spices and breads of all sorts. And his description would go on, the eyes of his fellow students glazing over, in these years between the sixties sensibility and the eighties mentality. No one they knew cared as much for food or the availability of those difficult-to-find items. And it was funny to think that later in life, when food turned faddish (Kiki and Henry used to laugh at that notion—it was like sleep becoming fashionable, or any other necessary function), these same former students would recall Henry as a "visionary" without ever understanding or remembering that Henry simply liked food. That is to say, he always remained secular in his approach to it, even if others did not. As he often said, food was purely sensual.

Basically, Kiki found herself drawn to a man of ambition in those aimless days of school. Henry never thought of himself as ambitious; he just knew, in his case, that the road to his heart was by way of his stomach.

They were in love, then out of love; then out of touch, then back in touch, making their way toward a close friendship. He brought her chocolate and strawberries because those were her favorite things, not the most exotic things he could supply. He tried to give Kiki what she liked, not what he wanted her to like, and she would listen to him talk about this girl or that girl; or the brief marriage that failed; or his indecision regarding children; or his three beautiful grocery stores, and they would laugh to think that Los Angeles ever became a place that grew to love food.

He knows that Kiki usually calls if she has something troubling on her mind. He will usually come to her because she is a girl who does not make requests lightly or often. And because he knows and loves her.

Kiki wants to ask him if she is looking less than herself these days, but decides that she will wait to see if he notices anything on his own. These birthday blues that set her to thinking about things like plastic surgery, wondering if she passes on having something "done" she will cease to look like her contemporaries.

(As Collier says, "You should come into my office once in a while. It is turning very odd. More of the women are getting plastic surgery—you know, bigger tits, wider eyes, smaller hips, fuller lips, more prominent cheekbones and chin, lifts and tucks. And you really notice the difference after someone's vacation or a holiday; or they try to tell you they "walked into a door" or some such thing. It is strange seeing these women shrinking and expanding all around, or slightly swollen and bruised from an operation—as if they were all in some terrible, unnamable accident." Kiki laughs to herself, "Yeah, the accident of getting older.")

Will they whisper behind her back that she looks tired, beat, weary, and why doesn't she take care of those dark circles beneath her pretty eyes? People may say, "Doesn't she care about her looks?"—as if it were some sort of minor sin to be less than perfect. Will she be thought slovenly, asexual, silly and cheap if she decides to remain as she is? Or will someone approach her one day and (she hopes not) label her "brave"?

So, Kiki, whose foot can pass through a cat or an oak door, if she moves fast enough; who sometimes catches her reflection in the glass and sometimes does not; who can dematerialize in her office without warning, now sees her body turning into gossamer, an outline, a veil, a silk stocking, the brilliantly worked lace of a wedding dress; a wraith, a ghost, a thought. She waits for Henry impatiently, pacing the length of her small house. Most of the time she thinks whatever romantic interest he ever had in her is gone forever, then he'll say something that causes her to look up from her cards to see him calmly watching her. As if he wants to say something to her but then catches himself, thinks better of it.

He will say something like, "I wonder what you were like as a child," a remark that makes her shy, off-balance; she cannot speak except to change the subject (although she is certain that this is not the thing he wishes to say to her, as much as it affects her). So intriguing, she thinks, to have someone curious about your childhood, that person you once were, or that still may bleed through, like pentimento in a painting.

The Floating Woman

During the *fin de siècle* women were sometimes portrayed as weightless and floating, held aloft by invisible forces that freed their feet from the earth and directed their paths. Yet women were believed to be strongly connected with nature, almost indistinguishable from it, fertility depicted on canvas by the male artists of the time. Such fecundity and sexuality was frightening; it was much easier on the mind to imagine women light as air; drifting on water; or angels perched on clouds. Walking was too deliberate an act—it was action itself—but to float was to surrender, to release your fate to something stronger; even the breeze could be rendered as forceful in these pictures. To hover above the ground is to admit that you are without will. To walk is to have an opinion, a mind of one's own (in the sixties, for example, many women were said to have "walked out" on domestic life).

Kiki pauses at her computer, her pencil clamped between her teeth. How can women be embodiments of nature and thereby threatening in their lack of humanly imposed "morality" and, simultaneously, easily blown about by the natural elements? These nineteenth-century painters, Kiki says to herself, make up your minds already. Of course, she reasons, this may be the logical result of being interpreted by someone outside the realm. She continues:

Ghosts float. Phantoms hover. Spirits allow the wind to carry them. Weightlessness, then, is the giving over of one's self. Curious that so many women strive to shed weight; is it seductive to be borne on a breeze?

Collier Grey spent her entire youth, her twenties, directed by currents of air. Like milkweed, as if she were a bundle of small beautiful seeds undone by the atmosphere; spread and soothed, laid upon the earth but never taking root. So here is what her shrink once told her as she sobbed in her office; when Collier was thirty, unclear, unsure, unestablished and knowing only that she was somewhere unfamiliar and could not recall how she got there. The shrink said to Collier: *Just chalk up your twenties as lost years, when you did not ground yourself* [those were her exact words, *ground yourself,* as if she, too, understands the attraction and danger of weightlessness] *for your thirties and now it is time to get on with it.*

"What she said," Collier told Kiki, "is that I should forgive myself."

"For what?" asked Kiki.

"For letting myself think that doing nothing, that moving from job to job, place to place, man to man, indicated a life. That I mistakenly believed that one could simply pass along with each moment and, when the time came, have a meaningful life."

"Your life did not have any meaning?" asked Kiki, in these years before her own ghost life, when she was trying to understand this idea of a woman without ballast.

"It wasn't my life," said Collier. "It belonged to someone or something unseen; unseen and moving me as if I were made of nothing; as if my own youth could not possibly be used up—this endless thing—"

"Look," said Kiki, "I'm not sure about how the twenties are to be spent, but I think thirty is like a second adolescence, that Awkward Age. All I remember thinking when I was growing up was what my thirties would be like; then I'm there and it is not at all what I pictured. Like when we were sixteen and thought we should resemble some blossoming starlet, only all I looked like was me, and all you looked like was you—it was us, only strangely us.

"It is a matter of expectations, I think. No blame, no forgiveness," said Kiki as she crossed her arms.

"Why is it," asked Collier, "that we are the same only no one sees us in the same way? Because we got older? Christ, I am so afraid of being 'cute' when it is no longer appropriate or, well, *becoming*. Does personality define age or does age do the alteration for you?

"Well," continued Collier, "what I think is this: Your thirties are confusion and tragedy and everything turning just a little bit poignant."

Kiki laughed. "Isn't that a bit much?"

But then these two young women had experienced loss: Collier's father died; men they thought loved them truly walked away; time had been lost as well, not misplaced but gone for good. And there was the matter of their mothers' aging, a thing that they could not even discuss, not with anyone. The topic commanded a silence from the women, still young and ego-strong, as it threatened to open up a world of more loss, more passing time and a general uneasiness during the unfamiliar territory of their thirties.

Now they are both wandering around outside forty

and Collier is involved with a man who is not good for her and Kiki is coming to understand an aspect of weightlessness previously unknown. As much as she wants to tell what is happening to her, to say the words that have brought her to this place, it is still Other Lives she relates. Maybe Collier is correct about tragedy and poignancy.

However, as Kiki knows, Collier's lesson was learned. She no longer saw the shrink. Turning thirty galvanized her toward a career. Though the path was not without an occasional detour, Collier Grey finds herself, on the eve of forty, working as a producer in a video production company she co-owns. "The eighties," she likes to say, "invented my career." Getting in on the ground floor of a profession held a certain appeal for her; it meant that she was not competing along established lines as much as she was new in a new area. It meant only going up, so she did not have that sense of vertigo failure: that she could fall from her climb.

She does well at this job, which requires her to deal primarily in time and money; does not love it although it seems to suit her. There are days when she likes what she does, bringing together directors and artists and stories and minutes and cash.

Now it is only her romantic life that fails her and she is baffled as to how she possesses the ability to decide in matters of a career yet remains as irresolute and as unmoored as ever in love.

Collier was attracted to clear definitions of objects, activities, titles, words. In college she studied music because she loved math, time, rhythm, languages and audio color. In her work she likes intertwining time and money; likes the play between the two: *Ephemera,* she says to Kiki, *are things not meant to be kept.* Transitory. They are the abstractions that rule our lives and aren't time and money just another way of saying music and math?

But love, love she cannot think of as something "not meant to be kept" despite its being an abstraction. So this is the only part of her life that remains mysterious, unpredictable, maverick. My mystery, she calls it. She cannot seem to settle down to it, cannot do without it; cannot fathom whom she loves and why or, similarly, whom she chooses to leave by the wayside. Because she was comfortable with the logic of numbers and measurements of time, she is uneasy in a place—a love place, vertiginous—where no logic exists. Which, as everyone knows, is its charm. If romance obeyed any sort of natural or imposed laws it would be, on the whole, much more explicable to Collier.

She says, This is the duality of my life: Open, on her desk, is a green leather appointment book. As Collier laughs and flirts on the phone, she is writing something down. Now there are two entries on a single day: one for a midmorning business meeting; one for an assignation with Gordon. Each to take place at the Old Huntington Hotel; the meeting in the Water Lily Room; then hurrying to find Gordon standing in the center of the Picture Bridge. She knows what will happen. She can almost feel the touch of his hand. His breath at the base of her throat.

Gordon, who is married to a woman named Les.

Language

Kiki, as with the rest of the staff, is periodically asked to compile a *Language* category. Kiki once asked if she could skip it and work on a similar topic called *Tongues*. She was told no. She types:

(For $200) Cordate: Heart shaped. An essentially feminine outline, the heart is. Round, voluptuous, generously curved, appearing to be fairly pliable—as if its form could be altered by a small push here, a little prod there; as if it could not be broken at all. Unlike, say, the star, with its five sharp points and glittering edges; "masculine" in the sense that the heart is "womanly," this configuration. It is seemingly crystalline, fragile, brittle, a cutting precious metal. One feels that if it fell from the sky it would burst into a thousand pieces, littering the landscape with a glinting waste of gold and silver. Beautiful and shattered; more beautiful because it is shattered.

All this, naturally, is illusory because the heart is not as accommodating as it seems. It *can* be broken; it can one day find itself beyond repair, still beating; it can

cause trouble in mind and ache in soul. Because a fissure in the heart extends like a fault line throughout one's very being. It knows no borders.

And a star could very well slice through any earthly obstacle or inflame a field of dry grass and eventually find repose on the ground; sharp, unapproachable and basically intact.

Kiki's fingers move so quickly they blur. An enormous run of words crosses her mind; why she settled on *cordate*—love!—she is not sure. Her first word could just as easily have been: *era, epoch, aeon, clepsydra, chronology, isochronism, metronome, passage, old, ancient, evanesce, vanish, eclipse, good-bye.*

That is, if she wanted to make her thoughts known.

Magic, Tricks & Illusions

Kiki happens into a magic store and asks for a book containing magic tricks, only to be soundly reprimanded. "We do not carry books on magic *tricks.*"

The proprietor is not old and crotchety; he is young and nasty. She hastens to correct her mistake because she notices a number of volumes behind the counter and is certain one of them is what she wants. So she begins again:

"What about magic that can make a woman disappear?" asks Kiki.

The young man gives her a patronizing look. Says, "People don't really disappear, now do they?"

"I know that," she says although she is thinking he is mistaken. And he is also wrong on a global level as an unpleasant thought crosses her mind concerning certain individuals in Latin America called The Disappeared. Clearly, sadly, a society can accomplish what a magician cannot. Then she breaks the connection. She says, "I mean, a magician would never work again if he failed to bring people back from wherever he sent them. You'd have a pretty tough time if you were constantly losing volunteers and assistants to god knows where."

"Exactly," says the young man. Pleased with himself, Kiki thinks. "Look," he says, softening a bit, causing Kiki to think that it cannot be easy to work in a store that experiences bouts of popularity during specific times of the year and she is a potential sale. Or maybe he just wants some company; in any case, "Are you talking about using a box? A curtain? Let me tell you something, what you are interested in are illusions."

"Illusions," Kiki repeats. "A book on illusions," she says in a louder voice. "Specifically," she adds, "things that were once there and now they are gone."

He brings her a stack of volumes titled *The Tarbell Course in Magic for the Professional, Amateur and Beginner* by Dr. Harlan Tarbell, 1890–1960. Apparently, Dr. Tarbell was quite an influence in the sphere of magic and can be seen on the outer sleeve in tux and boutonniere. Arms crossed, gazing off into the middle distance, some mystical place, she guesses. Kiki says, "I don't know where to begin."

The young man suggests that she start with coins or scarves or small animals only to have her insist that her main interest, at this point, is human.

He shows her an enormous index and Kiki notes some of the headings: Money Magic, Rope Magic, Mental Magic (a possibility), Silk Magic—until she locates what she is looking for: Illusions. Dr. Tarbell begins by writing, "The dressing of an illusion is very important." And there is mention of a South American magician, a Richiardi Junior, who excelled at sawing a woman in half, replete with spattered blood (a crowd favorite), followed by an admonition from Dr. Tarbell, which states that "blood," profuse and copious, may be acceptable where Richiardi Junior is from but may not be appreciated here at home, as if Americans to the north were a little too squeamish, a little too pristine for such graphic displays. Or perhaps he thinks it is possible that they would not be able to discern the difference between real and fake. Again, the image of The Disappeared runs across Kiki's mind and fuses with Richiardi Junior's South American illusion.

Kiki reads that one must never cut corners when setting up and executing an illusion. There is the Girl in the Trunk Mystery; the Girl in the Audience; the Indestructible Girl; Sawing a Woman in Half (first performed in 1843) and comprised of a box, rope for wrist and ankle tying, two single-edge razor blades, a large lumber saw and, of course, The Girl.

Now who, Kiki wonders for a moment, ever thought of this illusion with its attendant items of violence—razor, saw, rope? Why a girl? What exactly is the point? To show that a girl can withstand any sort of treatment? Isn't that what girls are taught: If the boys hit you it is because they like you? And why shouldn't there be a generous spray of faux blood as Richiardi Junior was so fond of including in his South American version of this illusion (and which so bothered American Dr. Tarbell)?

Or are women seen as just so bloodless?

Illusions

The magic store and its volumes yielded nothing. The women who participated in the various tricks all remained as solid as ever; no one really left; disappearances were executed by distracting the eye, controlling the line of vision, which is altogether different from Kiki's problem. Magicians also used mirrors.

The illusion that caught her was The Floating Woman, during which the woman appeared to be asleep or in a trance as a magician passed a hoop from one end of her suspended body to the other. Not unlike Collier and Gordon, or so it seems to Kiki.

Not long after her trip to the magic store, while visiting in San Francisco, Kiki finds herself in a shop that specializes in rubber stamps, just south of Market Street. She is killing time, really, because she is meeting friends for a drink in North Beach later.

As she walks around the store she suddenly sees a small shadow box made of velvet and plywood, with paper figures inside, obviously rubber-stamped people, filled in and cut out. The paper man in the box wears a print tuxedo, a gold hoop held at the end of his extended arm as a paper woman in a flowing gown, under some sort of enchantment, floats on her back above a paper French provincial sofa. Presumably she had been lying on it prior to her entranced state. Her paper hair barely brushes the top sofa cushion as the man draws the hoop the length of her motionless, lazy figure.

"How much is this?" asks Kiki excitedly.

"Oh, I don't think that is for sale. It is more an example of what you can make yourself if you purchase our stamps," says the saleswoman.

Kiki is momentarily disappointed; it occurs to her that she could possibly re-create this box, but that is not her desire. She must have this particular object.

She picks it up. She sets it down. She holds it again as if it were already in her possession. "May I buy it?"

The woman says, "Really, it *is* a display," and Kiki realizes that this is not the first time she has been bent on purchasing a display item. Why, she wonders, do I always fixate on the thing that exists only to enhance the Real Things? But she must have this box. Kiki says nothing.

"Well," says the woman, "I suppose I could call up the artist [Oh, now he's an *artist,* thinks Kiki to herself. Already she knows this 'artist' business is going to be expensive] and ask him if he would be willing to let it go."

"Then call him."

Kiki cannot speak as the woman looks up the phone number, dials, waits for an answer. Obviously, there is a pickup on the other line. The saleswoman begins relating her tale, with great enthusiasm, about the woman who wants to buy his small velvet shadow box. When she hangs up, she says, "He told me to tell you that it took him two months to make [Kiki winces; it would take her far less] and that it really is One of a Kind." Kiki can only hear these final words capitalized and surrounded by dollar signs. The materials are pennies, she is sure, and the figures just colored-in rubber-stamp impressions. But the content! The scene of the floating woman is compelling.

She thinks of a lunch, in Santa Barbara, a month ago with Collier and Gordon. They were in fine and friendly form; the three of them laughing and reminiscing, not drinking, but passing a joint from one to the other, no one at the outdoor café showing the slightest disapproval or interest. And she thought, Why aren't you two together, without absent Les always keeping you inches apart? How long can you go on this way, without direction?

"He says he cannot let it go for less than a hundred seventy-five dollars." The woman now seems less pleasant, a little tougher. She waits.

Oh, you've got to be kidding, that is far too much, thinks Kiki, who only replies, "That will be fine." Kiki cannot help but notice the surprise in the woman's face as she says, "I'll wrap it up." She wants to say, I'm a little surprised myself. Kiki also imagines her thinking, Wait until I tell The Artist. He won't believe it! And Kiki envisions a chain reaction where the saleswoman and The Artist see potential for selling overpriced boxes that were nothing to put together; Kiki wanting to explain that she is not normal, that he should not quit his day job, that the box is unnecessarily expensive but a fixation, such as hers, will not listen to reason. The saleswoman takes her time boxing the box, as if it were fragile and dear—which it isn't—and all because Kiki, in her agreement to pay too much money, had inadvertently increased the value of this object.

Kiki thinks of Collier's drifting on tides, and notes that this often happens to her; that is, things coming together in a seemingly random fashion: the magic trick called The Floating Woman, the velvet shadow box and Collier. An action, an object and a life: all linked in Kiki's eyes, which, she supposes, is why she is suited for her profession. She cannot help observing that in the shadow box the paper man looks rather pleased, the paper woman just a bit willing.

More on nineteenth-century women:

One hundred years ago, male artists found themselves preoccupied with the fullness of the moon, its self-absorption, the roundness of the mirror, the unbroken line, the circle as "feminine." Even as they attributed these symbols to woman so did they castigate her seeming indifference to these representations. In fact, women were largely uninvolved with this twinning of a circle with the female essence (or soul) and many not aware of it at all.

The artists saw the woman at her glass as a scene of self-love, of cold autoeroticism, of rebellion. The female, they seemed to say, needed none but her own face and hands and body. Maybe press her own mouth to the mirror. She perches at her vanity table, wallows in her vanity. No longer content to be like the moon, she does not want to reflect anyone's light save her own. This narcissism, this refusal to see anyone but herself. Unfeeling, hard, white, cold like the lifeless moon. The men desired to shatter the mirror, to force her to shine with their light.

Kiki remembers that pleasant, sunny lunch in Santa Barbara, speculating on the possibility of Collier and Gordon's ending up as friends—old and good friends—with none of the complications of someone's being married and both having to lie. Since Collier and Gordon have known each other for more than twenty years perhaps the sexual element will lessen.

Kiki carries the velvet shadow box of the magician and the lady under her arm.

But the impressionable picture of that day is the one of Collier blowing pot smoke into Gordon's mouth in a long, lingering kiss.

Mirrors

In the mid-nineteenth century, in England, alongside the rise of capitalism, this happened: As men became more unscrupulous and corrupt (or so historians would have us believe) as the result of capitalism's demands, and its fairly cutthroat ethic, women were encouraged to be more "spiritual." More modest, more pure, more moral. At least, that was the expectation of a good middle- to upper-class wife. So untouched by the physical world that it was considered indecent to initiate sex with one's own husband. Any pleasure derived from the act was a perversion that could be and was sometimes corrected surgically. The beautiful angel of the house was the spiritual protector of home and hearth; the balance against her husband's living; since he no longer had the time for morality, she became his moral center, his ethics, his conscience, his ticket into the Next World. This state of affairs grew so extreme that eventually wives became pale, listless, submissive, with a constitution that literally wasted away until they were transformed into a host of spiritgirls entirely without physicality. And this angel, this essence of wife, became the ideal. The goal. To erase the unpredictable, faulty

body—that potential downfall of the Good Victorian Wife.

What is Les, Gordon's wife, like? During the early years of Collier and Gordon's affair, Kiki did not think about her. After all, due to the past, she was used to Gordon and Collier as a couple. As a matter of fact, it almost seemed mythical, this idea that Gordon *might be* married to a woman whose name *might be* Les. Collier seemed willing to ignore her. Certainly, Gordon was not overly concerned. So Kiki simply followed where they led.

These days she is not so sure. She finds this woman, this Les, this stranger skirting her thoughts. Perhaps because Kiki is surprised at the duration of this second, adult phase of Collier and Gordon's romance. Because of it, Kiki has expanded the circle of thought—previously holding Collier and Gordon—to include Les and wonders if Gordon's distance seems novel to her or if it has always been so and is without comparison. "She must know," Kiki has said to Collier more than once.

"Yeah," said Collier, "but if she does, then what are we to conclude?"

Even more interesting than the wife who lives in ignorance is the idea of Les with absolute knowledge, who still remains in the marriage. A woman like that, thinks Kiki, I would like to talk to.

As Kiki reviews what she has written about the Angel of the House, she thinks, I am nobody's wife. People used to ask if she ever wanted to get married; now they simply say things like, Since you've decided not to marry—then complete their thought.

Bill walks into her office and pulls a box of paper clips from her drawer, leaves without saying thank you or acknowledging her.

As if she ever talked much about marriage in any case.

She flexes a forearm that fades with a pulsing movement but comes back, hard, when she drops it to her messy desk.

Les, wife to Collier's lover, Gordon, sees herself everywhere. As if other women were simply moving mirrors. In her dreams, she keeps company with women who sometimes fight with her or confide in her, or flirt openly with Gordon, or kiss her surprised mouth as the most passionate and besotted of lovers. And, sometimes, in her dreamstate, Les thinks, This is the taste of true love, and wakes in the morning, disappointed, longing to be someone's inamorata. She does not necessarily desire the phantom woman as much as she does the sensation of desperate love. That, she decides as she sits across the kitchen table from her silent husband, is the thing in life to miss. More than youth or her children as babies, or her parents as she remembers them when they were younger; it was that one thing: an absolute faith in love. The way in which the stars thrill to the night.

Some folks, Les is aware, more analytical and educated along specific disciplines, might describe her dream as veiled lesbian desire or a variety of self-love. These would be the same people who have deromanticized the moon by being more excited seeing moon rocks on display in Texas than pondering its effect on the soul.

When Les first met Gordon, he invited her on a night hike, a very popular activity during their college years spent in the northern-most part of California. He said, "The moon will light our way." She found herself trusting him and the light of the woman moon for the same reason that anyone trusts: They want to. So, intrigued by

Gordon, flattered by his interest in her, ignoring the talk about other girls and Gordon.

They left in the easing dusk as the sky turned red and purple and the moon rose behind the hills and Les followed him along well-used nature trails, excited by the fact that she could not make out her own way and each footfall seemed an unlikely chance for her to take. When the path narrowed, Gordon reached behind and gripped her hand, guiding her over this strange terrain. Until, quite suddenly, she heard a small noise—a sneaker skimming the top of gravel. Gordon lost his footing and started down the side of a small hill. Les would have cried out except the sound was interrupted by her own slide at the hands of Gordon. She was going down with him and could not catch her breath. Each had forgotten that Gordon still held her hand within his. What had begun as protection and guidance now was swiftly turning.

Les thought he would release her as she tumbled down after him, but he did not and, later, soaking in a warm tub, bruised and scratched, examining the stitches on her ankle, which were too big and inexpertly done by a very young MD manning the town clinic, she could not think why she remained in his grasp. Had he freed her it still would have been too late, the fall having been set in motion, though it is possible that the damage was made worse by their physical contact.

Now, many years later, Les can still trace the pale-white scar on her ankle from their moonlight walk. She considers it a mark of their union, allowing her to both revere and disdain it; at times finding it so disagreeable it causes her to weep.

As Les grew older she wished that Gordon, too, had been marked by this misadventure. Despite his lead into the accident, he emerged amazingly clean of blood and bruises. Funny, since he broke her fall. But there you are. Sometimes, in a fury, she wanted to scream at him, "Where is your scar? Where is the evidence of me carried on your body?" And maybe because he was uninscribed, her eyes would involuntarily scan the flesh of other women. In evening dresses, shorts, sleeveless blouses and bathing suits. Les would perform a visual sweep of them, becoming quite fast and private at it, checking for similar scarring, wondering if any of them were as she was: marked. She needed to know that she was not alone in her peculiarity.

Simultaneously, she wanted to display her white scar to let other women see that she and Gordon shared something—a moment or a life, she could not say which—in this permanent hairline mark as pale and curved as the moon, engraved on the flesh of her ankle, which embodied a sense of belonging that these other women (whose bodies held no public marks) would understand as Les's connection to Gordon and turn from her husband. Even if he made them feel as if they were the only thing on his mind; they would not be fooled and would see beyond the flirtation.

Les did not believe this would happen; it was a matter of her wish colliding with reality. She was fairly certain that he was seeing someone else. She wished she'd listened for the names of the other girls he was linked with in college. Even as she was unable to prove or truly determine it, this intuition that hovered (and never quite arrived); that lingered (and never quite became explicit). And because she felt the other woman's presence so powerfully, she began to act in such a way that Gordon accused her of being "irrational."

He said, "Christ, even the shrubs in the garden aren't safe from your temper."

Gordon's shirts were left for weeks at the dry cleaner. "No, no," she told him, "don't bother picking them up. I will get them for you." Then she would consistently renege on her promise. The trash he took from the house was mysteriously brought back inside; she would drive separately to parties and dinners, excusing herself to go to the ladies' room and never reappearing; the children were granted every whim—even the passing, unserious ones that were mentioned one moment and forgotten the next—all Les's household cash and then some was spent to fill their rooms with the aforementioned things.

She told Gordon they would have to think about moving soon because they were outgrowing the house. She said, "We simply cannot go on living like this and you know it too. We are too much and too many for this home."

And he would answer back, "Maybe if you would curb your spending, we wouldn't have so much crap. And spoiling the kids on top of it."

Which, in turn, caused Les to pull her mouth into a line as thin and white as the scar on her ankle and fall completely silent.

When Gordon caught her ripping out the plants in their garden he demanded to know the source of her anger. And she turned to him, her eyes so disturbingly bright that it took his breath for a minute, said, "Nothing. They just want me to love them all the time."

Les was dead certain that if she ever came in contact with Gordon's girl she would know her instantly, because she was without doubt that she (the girl) would appear as a mirror image culled from Les's terrible dreams.

The moon, the mirror, the enclosed circle, the rounded curves of the female body; all completeness and self-love, Kiki writes of the *fin de siècle* painters, **forgetting that**

narcissism derives from a man who was taken with his own reflection. Kiki continues, **In her way, Les is Echo, not to Gordon, but to a world of women attracted to her husband.**

When she thought about Gordon's leaving her for someone else (a notion both possible and impossible), Les grew afraid. *If he goes,* she would announce to the empty house when the kids were at school and Gordon on the road, *I shall be left with nothing, I will almost be nothing* and it was her "nothingness" that made her cry into her bent elbow as she sat at her desk in the den figuring the household expenses; the checks and balances of their lives. Les recoiled in natural human horror at the notion of being in the void; a darkness so absolute that she would be unable to see shades of nighttime.

How had she arrived at this point? What had moved her to the midnight path with Gordon, into marriage, into worry regarding her marriage? She did not know. She only knew that she was forty-four and that number was beginning to seem as overwhelming as a sheer mountain of blue ice. It could not be climbed or melted or moved. For Les had always suffered from "age sorrow"—that is, she always seemed to be too old (and, therefore, a step behind) for her place in life. She graduated from college at twenty-four; had her first child at twenty-eight; contemplated a career when all the kids had begun school only to remind herself that being in her late thirties made that seem impractical—to begin such a life at such a time. And now she was looking at being single again in her forties and it frightened her. After all, Gordon did not want her, she thought, and he had seen her at her best; so young and untried and now, in her middle age, he might leave her. It truly seemed to her that once she became a mother, both as job and passion, she ceased to be Les at all. She could not recall the last time a man flirted with her.

That she was a very attractive woman—"good" legs, fine arms, her figure actually better than before the three kids because of her determination to win back her old body through exercise following their births—seemed lost to her. Her hair, alternately coarse with gray and still an ashy brown, was less controlled, more touchable-looking. Her eyes carried increased depth; they had seen more and turned away from as much.

But she was not twenty-four and she knew that her youth was gone and would not come again. In the quiet of her own thoughts, she really did not mind its passing but in the Real World, youth counted heavily.

And the reassurances of family and friends, even of Gordon, regarding her looks, were tiresome and lacked comfort. Of course, she reasoned, they found her pretty, but they had stopped "seeing" her years ago; for them, her exterior was being judged alongside a close knowledge of her interior. It certainly was not their fault that they could not distinguish her heart from her face. It was a simple matter of spending years and years with people, intimately. They could not see you.

That seemed to be the crux of the situation—this confusion of inside with outside—Les knew she was a wife and mother and certainly these two roles comprised a large part of her, but they did not, she felt, sum her up in a sort of social shorthand. Now that she might one day find herself "free" of Gordon, unmarried and past forty, she worried about all those strangers out there and the desire to charm at least one or two of them grew within her.

Did this make her shallow? Should she be concentrating on holding her marriage together, persuading Gordon that he did not want anyone save her? Instead, she became aware of the time she was spending thinking about the possibilities of a life without him.

A life without Gordon. She has to laugh at herself when she remembers all the separate vacations and tours and business dinners that she was too tired to attend, too bored by the prospect; Gordon more socially at ease and well known than she, anyway. Or when he said, "Why don't you take an evening for yourself?" An offer that, at the time, seemed considerate (allowing her a measure of aloneness) now took on a look of being an opportunity to do as he pleased. The difference between trust and mistrust is this: Trust says, How thoughtful to think of me in that way, while Mistrust says, You never thought of me at all.

Les mistakenly believed that the small separations in the course of their lives, due to his schedule, in part, and her disinclination to travel with him, gave strength to their marriage; allowing them to be less like a couple and more like lovers who would rediscover each other every time they came back together. But this was not the case. Collier once said to Kiki: The problem with being alone all the time is that you get used to it.

As with the Good Victorian Wife, Les stayed home and remained faithful while Gordon routinely left the house and fell from grace. She, his moral center, because he could not resist the offers of an amoral world.

Les lost belief in the white crescent on her ankle. Les loses herself in the past and wishes she had listened closer to the names of the girls whispered when Gordon was mentioned.

Sometimes, when the *fin de siècle* painters depicted a woman before the mirror, the subject would lean close to the glass, laying full lips upon the cold image, gentle in approach so as not to scare away the woman in the mirror. Sometimes the women were nude or in partial states of undress. The one thing all the women shared was that they never looked away. Their gaze was steady, fixed, unflinching; the direct look of a lover.

Only Les knows that the gaze of love can cause her to avert her eyes and that the face in her glass may not be hers at all—it could just as easily be one of Gordon's other women or Gordon himself; her own expression may cease to exist; the mirror empty of her. So, in this way, she keeps searching for Gordon's girl without truly looking for her.

Hobbies

Nora Barrie has remained stolidly single. Some people who know and like Nora find in her a decency and intelligence and good humor ("I'm cheerful," Nora says, half joking, half serious), leaving them confused as to why she is not married or otherwise attached. During college, she moved in numerous social circles, occasionally bringing one or two of her acquaintances together. Gordon and Les, for example, or Kiki and Henry. Still, in the middle of the night, when Nora awakens with pounding heart, she, too, wonders if there is something "wrong" with her.

Certainly, she dates men who appear to enjoy her cheerful company; some even confess to a little love. And then it all seems to go south. Except for a man, L., who is part of a secret in Nora's life; a hidden corner that only her mother knows.

Nora could compose a list of the men with whom she has spent time as well as a list of their correlating hobbies and professions. The reason for such cataloguing is that Nora saw each man as a book to be read; a skill to master; a teacher by whom to be taught. It was as if she truly took to heart the notion that a woman must show exceptional interest in a man (or in his interests) for him to notice her. Now she is her own walking, living history of passion. She explains it by saying, "I want them to have something they can discuss with me."

"And what do you discuss with them?" asked Kiki.

"Anything. Everything." And it was true. The more men Nora dated, the more information she gathered. Her sentimental education through love.

She did not view this tack as submersion in another; she did not see herself as secondary.

From the carpenter she learned how to build shelves, align a door and use a level. After the chef she could whip up a terrine, a crepe, a Tuscan bread salad, and a Queen of Sheba; from the stockbroker a rudimentary understanding of investment and risk; from the drug dealer a certain discretion and knowledge of weights, measures and market values; from the lighting director a sense of opera and drama. From the landscape architect a visual sense of nature, seasons and color. And so on. However, none of these relationships lasted. They were all of different duration and depth with the ending coming slowly or quickly but arriving just the same. If you were to ask any of Nora's ex-lovers about her they would tell you what a fine person she is, without question, regardless of who desired the split, that they are still in touch and most would not be averse to spending a little time in her company, but not enough time, as Nora would say. And that is her best gift: that when it was over they still liked her. One or two grew slightly protective toward her.

All this running around was fine in her twenties and most of her thirties, but when forty was upon her, she began to feel something she had not felt previously: loneliness and a certain regret. Kiki knew that her friend had really much preferred when forty had passed.

. . .

"What I truly dislike," says Nora to Kiki on the day they are meeting for lunch, "is when you are hired as a secretary but actually seem to transform into some sort of Office Wife. And it gets tricky because you are asked to do many small things but never the same things, so how can you complain if you were asked to do that thing only on a single occasion? Forgetting that all those moments add up." Nora is late due to her boss's last-minute request that she wait at her desk until his own lunch was delivered.

"It isn't only me—all the time I see men trooping into their meetings, leaving their secretaries (all women, I have to say) various instructions of what to do or say if So-and-so calls, or comes in or delivers a package. Or when to interrupt them—or when not to interrupt them—and sometimes they don't let you know at all and god knows you don't want to screw up. As if you were preparing a family vacation together. Or you see them going to meetings together or seminars or lunch and their functions are so clearly delineated. He takes care of the decisions and she manages the little details that keep the mechanism running smoothly."

"Isn't that the nature of a secretary?" asks Kiki, who has always been her own secretary at work and, in the way that working women sometimes long for a "wife," she has found herself daydreaming about an assistant who watches the same scattering stuff that Nora is going on about.

"Here's the funny part, I think. We spend years trying to determine if So-and-so is the right man for us. Do we live with him? Marry him? Break it off and cut our losses because we are only trying to make it right and if we are honest with ourselves we will see that it is all wrong?"

Nora stopped talking long enough to order a sandwich. And continued:

"Lists, Kiki, we make all sorts of mental lists. We talk to friends for hours. We spend months dating. Do we take this a step further or not? Introduce him to the family or not? What to do, what to do."

Kiki still kept the copies of Collier's, Nora's, Gen's and her own lists of desires in her desk at work. Which Bill, her co-worker, had probably read. Since Kiki had begun to disappear spontaneously, she discovered that when Bill thought she was "gone" he would simply help himself to whatever he needed in her office.

"The funny part is," Nora says, discarding the top slice of bread and flattening the lettuce in its place, "that we will end up spending significantly *less* time with him than we will with the people at work—to, for and with. And all it takes is one newspaper ad and an interview to say, Yes, we will be in your company, day in, day out, forty hours a week." The lettuce crunches as she bites into it.

"How does that relate to my secretary question?" asks Kiki, who, observing Nora, is now guiltily eating tuna salad heavy with mayonnaise.

"Who takes care of the details at home? A wife. Who takes care of them at work? A secretary. What is the difference between 'Where's my file' and 'Where are my socks'?" Nora shakes her head, smiling. Reaches across the table, snapping the pickle on Kiki's plate in half. Nora has always helped herself to Kiki's food; it is almost ritualistic within their friendship. "Both, if I am not mistaken, are generally women. I cannot explain it any better than that. Of course, maybe I have just been out there working too long and everything is beginning to blur."

Nora and Kiki have known each other since college and one of the things Kiki enjoys about Nora is that her friend can shake her head at the world and still laugh at it. Even her secretary monologue is spoken in a tone more of wonderment than of anger. Nora has been with this boss for eight years. "The longest relationship I've ever had," she jokingly tells Kiki. Her undergraduate degree in English literature and master's in French mean nothing in the workplace.

"What did you think about turning forty?" asks Kiki, midway through lunch, watching Nora watch the clock so as not to be late returning to the office. Nora is punctual by nature.

"My reaction took me by surprise. I mean, I thought I didn't give a damn—age being a relative thing and all that. Then suddenly it was approaching and, well, I guess you could say, I went a little crazy. Acted rather foolishly." Nora looks at the clock again, signals for the check. "That," she says, "caught me by surprise as well. Much better to be forty-two. Really."

"How so?" asks Kiki.

Nora stops, looks at Kiki as if she were trying to weigh out something in her own mind. Kiki thinks that her friend is preoccupied by this matter of time and lunch hours, until Nora says, "Do you remember when we were barely in touch? About two years ago?"

"I guess," answers Kiki, who has never been consistent at keeping in touch with her friends during the intervals between social engagements.

"Walk me back to the office," says Nora. "I have something to tell you."

What Nora told Kiki was the secret that previously she had shared only with her mother: the secret of Nora's marriage to L. Virtually no one knew because Nora's husband did not want anyone to know. Oh, he said he did, but deep inside, he did not. Now, this clandestine arrangement had more to do with his personality than with Nora; the point is how easily and willingly cheerful, likable Nora fell into it. L. did not want anything to do with any part of her life that had come before him. He wanted her to be the tabula rasa girl of his dreams, despite her being forty; that he was powerless to alter her sexual history nagged at him but he kept his irritation hidden during their courtship. Though Nora was not one to discuss past loves with current loves—it was too indiscreet. When the marriage began to fail, he ceased sleeping with her as if to say, *Since you were with them you cannot be with me* (these men that he imagined lived in his wife's past). *You made your choice before we met.*

Kiki says nothing. She is listening, thinking, wanting to ask a dozen questions and knowing that, if she remains quiet, Nora will eventually explain everything. This is Nora's way; she does not harbor secrets as much as she is selective in what she will and will not reveal. Not unlike her silence about her romantic past. "Nora—"

Her hands went up, open, in front of her, as if being held up. "I know, I know—How? Why? Believe me, sometimes I'm inexplicable even to myself." And her story continues:

L. owned an expensive bicycle and he purchased a second one for Nora, who was only too willing to explore this new hobby. They could often be seen riding around Los Angeles, stopping at Farmer's Market for lunch and smiling at people's surprise that they would ride at all around L.A. "Doesn't the pollution kill your lungs?" they were asked. "What about the traffic? Aren't you scared?" And Nora looked over at L. and said, "If he can do it, I can do it." L. made her feel safe.

. . .

The problem was that now Nora had time only for work and L. and cycling. She missed her other hobbies, the legacies of her men friends. She missed the men as well. When she tried to engage L. in some of her hobbies, he told her that they lacked the time for such pursuits since he had started them on a training program: They were to ride up to Oregon for their honeymoon.

"Honeymoon?" asked Nora. "Are you asking me to marry you?"

"Yes," said L. "I am."

Nora experienced conflicting feelings of relief and happiness and apprehension. All the things she thought of as "normal."

"Yes."

Nora found she had a difficult time keeping up with L. He would speed ahead, leaving her puffing up a hill or careening wildly down an incline, frightened of the momentum gained. When she complained that she was being left behind, L. criticized her workout habits, said, "If you would quit puttering around the house, fixing this and that, or gardening, or trying out new recipes, you'd have more time to work out. It is your own fault." Nora, so ready to accept the personality flaws in her men, was equally willing to overlook her own shortcomings and thought L. should, too.

Nora let go of her hobbies and concentrated on the bicycle trip. She worked out with weights, went for very long rides, welcomed each hill, ignored her fear when racing downhill, told herself it was exhilarating. Her body became toned and sleek and strongly muscled. L. became more distant. Now, having inadvertently erased the men from her past by discouraging all interests but his, though he did not know that these were inherited interests, he began to complain about her friends and family.

"I don't understand what you don't like about them," Nora would say, to which he would reply, "I don't understand what you like about them." Nora thinking just how little she had seen of Kiki recently, or anyone else for that matter. And then L. set about pointing out her friends' weak qualities as he acted with friendship toward Nora. She became confused and questioned her own judgment of people, except for L. At times, she disagreed absolutely with L., but somewhere along the line he had grown stronger than she and eventually she kept her objections to herself.

In a final attempt to please this difficult man, Nora married him at city hall, where he did not smile and actually acted as if she had railroaded him into this situation.

What Nora told Kiki about her romantic past is that she began to see that in each instance, as she molded herself more to her loved one's life, he turned just a little bit colder, as she, Nora, disappeared piece by piece.

Disappeared piece by piece, Kiki repeated to herself.

Nora could only prop her chin in her hand, sigh loudly and wonder what in her female education had encouraged her to take a less active role in romance and she laughed when she saw what it had gotten her. Because it had, finally, gotten her L. And, she added, happy wasn't part of it.

At work, she was an Office Wife, seeing to details, running her boss's professional life until the evenings when she would hand off detail duty to his real wife. And what if he was fired? Or transferred? Or demoted? Wonders that her fate is so tied in with his and, suddenly, she is so tired out by all these roles that she thought were the correct ones to play. And how she hates them all.

Kiki asks Nora, "Why did you marry him?" They have stopped in front of Nora's office building.

"I honestly don't know. I guess I was scared because boys were starting to call me *ma'am* and my mother started staring back at me in the mirror and I hated my boring job and I knew I needed to change something but I could not figure out what that thing was. It is so dangerous to reach that point; you feel as if you'll say yes to anything and nothing your brain tells you will prevent it. So, I thought, 'I'll get married.' It all sounds so silly when I tell you that I thought it would change things."

"Did it?" asks Kiki.

Nora laughs. "Actually, yes, it did. L. seemed to dislike me. The more I did what he wanted, the more he wanted me to do until there was nothing left—for me to do or *of* me. I looked back and tried to figure out how I got there. I felt I was disappearing."

Kiki, without looking down, can sense that her feet are fading and the pavement is visible from beneath her shoes. She thinks, There are so many ways not to exist, and it seemed a number of them belonged to women. Was it their own fault? Surely no one forces Nora to immerse herself in a man; no one forced her to marry L. Or was it society at large? A world in which a woman's age can assume a strange proportion and move that woman to behave in inexplicable ways. She'd have to think about this.

Kiki turns to Nora, wants to tell her that she missed her during that year and is so happy to have her back; instead she says, "What did you do?"

"I walked," says Nora.

To walk is to act.

Language

(For $400) Ex-Voto: An object presented at a shrine as a votive offering. A *milagro* is a small metal or silver charm often depicting a part of the body: hand, face, leg, torso or an internal organ such as heart or lungs or kidneys. It is used in prayer when one needs something seen to; fixed, healed. Something that is damaged or failing.

Women in all countries, of all classes, are often seen wearing a variety of heart jewelry: in their ears, on their wrists, circling a throat, on fingers, around ankles. (Recall that Gen herself wears a gold anklet of interlocked engraved hearts. *Gen & Walt 2/14/52.*) In silver, gold, diamond, brilliant gems of all colors and pearl. Women drawn to the cordate shape and men offering up these various *milagros* as symbols of devotion. Tokens of the most elemental guileless adoration. This most sacred organ, as hope and promise; these ladies with their *milagros* that pass as ornamentation.

Does this fall under the heading of *Ex-Voto*? "An object presented at a shrine"? Does he worship you? Does he tell you that he cannot see anyone else but you? That he loves you as he loves no other? Are you his reason for being? Is his offering in sapphires and rubies, emeralds, turquoise or glass? Do you reach with your small hand for the charm, this heart, passed from him to you, in the belief that it will protect you from loss of love?

Or is this the last thing on your mind?

Gin #1

Henry, Kiki's friend and past romance, shuffles the cards and fans them across the table croupier-style. He is saying, "It was like she flew from my hands."

He is in the midst of a story called *Vacation with My Girl.*

Kiki concentrates on her cards as he speaks, notes the possibilities for gin, tries to decide what card should go into the discard pile. She hesitates, thinks, Maybe this card will serve me well later. I should hold on to it. Then reminds herself that since it is a lone card, complementing no others in her hand, it would be a sentimental and wishful choice to hope that more of the same suit will come along, revealing its bit of luck to her. Letting go, on many levels, is not Kiki's strength.

Henry, in his kindness, is aware of his partner's strategy and usually does not use it to his advantage. Sometimes, though, he grows impatient and pits it against her because some evenings he cares more about the game they play; more about winning.

They each know that he is here tonight because Kiki called, out of sorts. And when he arrived with expensive fresh peaches, which looked better than they tasted, she only said, "Please tell me a story. It can be about me, but me disguised. Or it can be about you. My only request, my single desire, is that it sound like a, you know, *tale.*"

"Let me think of an opening line," says Henry. "Give me a minute."

Kiki loves the sound of Henry's voice; the shape it takes in her own heart, fusing with her. As with numerous lovers, Henry and Kiki early on spoke in coded language. In fact, she occasionally wonders if her *Language* categories are not just an excuse to experiment with elaborate shrouded words of love; either creating a code or breaking it.

And so stories—read, repeated, invented—figured into their affair and remained once the affair diminished. She thinks, I cannot decide if he sounds more or less like himself when he relates a tale, yet she has always loved the way Henry tells a story. She can wrap herself in the warmth of his voice; listen to the words and let her mind wander.

She starts to ask him if he notices anything different about her, but refrains. "I need to put it all in order," she says finally.

"What, exactly?"

"I'm not sure."

Since Henry, too, without saying anything to Kiki, needs to sort something out himself, he continues, "So," says Henry, "shall I tell you about you, then?"

"No names, please."

"That's right. 'A tale' you said. How about a roman à clef? *'Vacation with My Girl.'* "

Kiki smiles. "Nothing too fancy."

He catches her gaze across the table and holds it, matching her smile. "You are very strange, Kiki Shaw."

"Stick around," says Kiki, "I may get stranger."

And so he begins as he plays his cards. "It was like she flew from my hands."

. . .

"We went to one of those fancy resorts—you know the type of place—surrounded by honeymooners and couples trying to rekindle something. I don't know why we were there except that we had promised ourselves a Real Vacation and not one of those trips that involve a lot of work. You know, traveling from place to place, searching out new lodgings each night, getting lost, misreading our maps, if we were fortunate enough to have one once we got to town. Fighting occasionally because of the tension that accompanies the newness that confronted and confounded us each day.

"And it's funny—the strangeness of each place, every day—I mean, there are days when you want exactly that and to follow where it leads; other days when you are too tired and crave only the familiar.

"Well, that was us, amid the newlyweds and silent couples, but I have to say that we were truly unto ourselves. It can be like that, you know, two people strongly connected. It can be just that powerful."

Kiki can almost see the images on her cards through her opaque thumb, which holds her gin hand. "Do you mind if I smoke a cigarette?"

"I thought you gave that up."

"I did," she says, flexing her thumb. "It came back."

Henry sighs. Kiki knows he hates her smoking, no matter how infrequent. But she also knows that he will not bother her about it; he understands that she is troubled.

He continues, "My girl"—he stops, looks at Kiki, who says, "Okay"—"had a pleasing figure, fine I thought it was; however"—he arranges his cards—"she did not agree. As usual. She used to say, 'I'm just so uncomfortable in my own body,' which always cracked me up because it presupposes she had other bodies with which to compare this feeling. As if she were only *recently* inhabiting this one. So, basically"—he discards—"I found her beautiful."

Kiki smiles at the body remarks. Says, "But that did not mean she was." Throws down a card.

Henry looks at her squarely. "Yes," he says, "it does."

"Right. Continue."

"We had flown into different time zones that altered our sleeping patterns, making us feel even more isolated: chocolate cake for breakfast, dinner in the middle of the night, rousing ourselves out of bed at any old hour."

"I rather like that myself," says Kiki. "That strange sort of timelessness. It makes life very still."

"Yes. Anyway, the sun was hot in this tropical place and the water bluer than any we had ever seen at home. And warm. Well, you know how icy the Pacific can be in California; it changes when you move to the tropics. It is clear and pleasant and so clean."

"I thought there were about only two places left in the world that weren't polluted," says Kiki. "Gin, by the way."

"I meant that *seemed* clean. A nice illusion if you can get it, I guess."

Ah, Dr. Tarbell and his nicely dressed illusions, thinks Kiki, in time to glance down at her cat rubbing against her leg, then passing through it to loving the chair leg and, as her leg solidified, feels the fur once again.

"Look," says Henry, putting down the pencil he uses to keep score, "the point I am making, rather, the reason I am remembering this—"

"Did you argue?" asks Kiki.

"No, no, I don't think we—"

"You were happy together then?"

"Very."

"And in love? And she was beautiful?"

"There was no one else for me. At that moment, in that uninteresting resort, in that tropical place, with its ceiling of a million nighttime stars and flower-sweet breeze."

"Gin," says Kiki, smiling. "Again."

Henry is tallying points. "As I was saying, it must have been two A.M.—"

"Were there other people at this hotel? Did you make up stories about them?"

"You know we did. We were storytellers."

They are quiet as they play the next hand, until, "Before I gin," says Henry, "I want to finish telling you what I set out to tell you."

"I'd much rather hear about some of the people you met. Like the androgynous couple who seemed to constantly be swapping gender identities."

"I don't think so," says Henry. "I think you want to hear about my girl."

"Perhaps you are right."

Henry holds up his hand for silence, his lips moving as he records the points with dollar signs in the very full, frayed, blue-lined notebook that they had been keeping for years.

"I think you owe me something like twelve hundred dollars," says Kiki.

"No," corrects Henry, "you owe me."

Kiki establishes serious debt when she is sad.

Henry continues. "It was two A.M., but roughly afternoon by our own real-life schedules, hot and fragrant and starfilled and moonfilled and flowerfilled and we decided to go for a swim. She agreed because, well, it was dark and she had that body thing that I mentioned—her pretty figure, white and pale and showing itself only to the moon. We were in the water of the hotel's swimming pool. One of those weird affairs with a bar in the middle of it and waterfalls and a slide made to look like natural rock. And this is what I did." Henry lays his cards face-down in front of him, turns his palms up, touching the sides of his hands, flush. Then, "She stood on my hands, facing me."

Kiki imagines this shy girl standing shakily on Henry's open hands, balancing, with her own hands on Henry's shoulders. Henry's girl, whose beauty is proclaimed, by Henry, as a fact.

"She arched her back, arms above her head, throat curved and executed a back flip. I lifted my hands at the correct moment to allow her more lift. And it was perfect, awkward; my girl entering the water with a great deal of noise.

"When she rose from the water, she cried, 'Again!' Soon, we could be found by anyone wandering out pool-side—me, standing in the water and she flipping backward off my palms, over and over, until she was a circle of pale moon-hued skin. Almost like those tigers that churned themselves into butter, only I was reminded more of spun silver. We continued in that way until the other side of three A.M. and I found myself thrilled and exhausted. Much like love in a very general respect, of course.

"So you can see why I know her beauty was true. I mean, who could not be made beautiful by the circle of her own body in the moonlight, in a tropical place where she neither fit nor belonged, with all those honeymooners and couples trying so hard to renew old emotions?"

"Was that the time you loved her most?" asks Kiki.

"No, I always loved her 'most,' " says Henry.

"Do you really believe that?" asks Kiki.

"Do you?" asks Henry.

The Past

Collier Grey used to live in Gordon's past until circumstances brought them again into contact; only now things were quite different for them since they are much older and Gordon had, during the interim, married a woman named Les.

Recently, Gen had said to Collier when told that, no, Collier was not "seeing" anyone, "I just can't imagine that. You're such a wonderful girl"—this girl of forty—"I would think any man would want you!" Collier smiled her pretty smile and mumbled something about "my generation," as if a generation were another country with its own attendant customs and clues, and how things had changed since Gen's youth. With Gen replying, "You know what you are, Collier? An unclaimed treasure. That's all."

She halfheartedly dates various men, sometimes boys, some who love her and others who like her company but without any sort of urgency, as well as Gordon, who used to love her and tells her that he still feels for her. This is the romantic summation of her rather disconnected life. She says the balance of these men is good and bad for her, when, actually "good" and "bad" are embodied in one man, Gordon, who calls her when his wife is absent.

"For example," Collier says, "he calls me on Wednesday when he goes to that one rehearsal hall downtown and his wife drops him off and picks him up."

Then she says, "I never hear from him on Mondays, so she could be an Italian chef."

"How's that?" asks Kiki.

"Italian restaurants seem to traditionally be closed on Mondays. As I said, he does not call me when she's around. Of course," she smiles, "I don't hear from him on Fridays either, so she could be a rabbi."

"If Gordon drops out of sight for the summer she could be a schoolteacher," Kiki says, understanding this game of knowing as little as possible about The Wife. Collier believes the less she knows, the better it is. No contact, no asking what she looks like or acts like or how she thinks or what she does for a living. Collier, flexible in some areas of her life and diligent in her work, adheres to this fairly complex, immutable code as a means to "save" herself; as if anyone can truly save herself.

Kiki has known Gordon almost as long as Collier has; remembers him years ago, in the course of their college years. She does not tell Collier that Nora Barrie knows his wife. They are all so loosely linked—Kiki to Henry to Collier to Gordon to Les to Nora to Kiki, a great, sparkling circle. What Kiki recalls is the time before this reacquaintance of Gordon and Collier, when their romance was paramount in their lives. It took precedence over everything and displayed itself with alarming fits of love and anger, these willful, strong emotions that were new and Collier and Gordon went at each other with all the carelessness of fighters in a ring. Never dreaming that any sort of injury would be permanent.

When Gordon left Collier that first time, in their early twenties, and ended up marrying Les shortly after, Collier said, "I've lived so long with my gloves held high to protect myself, then I lowered my hands. And was sucker-punched." She shook her head in wonder; this girl who later in life rejected knowledge of Gordon's wife in an attempt to spare herself. Collier thought, We gave each other our youth. We were together for years; adored each other and were faithless and made the mistake of believing that surviving such things renders love stronger, the two of us more powerfully joined, when all it did was diminish what we had.

"Oh, I can't imagine him with a schoolteacher," says Collier.

"Frankly," says Kiki, "I can't imagine him with anyone but you."

"I know her name," says Collier and Kiki is still.

"You finally asked Gordon?" asks Kiki, knowing Collier's Rules of Apartness.

"No, I wouldn't do that. But I believe it is Ella. I dreamed it. One night, Gordon was there and I was there and his wife was there, in my sleep. I dreamed it."

Gordon first noticed Collier Grey in his high school music class; bored, his attention often wandered and one day it set upon Collier. He liked her walk, which he classified as young-girl sexy, though he would not have put it that way at the time because, after all, he was a young man himself and did not think in terms of young girl as opposed to mature woman, sexy or otherwise. He was too full of his own youth. This distinction became apparent much later in his life. The way she threw her shoulders back and turned out her toes gave her a sort of balletic duck walk. Her body was in flux; girlish and grown; breast, waist, hips and backside, all unsettled. All of which was unconscious, this connection to Collier's body. All of which made her more compelling. He liked to watch her approach the piano, arrange her shoulders, squint at the music, her hands really somewhat short-fingered for a graceful reach.

They ended up together, with their similar musical tastes and the same heavy ash-brown hair, enormous smiles. People began to mistake them for siblings. His build straight and slender; hers curved with all that entails.

The sibling thing only added to their attraction for each other.

Gordon played classical piano and toured and was becoming known; Collier wanted to play piano. Now a curious thing happened years later, after Gordon married Les: Collier found herself in a restaurant, meeting the parents of a fellow she was currently dating, answering questions about herself. The parents asked, "What are your hobbies, your interests, your ambitions?"

She did not yet have the production company, was still drifting, weightless in her twenties. She answered, "I used to play classical piano and I was quite good." Then caught herself, forgetting for just the smallest moment that it was Gordon who was the pianist, not she.

In silence, she stopped and wondered if the people at the table noticed the violent internal reaction she was experiencing; turning cold, icy cold, then flushed and trembling, so certain that she trembled at this horrible minute when she forgot where Gordon left off and she began—even then, years apart and estranged. Curious if this was only some sort of weird aftershock of affection and intimacy or if her love for him was as active as ever.

It all happened very quickly, with the sequences of emotion firing off like a string of firecrackers. Satisfied that no one saw anything unusual in her face, having only just met her they really had nothing to compare it to, she finished by saying, "But then I gave it up."

Photography: Snapshots

"Here," says Henry to Kiki one night over cards. "I have a picture of her."

"God," says Kiki, "do we have to do this?"

"I want you to see my girl."

Kiki, at her desk, types:

Roland Barthes says that the photograph "reproduces to infinity what has only occurred once: the photograph mechanically repeats what could never be repeated existentially." He also says, "Cameras are clocks for seeing."

One of the first photographs ever taken is called *Two Views of the Boulevard du Temple, Paris, Taken the Same Day, ca. 1838* by Louis-Jacques-Mandé Daguerre. In this picture one can see the streets, the buildings, anything that is stationary because of the extremely long exposure time. Anything moving is not impressed. For example, evident are a man's feet and legs though

the body is entirely absent. His body was in subtle motion while his legs and feet were still, due to having his boots polished. Stillness can preserve an image, while activity causes it to disappear.

This interests Kiki, who experiences a pang of familiarity at the picture of the partially absent figure. Briefly, she turns from her work, places her fingers to the bridge of her nose. Eyes closed.

As the photograph that Kiki likes is, in a rough sense, a "clock for seeing," so might Collier's interest be piqued by Barthes's notion of image reproduction in light of the reprise of her affair with Gordon. It occurred once when they were quite young and is recurring in middle age. However, one could quibble, since the "reproduction" is not exact. There is, after all, Les, Gordon's wife, to take into consideration.

When Kiki first knew Henry he used to ask her, Why do you love me? This question bothered her because she did not know how to answer it. Certainly, it is one of life's mysteries as to *why* we love this person and not that person. It is possible to list all the things that are "better" or "worse" about someone with the balance weighing heavily on the "worse" side and still love him. If we could talk about love without involving the heart but only the mind, we might see clearly for the first time; but who has the will or desire to separate mind and heart; who really wants to understand the logic behind the attraction?

Kiki did not want to analyze it; she simply loved him; as if attachment just *existed,* the sole fact of her life that did not beg for scrutiny. She tried to shrug it off when Henry asked. She did not wish to break the spell of romance.

However, Henry was a practical fellow and needed answers.

So she countered by saying, Why do you think I do?

I really don't know, he said conversationally. I'm not all that special.

Kiki wondered, Do only "special" people find themselves deserving of love?

Think about it, Henry continued. Think objectively about *me;* not who you think I am, but who I *am.*

Kiki fell silent. How does one go about objectivity in matters such as this? Now, if she lists his fine qualities (one of which had to do with kindness, another with his quirky ambition), he will shake his head, say, No, you have only invented these qualities and hung them on me like a coat on a hanger.

(Not long after a conversation along this line, Henry mailed her a card. It was a photograph of two coats—a man's and a woman's—hanging side by side in a closet, wrapped in each other's embrace.)

When Gordon calls he says, Miss me like crazy? as a form of greeting to Collier. Depending on her mood, this salutation either pleases or irritates the hell out of her. It just depends.

"Miss me like crazy?" asks Gordon, then, "I'm performing downtown next week and I'd like you to come hear me." Collier hesitates and he takes her hesitation to mean yes, so he says, "Can you come by and pick me up?"

"I don't know," says Collier, slowly, trying to recall her schedule: meetings, shoot, overtime.

"I'd like for you to be there."

And Collier is not sure he means to pick him up before at the concert. Somehow, she is set to meet him at the home he shares with Les. (Or, Crazy Les as he has taken to calling her since her recent behavior—the plants, the laundry, the trash.)

"Come with me," says Collier to Kiki.

"You're on your own with this one," says Kiki.

"Don't make me beg," says Collier.

But Kiki can only shake her head no.

In truth, Kiki is curious about Les even if Collier claims not to be. Without telling Collier, Kiki has asked Nora about Les: What is she like?

"I've always liked her," said Nora.

"You like everybody," said Kiki.

"No. It is usually the ones I don't know very well that I like." Nora lightly punches her friend's arm.

The question, of course, paramount in Kiki's mind is: Does Les know about Gordon's Other Life? She cannot ask it because it would mean revealing Collier and that she cannot do. So instead she asks, "Are they happily married?"

Nora laughs, reaches into Kiki's refrigerator for a beer. "We are talking about *our* Gordon, right?" Then, "How is Collier these days?" Kiki lets it all drop, not knowing if Nora is referring to the past or the present.

In this way, Collier finally learns the name of Gordon's wife, which is Les, not Ella. As she enters Gordon's house it crosses her mind that there may be other women in attendance at the concert who are also involved with Gordon. It would, Collier thinks, be very much like him. Sure, she tells herself, he says he loves me, but coming from a faithless man, what does that mean?

The first thing Collier notices is the barrage of glow-in-the-dark stars flung about the ceiling and walls in the entry hall. Collier, it must be said, is caught off guard by the presence of the stars; she has hundreds of them pasted all over the walls and ceiling of her own apartment. Recalling Gordon's pleasure when she turns off the lights allowing them to reflect in the dark, as Gordon lies beside her, she feels a woman's hand on her arm.

Startled, Collier turns toward Les, who, noticing Collier's interest in the stars, says, "Oh, these. Look," and shuts off the lights. In the dark, Les says, "Gordon's idea. What can I say?" She flips the switch back on, extends her hand to Collier, introduces herself. "I'm Les. You must be Collier." Calls for Gordon to "Come down. Collier's here."

Neither woman can take her eyes off the other. Collier senses a vague sort of recognition in Les's face; as if she can almost, but not quite, place her. Had they crossed paths in college all those years ago? Then Collier notices that Les and she could almost pass for family: similar height, build, coloring, but not exact, not twins. They look, instead, related to each other. It is Collier who breaks the eye contact. "Les," she says, gently balancing the sound of her name on her tongue. And still she cannot remember. "I feel—" she begins.

"—as if I know you," finishes Les.

Les looks as if she were about to say something more with a glance that does not back down. And then it is gone, the scrutiny, replaced by the gracious hostess whose task it is to make her guest comfortable. Collier wants to shake Les. *Why don't you just say it?* Maybe she doesn't know. And Collier is not sure what has just taken place except that maybe Gordon is right, that this is one of Crazy Les's moods; all darkness and light.

As Collier stands with Gordon's wife, stargazing, she is struck by the unwholesomeness of the affair. No matter that she was first in his life; he is with Les now. This hallway with its confrontation of stars, the unmistakable evidence of her, Collier, echoes of her own home within his home, permanently affixed to the walls, in this place that partly belongs to the woman next to her. It is all she can do to hold back from weeping.

As she watches Gordon come down the stairs all she can repeat in her own mind is *I'm sorry, I'm sorry* and it is only when they are on their way that Collier realizes that she did not say good-bye to Les.

At the concert, as Collier scans the crowd before the show, she is astonished to see Les, sitting toward the front. Wonders if she should say hello or offer to keep her company except that it strikes Collier that Les may not want anyone's companionship; that actually "alone" seems to be a highly natural and comfortable state for Les.

After the concert is a get-together at a local restaurant. Collier sees a few people she knows—a video director, a couple of record company people—no Les. When Gordon asks Collier why she did not come backstage, she replies, "Les was there."

"I'm not surprised," he says.

"I'm not going to the party," says Collier. "Enough is enough for one evening."

"Why not? It's not as if she'll be there."

"How do you know?" says Collier, who cannot believe his lack of surprise at Les's random arrivals and departures. Whose appearance at the concert, unexpectedly, has unnerved Collier.

"Because I know my wife," he says, pulling the inside of Collier's wrist up to his mouth. She is taken aback by this admission of intimacy and all she wants to do is get to the bar; where she begins knocking back Kahlúa and creams, white Russians, Ramos fizzes, whatever sweet drinks the bartender makes up. She experiences her usual love vertigo as she subconsciously awaits Les's unannounced presence.

A professional photographer, who had sent her his book recently, looking to "get into video," roams around snapping pictures of the guests. Collier, a little warm from the alcohol, enthusiastically flirts with him, and patiently allows him to take a number of pictures as he talks her up: She is sitting alone by an open window; chatting animatedly with Gordon's best friend; laughing with her fingers to the bridge of her nose; Collier having another drink.

Gordon calls Collier a week later, asks, "Did you see today's paper?"

"Which section?" she asks.

"The party page," he tells her. "You looked like you were having so much fun that, compared to the other guests, it was as though you were at a completely different party."

All she can think about is Les's seeing it, though clearly there is "nothing" to see; she does not even appear next to Gordon. Still she asks, "Did Les see it?"

"Yes," he says. "She said, 'Oh, there's your little friend.' "

. . .

"She called me Gordon's 'little friend,' " Collier explains to Kiki as they eat sandwiches while sitting on the foundation that is part of the ruins of a Hollywood mansion which had once been in the possession of some Golden Era star. Also on the grounds is an empty, unusable swimming pool, cracked and overgrown with weeds. It is secluded and peaceful and the people who come up here, to make out (nighttime) or smoke a little pot (daytime), generally have a respect for privacy. "I wish that guy hadn't taken my picture. It is as bad as those goddamn stars in Gordon's hallway." Collier is breaking apart pieces of her sandwich and flinging them to the greedy birds that have gathered near them.

It is true, thinks Kiki; Collier has entered into Gordon and Les's shared life. It is an odd flipping of appearance and disappearance: Collier is imprinted, a memory due to the photographs on the night of Gordon's concert. As his mistress, she is meant to be socially invisible. Les, on the other hand, is not in any picture, but is always acknowledged as his wife; even if she attends the concert but refuses the party, she remains visible, known.

"I want to tell Gordon that I can no longer see him," says Collier.

"Why don't you then?" asks Kiki. Funny, that phrase, *I can no longer see you,* as if sight has everything to do with love. As if we cannot control how we behave in regard to what we see and can dismiss temptation only if it is not set before us. As if we were enslaved by our own vision.

Collier looks down at her hands, throws the remainder of her lunch into the wreckage of the swimming pool. "Because I cannot," she whispers. Then, after a moment, "Because in some remote, unreachable place inside of me, I don't want to." To herself she wonders if she and

Gordon would still be friends, then thinks better of it. There are times when she does not think he is much of a friend to her now; moments when she is not certain she even likes him. Doesn't like him, still loves him, hates it when he calls and says *Miss me like crazy? When can I see you?* Or, *I can't get away next week owing to my peculiar set of circumstances* (meaning his marriage). Or, *I can't see you because of my strange situation* (meaning his marriage).

"Well," says Kiki, "if you can't, you can't."

"And, you know, there's love and history involved," says Collier. She knows that she keeps seeing him because she cannot shake off the past; she is afraid to say good-bye to the young girl she was once, who captivated Gordon with her walk and their physical resemblance. Her early self coolly assessed the road before her with an even, expectant gaze, while the Collier of today, the woman who falls prey to nostalgia at the sound of Gordon's voice (not the Collier who successfully and competently runs her own company), is more like a confused person perched on a shabby suitcase by the side of the road, hoping like hell that a bus passes by here or a car that might stop.

She stays because Gordon tells her, You are still the prettiest girl I know. You turn heads.

The women rise, brush crumbs from the front of their clothing. Kiki saying, "Look, I think you should do whatever makes you happy," and Collier answering, laughing a sad little sound, "I don't think anything to do with Gordon makes me happy—" when she stops speaking, watching in the distance.

Kiki turns to see Gordon approaching them. As he draws near, he breaks into a waltz, his invisible partner reclining in his arms. Collier shakes her head, laughs, the sadness of a moment before erased. "That nut," she says as she moves slowly toward Gordon, through the ruinous landscape. When she reaches him, he spins her once in his embrace, then lifts her off the ground, still twirling, around and around and around.

Beds & Sleep

Women, it seems, like sleeping more than men do. And eating. Because sleeping and eating are so pleasurable, sensual, it is no surprise that these preferred activities are often accompanied by guilt. Strange to think of eating and sleeping being a point at which necessity and indulgence freely cross.

Dreaming is the best component of sleep since one can force action and fall helpless at once. Sometimes, it seems that dreams are laced with waking life and not the other way around.

Collier, so taken by its beauty, spent nearly three thousand dollars on a double bed, cherry wood with carved roses and inlaid mother-of-pearl. Since she then needed to purchase a mattress and box spring, she found herself spending three hours one day lying on mattress after mattress in a department store. She was there so long that she became quite friendly with the salesman, Gerard (grandfather to four children, ages twelve to four; married thirty-six years to Rosie, love of his life; vacations only in tropical places; drives an imported car, five years old and never a minute's trouble; had another career in a less prosperous country, import/export, "Perhaps you've seen sandalwood screens here and there? Painted pottery with whales and saints on the sides? Cinnabar bracelets? Boxes of soapstone? Well, that was more or less my line''; his neighborhood is not what it used to be; he doesn't understand the kids today).

Collier stretches her body across these many beds, imagining dreaming upon them, when Gerard finally says, "Look, you have thirty days to decide. So buy it; if you don't like it, send it back."

"I worry about long-term comfort," says Collier.

"But you are so young. You shouldn't be thinking about anything long-term," he says.

"If it's too soft, I feel as though I haven't slept," she tells him.

Gerard gives her a tolerant look, as if to say, I see this all the time and generally it is from young women like yourself—only he would never say this. Instead, he goes to his desk and returns with one of those cutaway mattress and box spring pieces, allowing the buyer to view the construction of his bed. He says, "Listen, spend a little more and I think you'll be happy."

"I need to think about it," she replies. "Is there an ice cream store nearby? Or a café?" She always punctuates large purchases with a pause for ice cream.

When Collier returns, she finds a young man looking at mattresses. He does not sit or lie upon them, as Collier did, only runs his hand along the foot. Nods seriously as Gerard enumerates the benefits of each model and make. Gerard catches Collier's eye, says, I'll be with you in a moment.

Collier, however, approaches the young man and asks him to lie down on the three mattresses she is considering. Because she has taken him by surprise, the young man acquiesces and soon they are lying side by side. "This one, I think," she says.

"I'm not sure," the young man tells her, "but I think the other one is firmer. That is what you wanted, right? Something with little give?"

"No," she says, "I think this is the one I want."

The young man shrugs his shoulders, says, "It's your bed." Gerard smiles.

Then, at the last minute, after Collier has decided and the young man is walking away, she tells Gerard to please write up the other one. "I can send it back if it isn't right?"

"That's what I told you." Gerard sighs.

Collier buys white cotton sheets and comforters for her new bed, bringing the cost even higher; she shrugs, What the hell. Imagines Gordon stopping by and burying himself in the luxury of the linens, only to discover she does not want him touching any of it. She wants these things that she has decided upon clean of Gordon's touch. Why can't he be more like the young man who helped her with the bed? Or like me, she thinks, a little taken with her final decisions, even if it is just bed frame, mattress and linens.

She resists the impulse to track down the young man, who must still be elsewhere in the store; surely, he is not like Gordon: involved, not involved, in love, not in love and dangerous with indecision. He seemed a decisive young man.

Naturally, Collier does not want this stranger, who, in truth, appeared a bit annoyed by the mattress testing, not charmed. Collier wonders if it is because she is not as young as he is. She does not know. He could be crazy. Or mean. Or mean and crazy. She's a little mean and crazy herself sometimes.

Or maybe she wants somebody new so she can be somebody new. The lust to reinvent herself is strong, fueled by her affection for movies and always wanting to be the latest character she has seen and liked. If she could begin again, she knows, everything would be different. Better, of course. Since she cannot (it is impractical), the only thing to do is to drop her current friends and make new ones.

Would she miss the old ones? If she were someone else, would her new persona miss her old persona's friends?

She sighs as she hands Gerard her credit card and suddenly cannot wait to get back to the office, to the new project she is putting together. Maybe she's fine and it is simply Gordon she no longer wants.

Gin #2

"How I met her is pretty unremarkable; that is, not a great story except that it preceded the story of us." It was Henry's turn to deal and he had brought some new cards, which were slippery and shiny and bore reproductions of famous paintings portraying lovers. "So," he says, "I'll tell you another meeting instead.

"A woman was seeing a friend of mine, my best friend, only he was living with someone. This was when we were all in college. I mean, she knew about it and it did not make her happy because she was thoroughly convinced that she was in love with this man. Actually, he wasn't really living with someone but he was one of these guys who invent a girlfriend or wife in order to gather some distance for themselves. You know? Even so, he was not seeing her exclusively—that much is true. He still had other women here and there; no one he was serious about, and he liked this woman better than the others, but not enough to hold on to her."

"Didn't she catch on that he lived alone?" asks Kiki.

"He was pretty convincing—never inviting her to his apartment; giving her a work number; keeping a low profile; every once in a while acting as if he were dying of love for her but, well, there was Someone in the Way. And since she had no other explanation for the lack of time together during holidays or entire weekends, no long vacations and all the rest, she, more or less, bought the story."

"Did she have a problem with his 'live-in' after a while?" asks Kiki.

"Sure. Guilt. Although she may have sensed the truth because instead of letting go she pushed a little harder and he kept coming back around, so perhaps she guessed something was amiss."

"Why would she want a man who played so fast and loose with the truth?"

"You might as well ask why do we want the people we want?" says Henry.

"I see."

"He was a little older, a grad student. And this girl was great—the best one he ever had, in my time of knowing him."

"Was she smart?" Kiki then smiled. "Oh, bad question since she couldn't figure this guy out."

"She was very smart. But smart had little to do with it. I mean, a person can be brilliant and it still won't rescue her from believing what she wants to believe and so it was with her. Did I mention that I actually met her through a mutual friend before I realized that she was his girlfriend? Nora did not tell me her last name, and so I wanted to see her again until we discovered that we had another mutual friend—my best friend. And all I could think about was why couldn't he be a better person. Just once in a while."

"Why didn't you say something? To him or to her?"

"She was dreaming her dream and the more I liked her, the more I wanted my friend to keep seeing her because she was bound to discover the truth—on her own—and when she did, I knew it would end for good. No going back; no nostalgia; no romanticizing what might have been, what could still be. I liked that about her, actually. Even though I one day found myself on the receiving end of it."

"You liked her ability to end an affair?"

"Exactly. It is a rare quality and very powerful."

"So," says Kiki, "this girl is dreaming her dream—"

"—and one day she wakes up." Henry shuffles the cards.

"Are you there?"

"Oh, no. Not yet. I don't want to intrude. But it's killing me because I am the impatient sort"—he smiles at Kiki, who smiles back, knowingly—"and I want to know her."

"You could've been her confidant. You are quite good at that."

"No. I wouldn't do it because I don't want to listen to her talking about my friend—no one really wants to hear about past love. They say they do; we are a confessional culture; we say, We care, we will be different from the last one, oh, if you will just tell me what went wrong with the last one, I won't hurt you like that. I personally hate it. It makes me uncomfortable and when someone is telling you these things—about failed love—you find yourself looking into a heart that is closed. Not like later, when she is interested in *you* and you find yourself at the edge, gazing into a heart that is open. And, well, I wanted this girl's open heart."

"So you could fall into it?"

"Yes."

"Wait a minute. I think I saw this movie. Or maybe I read the book." Kiki narrows her eyes with mock suspicion. "I think this plot is not new."

Henry laughs. "I told you our meeting wasn't much. I

said I would tell you a story: *The Story of How I Met My Best Friend's Girl.*"

"You are trying to confuse me," says Kiki, laying down her cards. "Did you or did you not tell me how you met? Or do you mean this as some tired plot you are repeating?"

"Ask yourself this: Is there any meeting plot I could relate, real or otherwise, that would not seem familiar? I mean, how many ways are there?"

"Millions," she says, picking up her gin hand. She glances over her cards. "You could do better."

"Okay. How about this: I was riding my bicycle and she was riding her bicycle and we collided?

"Or this: I was on the other end of a wrong number.

"Or this: During college, one of us was the professor, the other the student.

"Or this: Someone mixed up our mail.

"Or this: We watched each other from afar at the office for more than a year. Shared the same friend; showed up at the same social events until we laughed and gave in to the impulse to mate.

"Or this: Our parents were friends and we grew up together, lost touch for fifteen years, were reintroduced and went wild for each other.

"Or this: We were neighbors in a funky old building in some urban locale.

"Or this: Sat next to each other on a plane. She was terrified and began a conversation based on terror. Or, similarly, we met on a train, refugees from flying.

"Or this: We met in a class, at a meeting, at a party, in the theater, in a café, at a wake, at a wedding, in a hall, down the road, in a busy restaurant where we were asked to share the same table. Met on a submarine. Met on a blind date. Hated each other initially. Grew attached eventually."

"Okay, okay," says Kiki, laughing. "No more. I get your drift."

"What I am saying—"

"I think I know what you are saying."

"What I am saying," Henry begins again, "is that it doesn't matter how we meet; the true miracle is what follows. The recognition of self in another person, somehow—"

"Soul mate," offers Kiki.

"Soul mate," agrees Henry, "which seems to cure us of soul loneliness. The Greek notion of the other half of self. And this girl, whom I met in a very ordinary manner, because we had a mutual friend in college and because I was the best friend of her man, lifted me."

Weather

As occasionally happens in her job, Kiki receives an assignment. It is a dull category that tends to surface now and then. There are a handful of them (just as *Potpourri* is an old standby made up of the odds and ends of other categories). No one enjoys them because they do not distinguish you in any way, nor can they be made to be more than they are.

So there it was on her desk Monday morning: *Weather.*

Halfheartedly, Kiki makes notes regarding the

three types of wind systems (trade, westerlies, polar). Jots down such things as ***Dog Days*** **are warmest days of summer, which fall between July 3 and August 11, in the Northern Hemisphere. The Dog Star, Sirius, is brightest during that time. So named by the Romans who wed weather to stars. Hurricanes, tornadoes, Santa Anas, squalls, blizzards, hailstones like fistfuls of buckshot, lightning, thunder. And clouds, ten different types: cirrus, nimbostratus, cumulonimbus, altostratus, and so on.**

So it was with a great deal of relief and enthusiasm that Kiki accepted Nora's offer of lunch at the Farmer's Market ("and I am being given the rest of the afternoon off if I will stop by the Museum of Contemporary Art and pick up a book for my boss's son's school project," said Nora). They agree to meet in the parking lot and Kiki has already pretty much decided that she, too, is finished with work for the day. She'll say that she had to do some out-of-the-office research.

As she waits for Nora, Kiki leans against her car, her eyes to the sky, notes that the clouds are cirrocumulus, which is an indicator of unsettled weather.

"Sorry I am late," says Nora, startling Kiki, who was too preoccupied to be aware of her friend's approach.

"No matter—I'm not going back to work today, either."

It feels rich and privileged to have the afternoon to themselves. And the thing that strikes them—that always strikes them on days like this—are the sort of people milling about. People, they think, who either do not work or do not have to work or who have very flexible hours. Maybe artists of one kind or another. Even if the people they see are unemployed, just the fact that they can be wandering around Farmer's Market during the week in the middle of the day makes them seem, to Kiki and Nora, extravagant. Money, they always say to each other, comes and goes; time is only gone.

They settle themselves at a table, partially covered by an awning, Nora eating Chinese food while Kiki nibbles on falafel. And Kiki is telling Nora about her dull category, saying, "You can read messages in clouds, and so forth, and I find this all very uninspiring."

"Are you going to do any traveling this year?" asks Nora.

"I'm not sure I can. I wish the program would expense some employee trips. I could go to Egypt, for example, do a category about *Sand.* With my luck, I'll get assigned another one of those travel seminars, like the Scotland thing."

"I think a lot about traveling." Nora takes a bite of her meal. "All the time, lately."

"Where do you want to go?"

"Everywhere. I start to think, Will anyone miss me? If I simply leave one day."

This causes Kiki to take a closer look at her friend. She scrutinizes her movements, searches for signs of physical fading, wondering if perhaps Nora, too, is disappearing and all this talk of leaving is a way of preparing Kiki for her absence. Then it crosses her mind that maybe Nora has noticed Kiki's own recent tendency to evanesce and is trying to discuss her observations. Finally, Kiki decides, no, Nora does not notice, that this conversation is about Nora.

Before Nora can say anything more, a rather tall woman with ash-brown hair approaches their table and asks, "May I join you?"

Nora turns to glance up, then says (as she stands), "Les. Of course. Sit down." Leaving Kiki to watch the two women embrace, smile, scratch back metal chairs and arrange themselves; Kiki suddenly wishing to be anywhere else, to be anyone else or to remain Kiki but a Kiki that did not have Collier for a friend. Maybe she could just disappear, allowing her to see for the first time the advantages of her recent troubles with tangibility.

"Les, this is my friend Kiki. Kiki, Les," says Nora. As Les takes Kiki's hand to shake it she says, "Hello." Kiki has the sensation that Les means to continue speaking, only she does not. Smiles.

"Hi," says Kiki, looks away. Unfortunately, she is completely drawn and repelled by Les. She would love to openly, rudely stare. As she sits there, Kiki is in the position of wanting to participate and wishing to observe at the same time so that she might better remember Les and think this all through later, in private. And, naturally, in her mind, Kiki cannot stop comparing and referring to Collier, debating whether to tell her about this chance meeting or to pretend it never happened. If she makes the decision to relate this lunch to Collier, she will be unable to finish her meal, or to remain in Nora and Les's company any longer; it would be too unwholesome, this situation.

And Kiki is a bit unnerved by Les's open appraisal of her.

"We are taking a sort of work holiday," Nora is saying.

"I guess that is what I am doing as well," replies Les.

"What do you do?" asks Kiki, who cannot help thinking about Collier's list of possible jobs Gordon's wife could perform.

"Actually, I'm a housewife," says Les pleasantly, "but since I am out of the house, I imagine that I am away from work."

"I thought you weren't supposed to use the term 'housewife' anymore," says Nora. She turns to Kiki, "You're the culture expert. What should Les be calling herself?"

"I'm not really any sort of expert," she explains to Les. "I work for a TV game show—you know, answers and questions—"

"Oh, I love that show!" says Les. "That's right, you probably would know some title like 'domestic engineer' or whatever. Speaking for myself, you can call it anything you want but it still adds up to wife and mother. I like what I do. I never apologize."

Kiki finds herself liking Les. Wonders if that constitutes disloyalty to Collier. And suddenly she has a vision of Collier's waiting outside a closed door in a dull landscape while on the other side sits happy Les and attentive Gordon and their beautiful children. Kiki sees herself as an observing little ghost in their lives who longs to stay in this circle of family happiness but knows she will pass through the door and stand beside Collier. Kiki works out of her reverie to the realization that Les is beginning to look vaguely familiar, in that way that they could have met before, or that Les resembles someone whom Kiki knows.

College, of course, seems the logical place, since they all attended the same school, though divided by two years, but it seems more recent than that.

"Do you live around here?" asks Kiki.

"Oh, no. We're about twenty minutes from here," says Les, which causes Nora to laugh and say, "Everything and everyone in Los Angeles is 'twenty minutes' from wherever you are." Kiki recalls how Collier particularly likes this notion; Collier most comfortable with increments of time.

Les continues, "I don't know why I came to Farmer's Market today. I think I just wanted to be around many people. It has been a long time since I was here. Usually I go to Navy's, closer to home. It has pretty good food and I never feel rushed. Maybe today I wanted to feel rushed." Kiki notices Les picking at her sandwich but not actually eating it. Les looks thin and strong.

Now Kiki knows where she has seen Les—at Navy's. It was Collier's idea to go, Kiki wanted to go elsewhere but

Collier said, "Come on, we've never been there." So there they were and now, Kiki realizes, there was Les. Kiki only remembers seeing Les because she caught Collier watching her. Kiki said of the stranger at Navy's she now knows to be Les, "She looks pretty good for her age." Commenting because Collier was staring at this woman whom Kiki might not have looked at twice, except that she vaguely called up Collier herself—the ashy hair color, the build and height. Upon noting this similarity, Kiki assumed this interest in the woman had something to do with recognition of a sort.

"Think so?" asked Collier. Her voice sounded both sincere and edgy.

"Don't you?" asked Kiki.

Collier sighed. "I don't know."

Kiki is feeling angry, betrayed. Collier, she thought, understood that Kiki wanted nothing to do with Collier and Gordon and Les, that to see Gordon's wife in person would be confusing, awful, and if Collier was forced to encounter her (as on the night of the concert), then she could go it alone. Kiki would not judge her friend, but she could not aid her in all situations, either. And now it seems that Kiki was unwittingly dragged, by Collier, into the circle that included Les.

As Kiki sits at an outdoor table in Los Angeles with Nora and Les, friends who have moved onto other subjects, catching up on current events, she is stricken by her desire to disbelieve Collier's behavior (the Rules of Apartness smashed) and her necessary loyalty to her in the presence of Les. She feels the drops of rain, looks to the gathering of clouds in the sky just as Les abruptly turns to her and says, "Now I know where I have seen you before.

In college. You had that friend"—looks to Nora—"you know, I used to see you together. Sort of light-brown hair."

Kiki is silent as the rain remains light but increases in volume.

"Collier," Les says finally.

Architecture

Kiki's mother, Gen, used to throw the kids in the car and drive downtown. "I just want to see some buildings," she would say. Although Los Angeles had relatively low structures and Gen's longing for Manhattan skyscrapers was powerful. Gen had no interest in architecture aesthetically speaking but her need was pure: skyscrapers. Something not altogether easy to locate in a land rocked by earthquakes and shifting fault lines.

Sometimes, Gen raised her voice and demanded (of whom, Kiki was not sure), "Where the hell are all the buildings? How do they expect a person to live like this?"

Kiki liked the La Brea Tar Pits. They bored Gen, who said, "Big deal, a bunch of fake prehistoric animals being pulled down into some ooze."

In the years preceding the Great War, millionaires from the East Coast traveled west to build winter homes where they relaxed in the sun, entertained guests and danced with women who were not their wives. They had names like Huntington, Gamble, Wrigley, and Chandler; they were from newspaper families or pharmaceutical families or, in the case of Baldwin and Huntington, were simply referred to as "robber barons"—a label simultaneously unflattering and curiously romantic.

They purchased huge tracts of land and constructed glorious monuments to themselves and their possessions. They were men of consequence. This old money ("old" being a relative term in California) found its way to the rolling hills, the arroyo and the oak groves of a little town called Pasadena, located at the base of the San Gabriel Mountains, eight miles from Los Angeles; far enough to maintain its aloof quality and close enough for convenience.

Pasadena was a place where guests vacationed in the moneyed Green Hotel, high above the Rose Parade route; they sipped tea and played tennis at the Huntington Hotel, which had ballrooms and bungalows connected by a wooden footbridge called the Picture Bridge for its series of paintings under the roof.

There were a number of churches that leaned toward a British appearance: red brick, stained glass, dark wood vaulting and stone angels weeping in the garden.

Pasadena is the place where Mildred Pierce's faithless lover and ungrateful daughter spent their time among the snob set, conspiring against Mildred as she toiled away in her Glendale pie shop.

And it is said that one summer evening at a party in a house on Orange Grove Boulevard, Beryl Markham and Raoul Schumacher's seemingly happy marriage showed signs of strain, culminating in Raoul's assertion that he, not his aviatrix wife, wrote her famous book. What he said was, "I want you to know that Beryl did not write one word of *West with the Night,* or any of the short stories. Not one damned word of anything." Since Raoul himself was a writer, one felt compelled at least to listen.

Pasadena is also where Albert Einstein lived and taught

at Cal Tech. His house located on a tree-filled street; his office on a tree-filled campus; who said his favorite place to think was the Princeton men's room, third stall from the left.

So, in the years before The War, there was a boom in custom residential building; never before or since have there been so many homes of such pleasing style and fine quality. It was the Arts and Crafts movement and no one executed it better than the firm of Greene & Greene, two brothers, Henry Mather Greene and Charles Sumner Greene, who, like everyone else, migrated from the East. They had come to Pasadena to visit their parents and ended up staying, charmed by the landscape and all the money that was floating around. Eventually, they perfected a style known as the California bungalow, a term that in subsequent years would conjure up images of squat inexpensive housing; the sort of place that would shelter some movie star hopeful.

What interested Kiki was the cluster of Greene & Greene homes situated above the Arroyo Seco in a section known as "Little Switzerland" for its hills and deep valley. The bungalows reflecting both Swiss and Japanese influences, incorporated with a personal philosophy based on the principle that a structure must be "organic," characteristic of its environment, as if it had always been there, grown from the landscape. For themselves, the Greenes had a reputation for being slow, obstinate, costly and talented. Very talented.

When Kiki first acquired her driver's license, she would "tour" Pasadena; cutting classes, driving around discovering all those prewar homes by the Greenes, Wright,

Brown, Hunt & Grey. Trespassing, really, up someone's driveway, wandering across someone's lawn, risking discovery by the owners, Kiki thinking—if she got caught—that they would not begrudge her a glimpse of something beautiful.

When Kiki left home for college, she would return, ask for the family car and drive around Pasadena on her personal route. Even later, when she fell in love, she brought him to Pasadena, showed him house after house, discussed the merits or lack in each, until they had been in the car for hours.

All those high school and college years with her parents' never quite understanding where she went or how it was that she always returned with an empty gas tank. It sometimes made her feel akin to one of the Twelve Dancing Princesses who, night after night, mysteriously wore out their slippers until they were paper-thin.

Kiki's tours always ended at the Gamble House.

David Gamble, second generation Procter & Gamble, retired with his wife, two grown sons and maiden aunt in Pasadena in 1895, an arrangement that always called to Kiki's mind some nighttime soap opera where all the family members have more money than God but insist upon living under the same roof. Not long after that he commissioned the Greene Brothers to build them a home. The location he chose was Westmoreland Place, above the arroyo and just off the same Orange Grove Boulevard where Raoul would eventually end up denouncing Beryl.

It was walking distance from the Colorado Street Bridge, known to locals as Suicide Bridge; a Gothic, late-Victorian structure that, to date, has been the site of approximately seventy-nine suicides. As with many cities with an extremely high bridge, the true number is never revealed out of fear that when it reaches ninety-nine, people will literally begin killing themselves to be number one hundred. Kiki thought that people who killed themselves by jumping from a bridge were a different breed from other suicides; something about a human being's instinctual fear of falling, combined with flying, and the attendant notoriety, and being in a public place, and that desire to be a round number, all figured into it somehow. She even proposed a category at work called *Bridge of Sighs/Notorious Bridges,* but her boss said that it might appeal to a certain "element" that the show did not wish to court.

The Gamble House was less than a mile from Suicide Bridge, above the arroyo, in that area known as Little Switzerland, on a piece of land, eventually subdivided, with two giant eucalyptus trees that the brothers worked around.

The house is wood and stained a dark green, polished and smooth, accented by a huge front door inset with Tiffany glass depicting a sprawling California oak tree. The glass appears dense in color when viewed from the outside, but once one is inside, with the sun as backlighting, it is beautiful and brilliant. Inside, all the wood is joined by dowels; all the Tiffany light fixtures held by leather straps. The brothers designed the fixtures, rugs, furniture, masonry; the fireplaces and a few pieces of furniture inlaid with semiprecious stones, lapis and mother-of-pearl, quietly, so as not to disturb the expensive austerity of the house.

Upstairs and downstairs are numerous screened windows and porches. Kiki has never been inside when the house seemed too warm, despite the outdoor heat. Off each bedroom there are sleeping porches. On these open platforms, during hot airless Pasadena nights, the Gambles would stretch out on chaise longues and sleep with the smell of eucalyptus and honeysuckle saturating the night air.

Kiki grew up passing this house daily and visiting it with each trip to Pasadena until, as with many things one eventually comes to love deeply, each encounter charmed her more than the last. Her affection was so complete that it became impossible to visit Pasadena without driving by, getting out and walking across the grass. She liked sitting on the clinker brick wall or beside the irregularly shaped reflecting pool. It had become, this prewar house, her amulet, her talisman, her lucky star.

She supposed it embodied a number of things for her: her childhood, her sense of history, the man she loved. It was not her favorite Greene & Greene house—there is one far more grand only a few miles away—but it is the one she loved first and best. If we give nothing in our lives, we maintain a certain loyalty to that which we loved first and best; we always allow that thing a slightly magical quality because it transformed us into someone we were not before and will not return to, but now Kiki finds herself thinking of something not nearly as tangible as the house on Westmoreland Place.

So it was quite natural that Kiki should find herself parked in front of the Gamble House after saying good-bye to Nora and Les, since she was feeling fragile, afraid and wary of her own lack of substance. She walked the grounds—and was seen/not seen by a docent who mistook Kiki for a ghost—or maybe the docent had had too little sleep the night before—she cannot be certain she sees this wandering figure, strolling in broad daylight—Kiki thought about nothing, thought about this: She had once brought Henry to this house, oh, a number of years ago and he seemed to like it very much. He said, "I can clearly see the attraction," then snapped her picture.

"Can you?" she asked excitedly. "Can you see what I see?" It was important to her that he understand her affection for the place. As if we all have these tests, almost hoops, for potential lovers to pass through. Fairy tales, myths, folklore have all taught the Importance of the Task. With completion, we understand bravery and desire and the fact that these two things must always remain hand in glove. Bravery and desire and faith and love; like four corners that connect in an endless line forming a box containing a treasure.

Language

(For $600) Anamorphosis: Especially popular in the eighteenth century; it was a drawing or painting distorted or unrecognizable except when viewed from a certain angle or distance or with a correcting mirror or lens. Essentially an "artistic stunt." A face hidden in the landscape.

Most adults are introduced to anamorphosis as children when shown pictures that hide creatures and objects within a larger, unconnected scene.

In the case of Collier and Gordon there are many applications of anamorphosis:

Their affair. It is always there, ongoing but hidden; that is, Les can sense its presence and remain unable to *see* it. Friends and family, too, know that Collier is "seeing someone" yet do not know his name. Even when Collier and Gordon walk around town together, happening upon a person who knows (or knew) them, their current relationship is undisclosed. Invisible. In part because they are discreet; the larger reason for the invisibility of the affair is that no one truly wants to *know* it, or to see it. After all, Gordon is married and Collier single and there are those who do not think they should "carry on," forgetting that the majority of Americans have a rather loose interpretation of monogamy. It makes one wonder if this willful ignorance of infidelity, for a number of people, is a pure, innocent, almost wonderful act (a genuine bit of hope) or is it a cruel, jaded response, some sort of joke everyone is in on ("Yes, we know this stuff happens") and shrug their shoulders because, so what, nothing new under the sun.

As his mistress Collier is without substance; her role in Gordon's life does not register on any social scale. It is not that she is excluded from celebrations and important decisions; rather, she is never thought of in any case.

Further, she cannot call Gordon at home without pretense. If Les answers Collier must will her voice to normalcy; casually, Is Gordon home? like camouflage, her voice. Like camouflage, her face, no expression, when running into a mutual friend while out with Gordon—hidden, no attention drawn. This is how it goes.

And Gordon's friends are not privy to this extra woman in his life. They, he believes, would not approve. They, he believes, would react the way many couples react when they learn of a friend's marital faithlessness: immediately apply it to their own lives.

They look askance at the wife. Perhaps they openly stare, trying to see beneath the surface of things. Does pretty Les suspect anything? On *some* level, they tell themselves, she must know. They do live under the same roof. Unless she is harboring her own secrets. And, maybe, for a moment, they are intrigued by the expansion of one life—married life—into two lives—married life plus an additional illicit life.

But all this is a speculative way of examining their own coupled lives; they would want to know if their loved one was keeping company with another. It is too hurtful to think that you could be blind, ignorant, in love and unknowing.

Collier simply doesn't exist. How could she? Without other people to recognize her place in Gordon's life, she has no life *in regard* to Gordon. Certainly, he does not acknowledge her. Cannot claim her, which is sometimes hard for him because he thinks he loves her very much and how many things are worse than denying someone you love? To act as if affection, loyalty, *friendship* were a shameful thing. To admit adoration.

Anamorphosis because Collier does exist, is loved, not seen, by a society that will not and cannot see her; by a man who occasionally pretends she is not there; all that guarded, conflicted love.

A final definition:

When Gordon left Collier the first time, then quickly married Les, Collier experienced anamorphosis most acutely, unexpectedly: She saw Gordon's face everywhere. Because she returned to Los Angeles, where they had been together, while he settled somewhere else, for a period of time, with someone else, leaving Collier with no greater desire than to be done with this sad little haunting and a wish to be rid of this shade of love. She did not want to feel or see or sense or hear his careless voice speaking its empty words of careless love. Collier wanted Gordon gone.

So she grew irritable and sorrowed at the way his face blended into her world. Crying bitter tears, she reminded herself that as she was grieving for him and being continuously visited by his memory, he probably did not see her at all.

When he no longer had a need for her, Collier was sure, she faded away until she was gone.

Kiki shut off her computer, turned out the light and left the office.

Music

Collier once said to Kiki, "My parents were the recluses, the bookish ones, while yours were the socialites. I always imagine Gen with a drink in one hand and dragging on a Kent, saying, 'Kiki, darling, what a clever girl you are. So bright, so brilliant. Just like me, your mother. You are my best friend.' And there you are, this little eight-year-old adult."

Kiki's parents did travel, which was a pleasure for Walt for whom each new place yielded new interests. Walt, so continuously fascinated by the world; Walt who understood so little of its workings. He preferred the inanimate or nature vista or the brilliance of a city to the people they met. He could not fathom people. They obeyed no predictable code of behavior and were, therefore, maverick, rendering him uneasy and retiring. So, when it is said that Walt understands little of the world, what is meant is that he cannot figure out personality.

For Gen a trip was a success only if they ran across entertaining travelers. It upset her to glance over at Walt reading some plaque or guide book or examining some ugly bit of rock he happened upon; so clearly uninterested in most of the people whom she engaged in conversation.

They brought Kiki and Robert gifts with the name of traveled places emblazoned upon them: sparkling, breakable objects that would not survive their childhoods, or unsuitable clothing for children.

Collier's parents gave her books and sheet music. Her father said, "I was sorry when you gave up the piano," only to have Collier look at him incredulously and say, "I was never very good."

"You didn't practice enough," he insisted.

"All the practicing in the world would not have made a difference," she said, though she was more accomplished than she would allow.

"Well," he said, "*I* loved you when you played."

His choice of words was not lost on Collier, who tried to ignore the "I loved *you* when you played" instead of "I loved *it* when you played." She told herself that perhaps she was wrong and that his words ran no deeper than a carelessness of language.

Which may be why when Collier and Gordon were kissing in his car outside her apartment, she abruptly left his embrace and asked him inside, only to have him sit on the sofa to listen to her play "Time After Time," the theme from *Picnic,* and a beautiful *Arabian Nights*–sounding piece.

He sat quietly, half watching, half waiting, asked, Don't you know anything classical?

Right, said Collier, covering the keys. As if I'd play something classical for you.

When Gordon first noticed Collier, he could only recall the lines of a sentimental pop song. They played over and over in his head as he watched her day after day, concentrating less on what was being said around him than on waiting for her to speak up in class. Although he knew she never would raise her hand—she was not that sort—he strained to listen when she laughed with her girlfriend, who sat to her left and scribbled notes, which Collier answered back by whispering. Until one day Gordon passed Collier a note, which ended up getting kicked across the floor, ready to be retrieved when class ended, except that it was completely forgotten by the end of the hour. It contained the words to that song. It said: "Dreaming of your love and not knowing where to start."

Pregnancy

Les is sitting in the den, a book open in her lap, only she is not reading. She tries but cannot concentrate and is thinking of other things; things not in this novel she holds open. Gordon took the two kids out for the day to Travel Town, where they can climb around on the old retired trains and her younger child can ride the ponies. Gordon will allow them a ride on the miniature train, which is something the elder child, now a little rebellious, obstinate, will no longer do. All this leaves Les with unfettered hours to herself.

She relishes her time alone, believes she will accomplish so many things during the absence of her family ("If I only had a few minutes to myself, I could do it"), only she rarely does. Instead, she becomes so lost in the silence of the house it is almost like a reverie.

Gordon has been after her to "talk to somebody" since the day she abandoned the car at the market and walked home.

"It isn't as if I did it on purpose," she told him crossly.

"For me," he said. "Do it for me."

Les shook her head. Everything is for you, she thinks, watching the sun on the carpet before her. What would she say to a stranger? A *paid* stranger? That she feels the presence of other women pressing in on her marriage with its delicate scrim boundaries, so simply seen through, so effortless to tear? That her mind is beginning to form a notion like the setting together of carefully placed building blocks, the sort her younger child plays with, over and over? Les is listening to the names of girls in college; the names that sometimes placed themselves close to Gordon's that she refused to pay attention to all those years ago. And maybe it is seeing Nora and her friend the other day; maybe it was Collier Grey going to Gordon's concert.

That is Les: thinking, thinking. Troubled, analyzing and not wanting to be analyzed. I am comfortable with silence, she thinks; is that an unnatural thing? Does it require correction? Or maybe she just doesn't think she owes the world a window into her life.

One of the things Les loved best about her marriage was pregnancy. And what she loved about being pregnant was that it made her feel safe within her own marriage. There is something about Gordon that she cannot quite identify, she does not know, maybe he has other women, maybe he does not and yet she feels certain that during the time she was pregnant he was faithful to her. And maybe for a while after as well. So, when Les considers her life, those are the days, the months, where she found relief and happiness.

Gordon took care of Les, listened to her, was, in general, attentive, as if he, too, were awestruck by the wonder of having a child. It was almost as if he wanted to carry the baby and since he could not, chose to stay very close to what she was going through.

Les cannot say that he loved *her* more during those

periods or if it was a selfish thing of wanting to possess her experience. He used to round his hands on her belly, or listen, his ear pressed to her flesh. Or chat away to the baby. They actually felt married then.

That is the good side.

The bad side of pregnancy was feeling less and less human each day. Maybe Les should say "less female." There is an irony there, she knows. She never grew accustomed to being seen as "a pregnancy." No one flirts or jokes in any sort of base manner, as if people seem to cease regarding you as a sexual being, which is, of course, also ironic since sex is what got you there in the first place. Men are more respectful and the world treats you a little better. Friendlier, more interested, not in you, in your condition. Like a fragile object, like Les was a piece of pure crystal that no one could quite see through. So, everyone wonders about this baby who is hidden.

Gordon once said to Les that there must be something a little wrong with her because she did not like to tell people that she was pregnant until it began to show and even then she wouldn't always mention it and most people are too polite to say anything. What if she was just an oddly shaped fat woman? No one wants to insult anyone. So she spent her days fantasizing that some stranger, some sweet handsome stranger, would approach her and actually *talk to her* as if she carried the possibility for a romance, not a baby, because Les missed that terribly when she was about to become a mother.

A mother. As if she were being transformed externally when inside she still feels exactly like herself, only motherhood makes Les a little happier. She used to receive the usual compliments: glowing skin, thicker hair, she smiled more freely. A mother; as if she were no longer Les, stripped of her sexuality, a certain element of her femininity.

And bringing a baby into a culture that, she is beginning to believe, does not really like children and only tolerates them and keeps finding new ways to be unkind. God forbid she has the kids in public—a store, a restaurant, a movie, a park—and they begin Acting Like Children, all noise and motion and Les really is The Mother who should be controlling her kids and sometimes she gets so tense about it that she develops a terrible headache and they all have to leave wherever they are anyway.

Her first child, a boy, loved to look at the sky. Anytime they passed a window in that first apartment, which was set up quite high with views all around, he would become very quiet and serious and concentrate on watching the clouds and the sun and the blue of the world. Or the rain; he was born during great storms. Always Les watching him.

Then, when he was a bit older (though still an infant), she noticed him noticing the trees. If she took him outside and laid him on his back, he would smile and laugh and talk to the trees every time their leaves rustled or branches moved. Les looked into his bright eyes, noting this very clear sign of affection.

She became curious, then, about what sort of man would come from a baby who revered the sky and loved the trees. Les wanted him to be like Gordon; Les wanted him to be anyone but Gordon, a man she did not altogether trust. Love, yes. Trust? Maybe.

If they were hanging around the house, her boy and Les, they would dance in the living room. She led. And she could not describe the purity of her senses as she held him close, gliding across the carpet, sounding no louder than a whisper. For his part, it soothed him—all that mild rocking motion—she is sure that he did not think of their waltzing as together time. That is fine; he was too young to think of anyone but himself.

So, being a mother, past and present, has its good side: dancing with her son or holding him near the glass to watch the sky or lying beside him, talking to the trees; as well as its not-so-good side: that she is a mother and that title seems, curiously, to negate her womanhood while publicly confirming that, yes, she is a "successful" woman with her child—later, children—as evidence. In one respect, it does more for Les's credibility in this world than if she ran her own multinational corporation (people could always say that she did not earn it, that she "slept" her way to the top, never stopping to think that a woman "sleeps" her way to having a child; or that there might have been some form of favor involved). People like the notion of Mother. Even if she were a CEO she imagined being asked, until she turned forty, if she was "considering children."

But how can someone be lauded for a natural act of her own biology? And how can a woman be made to feel "less" if she cannot have or does not want a baby?

Some say things have changed; Les is not entirely convinced. One of the most subversive things she can do is to confess to not understanding the large number of women who will do anything to have a child. She does not think she is missing the point. It just seems to her that women are praised for that which they cannot control and punished for the same.

She thinks she would like to be a photographer and have people admire her work, maybe even have it shown or bought. In college she thought she would end up in that direction but her family competed for the time and affection that photography would require; well, it was not so much that she gave it up as that it never seemed to take hold in her life at all. Maybe later, she still tells herself.

Les sometimes worries about being wife and mother and not Les, to the larger world.

"Why not get a job?" asks Gordon when Les hints at these private misgivings.

"I don't really have any skills. I mean, what, exactly, would I do?"

"I love your pictures," Gordon says. "You should be taking pictures."

Les is touched by Gordon's stubborn devotion to her unrealized dream. It is sincere, she knows. He has always told her, "You have a good eye. Your own way of viewing the objects that make up the world."

Les sighs, "No one is going to pay me for that."

"Whatever," says Gordon. He seems to immediately lose interest in the conversation.

Maybe she could start as a secretary, or someone's assistant, though she finds the idea of linking her name to another's distressing. I want my name to stand alone somewhere, she thinks.

It is not as though she'd kept her last name; only her first name, Leslie, truly belongs to her. In marriage there are many nicknames, as if they were constantly renaming each other according to personality traits: They call their daughter Miss Drama and their boy Mr. I Want. Les calls Gordon Honey or Rabbit (reminiscent of Alice's white rabbit, always in a rush) or White Fish (which he would eat exclusively). Gordon calls her Honey or Ansel, as reminder and wish regarding her photography, she knows. Although lately he mostly calls her Les. Which she rather likes. Anyway, each year they all seem to add to the list.

Les has come to dread days like these when she cannot concentrate on the book before her for wondering exactly who she is.

Romance

Kiki writes: *There was an art movement during the thirties of fusing images of women and stone.* Her pen appears to be floating above the paper. Ghostwriting; she smiles to herself. Thinking about the silence of stone, of immobility and the romantic notions of some men, Kiki makes further notes: Approximately one hundred years ago the first fashion models showed up in our society. It is said they lacked status and were not beautiful by anyone's standards, so as not to detract from the clothes they modeled. One Parisian couturier, in 1920, who was lunching with his models (all dressed alike in semimilitary attire), said to a journalist who happened to address one of the women, "Do not speak to the girls, mademoiselle; they are not there."

MEN

If you really want to make a woman disappear, romanticize her. That will rid the world of her. Make her into such an untouchable incorruptible ideal that no woman (including the original woman) will ever be able to live up to her image.

Tell everyone that she was the moon and stars and the cat's pajamas. Say: She was brilliant, beautiful, sexy, spontaneous, just, kind, honorable, affectionate, generous, perfect. Say it again: She was perfect.

Once you have done this, shout out loud her perfection, repeat it to everyone you know and/or are dating. Making it clear to family and friends, and you will soon lose your need for this or any other woman. Oh, sure, you will "see" other women (though, in truth, you will not be seeing them at all as they stand before you, trying to get your attention) but you will never again have to involve yourself with them. After all, you must remain true to your dream girl; the one loved and lost (it does not matter if it was your fault or hers; it is as immaterial as she is).

This, you think, will make others find you very romantic; that you bear the torch and the scar of Real Love; that you are no stranger at the Altar of Affection. Some may even make the worst mistake of all and take you to be some sort of poet. With a beautiful ruined soul; brutalized by disappointed love.

The cruelty of the Romantic will not dawn until later when your current girl [Collier, Les, Nora, Kiki] screams at you that you are insensitive, cold, distant. You [Gordon, L., Henry] will look up calmly, say, *If that is how you feel, you must do what you must do,* smug in your own self-image as the fallen romantic. This angry girl, you think, has a problem. That is, she is oblivious to the rarefied atmosphere of longing. And desire. You need someone more like you; more willing to toss it all to the wind for a single glance. Your old love, you think, would instantly know this about you.

With this approach to romance, you will never lose anyone.

It is a sort of modern-day version of The Disappearing

Woman; Dr. Harlan Tarbell would be proud of such a successful and well-dressed illusion. Because, as he says, the object is not truly gone (the rabbit, the coin, the car, the girl); it is simply that something else has caught and directed our eye, so we are looking elsewhere.

There is a brief moment, when the woman has gone and before the man idealizes her, that she is still a flesh being, the cause of his fractured heart; when she still has faults and calls up anger, hurt, nostalgia; before he ditches her by placing her on a platform of stone. The platform, which grows cold to the feet, hardens them, turns them to stone as well, progressively makes its way toward transforming the entire woman, and there she is, forever young, unattainable and, finally, heartless. (Do not forget the pedestal of the Southern Belle and the bloodless American version of the Sawed Girl illusion.)

WOMEN

Whereas men seem drawn to the idealization of women [Henry's stories to Kiki; Gordon taking up again with Collier; L. believing Nora "fell short"], women often identify past loves as though they were a variety of "phases" (the moon, too, has phases):

High school: the jock, the bad boy, the scholar.

College: the poet, the graduate student, the professor, the dropout.

Postcollege: the young executive, the bike messenger, the pianist, the drug addict.

And so on.

They even believe that they were in love, once or twice. As they relate stories connected with men in the past, they will laugh about funny things ("The thing that was good about us is that we were both in love with him''), and sad things (''I mistakenly thought I was the only one''). Quite often they will say, ''Oh, he was my poetry phase'' or ''That was my motorcycle phase'' or ''He was my corporate guy''—as if romance can be broken down into a series of fads of personality; stops on the way to becoming the Real Me.

Women are seldom broken by love; in this way, they are slightly less fragile than men. They have learned from birth to ''make allowances,'' to carry a heart within their heart and never entirely reveal it. When it is over, they go on. They recover. Some can even smile backward at the memory of the man.

But lest it be thought that women are charitable and strong whereas men are bitter and damaged, here is something else to consider: Women may say (of a particular phase), ''How I thought I loved him at the time,'' not daring to call what they felt True Love. Everyone knows that true love is forever, and if it is not, then it isn't true love. Well. So, they call it a phase (''My poet phase''), minimize the love they felt, attach it to the person they were *at the time,* and, in this way, get themselves through romantic disappointment.

Divorce

Divorce escalated in the mid-sixties in the United States. Women entered the work force in greater numbers and feminism finally reached a substantial audience. Under its influence, some argued, women took leave of the home and marriage. That is to say, life in the work world led to dissatisfaction with marriage, culminating in the divorce increase.

Kiki is still moving about facts regarding women in the twentieth century, despairing of the notion that any of this information will ever make a suitable category. It should, she thinks; it is a natural and, most important, loaded with trivia. She is, however, utterly bored with her job. What would she do if she did not work here? Her skills, such as they are, are definitely limited and this job has only prepared her for other, similar jobs, and if she is going to find a similar job, then why not stay put? At least she has a few years here; likes her co-workers fine; and she has begun to wonder if her disappearing isn't somehow her body's response to anxiety. Maybe about this birthday, maybe her life in general. Why isn't she further along or more established at this point in her life?

Nora told her that her boss is getting a promotion, which is good for Nora. Now there is someone who dislikes her job and still stays a basically happy person. But that is Nora, thinks Kiki. Nora has changed very little since college. That is to say, she still keeps in touch with everyone, still remains very discreet when moving between friends. Though Kiki does not tell her about Collier and Gordon, she is sure that Nora knows. The question has never been, What does Nora know? rather, What *doesn't* Nora know?

One of the pressing questions in Kiki's life: Does Nora see that I am leaving this world; color being bleached by the sun? And if Nora does not see it happening, then *why* doesn't she? Odd to think that Kiki's closest friends are oblivious to her recent ghosting ways.

So Kiki thinks maybe the fading is an emotional response to a particularly bad day while working on the twentieth-century women category, coming to divorce. She wonders if Les will ever divorce Gordon, or Gordon Les.

She continues:

1. Did women's dissatisfaction predate feminism, rather than feminism fueling dissatisfaction?
2. On lonely mornings, a woman could be left with housework, which is endless and not appreciated. She could finish her day, count the completed tasks and still not have a sense of accomplishment.
3. Boredom within her own family. Her husband too worn from his own workday. The kids too young, disaffected, bored with her. As teenagers they will grow even more uninterested, unlike later, when they are adults and appear to awaken from some odd enchantment to rediscover and want to know their parents.

4. **The root of marital discord might be locked behind the front door and not waiting outside in the work world to ambush an unsuspecting wife and mother.**

Kiki concludes:

5. **Feminism and work did not cause divorce. It was unhappy marriages and boredom and housework and feeding the kids and wanting something else that led to divorce.**

Not in the case of Les. She wants to be home, and she wants Gordon to want to be home as well. Les is not easily lured by promises of a life outside the house; she already has a life.

Gen was different. Without putting too fine a point on it, Gen grew restless with Walt. That is to say, marriage and motherhood caused her foot to tap and set her to pacing her home. Work beckoned and, shortly thereafter, she found herself a new man, with Walt suffering by comparison, as he was part of her old restive life. He did not know that he was "competing" for his wife; marriage, he thought, had ended romantic competition. He created an illusion of until death do us part and forgot that he lived in a world of ceaseless birth and death, forgot that those two things are not limited to being physical occurrences. They can apply to the spirit as well. Birth and death and death and birth. A person may win love and not allow for the possibility of losing that prize. Funny to think of losing something that cannot be held in one's hand.

Walt and Gen moved to a more affluent section of Pasadena, Al and Jean, their old neighbors who never did divorce, having been left behind. And no one is really talking anymore. Oh, words fill the house—certainly Kiki and Robert make enough noise to be heard across town—and Gen and Walt keep the place running with Pick Up the Dry Cleaning and Ask for Another Quart of Milk from the Milkman and Did You Pay the Electricity? and The Kids Need New Shoes and Who Is Taking Robert for a Haircut? and Feed the Dog and Drive the Sitter Home and Perhaps We Should Redo the House.

What they do not ever discuss is their first child, who passed away in the early years of their marriage. Curiously, this is the one thing they will bring up with each other, time and again, but that is many years later when they have been divorced a very long time. Affection, it would seem, sustains itself on words; the bedroom whisper is the linchpin of it all. Without the vocabulary of love, spoken with a private tenderness, there is nothing. As the saying goes, when you've got nothing, you've got nothing to lose.

Gen ventured out into the big world and found a job. Also, a new husband; and it was out with the old and in with the new while Walt embarked, not willingly, upon a new life.

Unfortunately, it was the old one he wanted.

Gen wrote in her journal: *I am seeing a man who calls me sweetheart.* And on and on about this man and what he meant to her while neglecting to record a single observation about Walt. For example, she could've noted the terrible hurt in his face when she told him (in not so many words) that the old life was over. People like Gen have a difficult time imagining that other people may react differently from themselves. Gen believes that her emotional expressions are correct; any unlike hers are, by definition, incorrect. Or, in the case of Walt, she mistook his silence as proof that he simply felt no emotions. He was not a man easily given over to confession; he could not tell her how awful he felt. It was a blow to the body, he could say, a tightening of the heart and a hardening of the spirit that would not again fully yield, to anyone. Like a death of the spirit.

He maintained his animal silence, which led Gen to remark to Liz Beth, "Imagine, he is not even angry enough to fight for me. I suppose I never really mattered." A great insult to a woman who cannot conceive of not mattering to a man who never thought he mattered at all.

Gen's birth of new love necessitated Walt's spiritual death.

Now, there is a rough connection between love and violence and danger and revenge. There is also a connection between love and exhilaration and soul soaring. But to return to the first grouping of words.

With a baby, a parent experiences tremendous love (recall that love is always love; this affection is different, not greater), causing the parent suddenly to understand the world as such a dangerous, random place. Your child can so easily come into contact with any number of physical dangers: an open window, a sharp object, heat and cold, careless strangers who do not concern themselves with your child's welfare. Now this wondrous love lives uncomfortably inside you as it begins to coexist with world fear. Along with the knowledge that a child is just so small.

Then there is love between lovers and again the awakening to harm. There are almost too many ways for this to occur. Distractions, temptations, negligence, and more strangers, only this time it is not your child for whom they lack regard but for your very own heart. The harm is not physical; it is spiritual. Soul bruises.

When Kiki fell in love, then was left, she discovered that she held all sorts of violent fantasies which became confused with a sense of great tenderness and protection for her man. Sometimes she could not separate it all; this desire for revenge and equal longing for sweetness.

Across town and many years following Gen and Walt's divorce sit Les and Gordon and their two children: a boy and girl. Following her accidental lunch with Nora and Kiki, Les found herself making plans with Nora to go to the music center, China Town, the county museum, MOCA, Old Town in Pasadena, the Asian Museum and Pasadena Playhouse and Huntington Library, Hancock Park and so on. She crams in movies and meals and even a few tourist attractions; with Nora or alone.

All because she discovered something when eating lunch that day with Nora and Kiki: Les could very easily run into Gordon. Sometimes she wants to find him with someone and sometimes she does not; this running around Los Angeles and environs; this hegira from her own, much-loved home. And if she finds him somewhere he should not be, if she finds him?

Gen made a mistake, however, in trading one man for another. Divorcing Walt was another matter and could not be categorized as a mistake, but she should have left on her own, not to be with someone else. Gen wrote in her journal: *I love Fran to distraction.* And love him she did but it would have been equally true for her to have written: *I am marrying up.* Gen, at this time in her mid-forties, worried about anonymity. Having not distinguished herself professionally and feeling the frayed edges of home and hearth, she felt pushed to move on. Though she would not think of it this way. All she could recognize for the moment was that she had fallen in love.

Here Gen and Walt dovetail: They each thought that by marrying someone who had what they wanted those things would become theirs. For example, Gen believed that a wife was truly an extension of her husband: his profession her profession, his money her money, his friends and family hers as well. In this respect, Gen remains faithful to her generation. Walt was attracted to Gen's sense of fun, her ease with life, her expressiveness. He said to himself, I will learn these things from her. Instead of learning them, he remained as he was and allowed her to be those things *for him:* his social bridge, his warm heart. This was his undoing, not unlike Nora and her many "hobbies," because the thing we love in someone we may cease to love, or they are the things that will always belong to them and not to you. Ask Les. Ask Walt.

Science & Math

There is an equation of families. You begin with two; then, with children, two become four. And when the physical properties and chemical natures of the original two grow incompatible and one of the original two marries a man with grown children of his own, you must subtract one, add one, then carry over another two, the grown children who do not live with the man but are in the picture nonetheless. The two children from the Shaw marriage are remainders in the division that represents the now-defunct union.

Gen married the man, Francis O'Neill, who called her Sweetheart. They moved to a larger home more pleasantly situated than the one Gen had shared with Walt. It was located in Pasadena, across the arroyo from the Gamble House and, because of its age, was a house with many flaws. Gen and Francis were not the first owners, only the most recent.

As Francis stands on a chair hanging drapes, Gen is saying to Kiki and Robert, "I want your rooms spotless. I mean it, the bathroom, too. Anything not put away will be thrown out." Kiki narrows her eyes, but Gen does not notice since she is concentrating on Fran, says, "Darling, I think you missed a couple of hooks. They are hanging funny, toward the center."

Tall, good-looking Fran tries to crane his head to take in the total effect as Gen places her hand lightly on the back of his thigh. "There," she points out, "can't you see it?"

"Sweetheart, why don't you wait until I am finished."

"Oh," says Gen with Kiki listening to this exchange knowing that Fran *is* finished and is tempted to say, Nice recovery. Fran, as the family is aware, is not very good with household repairs or tasks, but since this is a new marriage, criticism is conveyed graciously, politely.

With her other hand, the one not touching Fran's leg, Gen tugs on the drapes, tries to pull them in order as Fran looks down and smiles. "I love you so much," he says.

"Me, too," says Gen happily. Then, "I want things to be right for Mae. I know you are excited about her visit."

Kiki cannot help but notice the pleasure that registers in her stepfather's face at the mention of his younger, absolutely treasured daughter. "She will love you as much as I do" is the daily pronouncement from Fran; he says this again as he descends the chair. Kiki, Gen and Fran examine the job he has done; the drapes look awful. "Wait until you see how pretty she is," continues Fran. "Not that she models much anymore. Still, she really takes care of herself. Even with Don and the kids, Mae has not let herself go."

Kiki recalls how unforgiving Mae was when Fran divorced his wife to marry Gen (Grace, another subtraction in the mathematics of human connections), even though she herself divorced a first husband, took the kids and married another man.

"Is your room done?" snaps Gen. "Am I not speaking a common language here?" Then, to Fran, "*Nice* drapes, darling."

It was a bit of a shock for Francis O'Neill to find himself, at his age, stepfather to two relatively young children: Kiki, twelve, and Robert, ten. His own children were grown with children of their own and, he notes, each on second marriages as well. And there is the wonderful surprise of Gen; his fine luck at finding and winning her. Who would have thought that I'd find myself as a father again, he muses, after all this time? He smiles, ruffles Robert's hair, says aloud, "I always wanted a boy of my own." To Gen, "You have given me everything I have ever wanted." Kisses the tips of her fingers.

Fran, now in his early sixties, tosses himself into his new life with great energy; pretty Gen by his side; Robert and Kiki, who was temperamentally a bit like her father, Walt, well, they'd get past all that. His Gen affectionate where his previous wife had been distant; Gen flexible where Grace was rather set.

What happened here? he wondered. He tells Gen, I am so fortunate. It is as if the gods looked down on me and said, Francis X. O'Neill, you deserve another life; you have earned a second chance. Without a doubt, he thought, they could just leave the past behind, begin again in this new place. They could simply let it all go.

Kiki, much later in life, close to forty, feels for both Gen and Grace, two women connected by marriage to the same man yet divided by the space of nearly twenty years. A generation. The "benefits" of divorce for women and children were limited; previous wives and children resembling so much excess baggage and their financial lives drifting into easy ruin. It was far likelier that a man like Fran, at sixty-two, could find himself again a family man while a woman like his ex-wife, Grace, would find herself very much alone.

Grace and Gen's generation assured them that social visibility could be secured through the right marriage, so in order for Gen to reflect Fran's light, Grace necessarily had to be moved into darkness.

"Mr. Blandings," says Gen, "do you think we can call someone to come out and fix these drapes before Mae arrives?"

"Sweetheart," says Fran. Sighs, picks up the phone to call the shade shop. Gen hears him say, "Can't you find someone to come out today? What if I pay extra? No, no, I tried that. I do not know what went wrong. Please don't tell me how easy they are to hang or that I should have thought of this sooner." He laughs. "I'm thinking of this *now*. Two days? Are you—okay, okay—fine." He turns to Gen. "Two days."

She shrugs her shoulders, says, "That's the way of it, then," and pulls Fran into her embrace. "My man around the house. My Mr. B."

Fran, so eager to seize his new life, bought this house quickly. He hired a landscape architect, purchased potted plants for the backyard, had concrete poured, sod laid, sprinkler systems rooted in the front garden. He had work begun on a swimming pool without figuring on all the inspections and codes, time delays, limitations of distance and safety ("Mr. O'Neill," said the contractor, "if you dig here"—he walked a few feet from the door—"then you have to allow for a wall there," which reduced the size of the pool). At the moment, the "pool" is an enormous hole swallowing up much of the backyard, patiently awaiting the next round of inspections. There are twelve inches of rainwater in the "deep end."

Kiki is in her room, a little petulant at the prospect of turning it over to Mae, a stranger. She lingers, randomly thumbing through the *O* section of her encyclopedia, reluctant to gather up her night things to move them into the guest room.

"Kiki!" calls Gen from downstairs.

"Coming," replies Kiki without looking up from an entry that reads: *There is an observatory located in Big Bear, California, situated in the middle of the lake because the earth is calmer above bodies of water than above land.*

Fran decided to wallpaper the guest room and Robert's bedroom and now the paper is curling down at the edges. The paper hanger is arriving tomorrow roughly the same time that Mae's plane lands at Los Angeles Airport. The newly painted walls of the master bedroom seem to gain color intensity daily and need to be muted. Two hanging lamps are lying on their sides in the corner of the living room; shelves mounted to the wall are useless, empty, so slanted that objects are forced to the floor.

Fran thinks all his projects are so simple, foolproof; the approach in his mind clear yet the execution sabotages him every time. Gen tells him, "Hey, at least we have love. At least we are happy." She seldom thinks of Walt, who was heaven-sent around the house; does not forget the orderliness of that previous life.

To which Fran agrees, My little family.

. . .

When the time arrives to pick up Mae, Fran is happy and anxious. He rises from one chair only to sit and fidget in another. He paces, he synchronizes his watch with the kitchen clock, he asks Gen to come with him. She declines, says, I think a little time alone with Mae might be a good idea.

But I will miss you, he says.

You won't be gone that long, she laughs.

Honey, he says, any time away from you is too long.

This is how they speak to each other, as if having found one another they cannot bear to be parted. They sit close in the car, in restaurants, at parties, like people much younger in the grip of a first passion. They lock eyes. They embrace.

Gen and Fran's enthusiasm is contagious; their desire for each other, for family, is strong and so overpowering that Kiki becomes infected, seduced by the image of the American Family without strife, where difficulties are settled with a word and a kiss. It renders her dreamy-eyed.

Walt, her father, and the weekend visitations are beginning to seem intrusive and irritating. Unnecessary in this new equation, Walt unbalances the numbers and she finds herself thinking, Wouldn't it be nice if Fran was my real father and everyone just thought we were happy all the time? Kiki believes they would be happy all the time.

So she thinks she might start calling Fran Dad. He would like that, she knows, very much, in fact. The attraction of such an arrangement is not lost on her.

"Why does Mae have to sleep in my room?" asks Kiki.

"Because it is finished," Gen tells her. The wallpaper is properly hung; the closet hinges repaired.

Kiki starts her protest as Mae walks into the house with Fran trailing behind, weighted down by a garment bag, cosmetic case and one very large suitcase. "Honeys," calls Fran to his family, "this is Mae." Then steps aside to retrieve one more bag from the car.

Mae is tall, athletic (all that tennis back in Florida), with soft gray eyes, an ample mouth. A perfected grace in all her movements. Kiki agrees with Fran: Mae is quite lovely.

"This is very nice," Mae finally says after glancing around, offering her cheek to Gen to be kissed. Gen responds by throwing her arms around her stepdaughter, saying, "Fran is always talking about you. Always. Of course, I feel as if I know you."

Kiki notes that Mae leans into the embrace without returning it. An odd curve to her pretty mouth.

"Excuse me," says Mae. "I need to use your phone."

Deduct Walt. Add Mae.

Kiki awakens the next morning to find Gen constructing an enormous breakfast; Gen, who rarely cooks, is placing eggs in the oven, along with steak, English muffins and waffles. There are sliced strawberries and cream; powdered sugar dusts her blouse, grease marks her sleeve. Gen tells Kiki to remove the orange juice, fresh squeezed by Gen the day before, from the ice box; ordering Kiki around in a way with which she is unfamiliar.

"Did you tell your brother to come down for breakfast?" asks Gen.

"He's not even dressed," says Kiki.

Mae relaxes at the table, dressed in her golf clothes, calmly watching Gen's hurried movements. She and Fran are heading out to the club to play a game after breakfast.

"Are you sure you won't join us?" asks Mae in a lazy voice that reveals nothing; no real invitation, no distance.

"Oh, no," says Gen, "I'd only slow you down." In her journal she wrote: *I am not built for sports. Even golf, much to Fran's dismay.* "I haven't been playing very long and Fran tells me that you are quite good."

Mae slouches in her chair and does not insist that Gen join them. Kiki says, "I'll go with you," which Mae ignores. Kiki understands that golf is a game for four, though, in fact, the players are not pitted against each other and the only competition is with one's self. There is no true winning in the traditional sense; it is more a matter of ranking and order of best to last. Therefore, her lesser, childish skill should not be an intrusion to the other players.

When Gen places a plate of food before her, Mae says, "Oh, I just want a cup of coffee. No sugar."

"Sure, fine. You have such a nice figure—I'm always fighting mine—sure, I understand," then eats very little herself as if in deference to her guest.

Fran bounds into the room saying, Wonderful, wonderful, honey! This looks great! Beams at the two women, says, My favorite two people in the world. Gen wrote later: *Fran acts like a man blessed.*

"Gen has been quite nice," says Mae.

The remark about the "two" favorite people is not lost on Kiki, who is still clearly in the room. Two does not equal three. She imagines writing a list that begins with Mae and ends with Kiki.

Mae pushes her coffee away from her. "Daddy, we should get going. I don't want to be late."

"Sure, sweetheart," agrees Fran.

"What happened over there?" asks Mae, tilting her chin in the direction of a water stain that has discolored and spread across the ceiling and partially down the wall.

"Oh, that," says Gen. "We had a little problem with the plumbing. It's fixed now; it just needs some paint."

"Fran tried to replace a pipe," offers Kiki to no one until she says, "We call him Mr. Blandings," which catches Mae's attention, causes her to stare at Kiki as if she cannot quite place her. Then turns back to her father.

"It's a joke we have around here," he says and smiles.

Mae says nothing; no comment, no interest.

"Shall we go?" asks Fran of Gen.

"I'm not going, honey. I don't think I'm ready."

The telephone rings. "Robert!" calls Gen loudly, her eyes glancing up toward the second floor. "That boy," says Gen. On the third ring, when Gen says, Would you get that? meaning Kiki, Mae pushes back her chair as well.

"Mae, Kiki will get it," says Fran, his hand gently resting on her arm.

"Of course," says Mae, her posture tight.

"You are definitely ready, sweetie," says Fran to Gen. "Ah, Mae, you should see Gen on the green. A very light touch." He quickly kisses the inside of his wife's wrist. "I think she's a natural."

Kiki returns to the table, notices Mae's lessening interest in Fran and Gen and sharper focus on her.

"Who was on the phone?" asks Gen.

"Nobody. Some friend of Robert," says Kiki, adds, "I have my own putter and driver"—but Gen cuts her off, saying, "Why don't we do something together today?"—then Mae turns to Kiki, says in a slow, deliberate tone of hers, "What sort of a name is 'Kiki'?"

Kiki resents being placated by Gen, challenged by Mae and forgotten by Fran, who, by his own admission, had only *two* favorite people in the world. Kiki considers making a small scene forcing everyone to acknowledge *her,* only it does not seem worth it. Fran says to her, We'll all do something together later, okay? And Kiki is reminded that she is not his "natural" daughter and only someone's kid left over from a failed marriage. All of this sends her quietly from a room where she does not count.

This was Kiki's first strong experience with invisibility. First, Gen did not regard Kiki in her attempt to please Mae with the elaborate breakfast and, second, Fran was too caught up in this meshing of old family (Mae) to new family (Gen). Third, Mae scarcely noticed Kiki at all, though Kiki could have pointed out to her that legally they were stepsisters. It was as if Mae viewed Kiki as some sort of temporary fixture in her father's life; as if she counted on having to reckon with Gen but anyone beyond that did not warrant any extra effort.

Here is another game for four:

It is the nighttime of that same day. Mae, having made two phone calls before she changed her clothes—"I have to check with Don and the kids," she explains—is now sprawled across the sofa, laughing and knocking back Scotch and sodas with Fran. Gen is there, sipping wine, struck by the physical resemblance between father and daughter; how they seem to match, fit, belong, reminding her that families are one part choice and one part blood. She is saying very little. In private she is writing copiously in her journal about Mae and blame and guilt and how she feels she is betraying Fran by not succeeding in a friendship with Mae. She writes: *I try to like her; I try to have compassion. Bending over backward is not enough and I am no contortionist. For anyone. I do what I do for Fran.* Much of the conversation revolves around memories of Mae's mother, Grace, and their shared past, always punctuated with little shakes of Mae's head and "Mother is such a super person." Gen tries to imagine Kiki years from now, telling Walt that Gen is a "super person" and hopes that her own daughter will find a less silly adjective to describe her.

Then, "The divorce was hard on her, Daddy. Who expects to come home after thirty years and find her husband has left her for someone else? After she's given him everything? And he leaves." Mae takes a long swallow of Scotch, then extends her empty glass. "Another, please." Mae leans her head back against the sofa. "Whoever expects to be left." Closes her gray eyes.

Gen says, gently, "I know it was tough on your mother. This sort of thing is never without harm." For the softness of her voice, Gen's posture is as rigid as Mae's is loose and she speaks only because she can see Fran's discomfort and is allowing him time to collect himself.

"She is such a wonderful person, I mean, she did not, really did not, deserve this," says Mae, accepting the fresh drink from Fran, their fingers touching in the exchange of the glass; Mae looking up: "She trusted you, Daddy."

"I know she did, sweetheart."

Getting to her unsteady feet, Mae wanders into the kitchen, reaches down to open a small cupboard (What the hell is she looking for? wonders Gen) only to have the door fall off in her hand. Mae stares at the door in her hand, which causes Gen to laugh. Mae says drunkenly, politely, "Oh, I'm sorry—" her words dissolving into the sound of Gen's laughter.

"I should have warned you," says Gen, "only I can't remember all the things that need attention. Your father meant to secure it—actually, he *did* fix it but, well, you know your father."

"No, I don't." There is a quiet as Mae sways a little, her

eyes glassy. "Why don't you tell me about my father? You seem to know something the rest of us don't. How about telling me how you got him to leave my mother? What is it she calls you? 'That wop thief.' "

Gen's smile remains on her lips but leaves her eyes, which, in turn, do not leave Mae. Her gaze is direct, even.

Fran says, "Don't do this, Mae. It does not become you."

"Let it go, Fran," says Gen. "I can take it."

"I don't want you to," says Fran. "Not in our home."

"Yeah, right," says Mae, splashing the contents of her glass as she gestures around the room. "Your *home.* Why don't you fix your fucking home? This place is a mess. I mean, what do you see when you look around here? Jesus, Daddy, is this what you wanted?" To Fran, "Oh, oh yeah, I forgot—you can't seem to repair a goddamn thing." To Gen, "Isn't that right? Isn't that the gist of it around here?"

"I'm going upstairs," announces Gen. "This really doesn't concern me, though I would appreciate it if you would hold it down—I do have children."

"Stay," commands Fran, as he grabs Mae's arm, opens the sliding glass door and pulls her outside, yanks the door closed behind them, cutting all sound; Gen watching them through the glass. Mae's Chanel No. 5 lingers in the room as Gen thinks how difficult it is to associate this sweet fragrance with the angry, drunken woman sobbing on the other side of the glass, her mouth bent with fury.

Kiki is upstairs at her mother's vanity table, brushing her hair, examining the contents of the drawers—colors, scents, little grooming implements—when she is interrupted by the sound of rough voices rising from the backyard through the open window.

"Mae," she hears Fran say, "I won't have you talking that way about Gen. She's been wonderful to you, welcomed you into our home."

"I'm a guest. I'm *family*"—and Mae makes a strange little mirthless sound—"she's obligated to be wonderful. It is not that big a deal."

"You don't know how she feels about your mother."

"Oh, please," says Mae, "spare me. If she feels so bad, then why aren't you still with Mother? Answer me that?"

Kiki hears someone walking, pacing, she thinks, then Fran's voice, "I thought you of all people would understand. Christ, you're an adult, Mae. What did you think you were doing when you and Don started up and you were both married? What did you think it meant when you two married?"

"Don't you dare compare your situation to mine," she hisses.

"You don't see what you don't want to see." Fran's voice softer, still tense. "Almost like your mother."

"I hope I am exactly like my mother," screams Mae. Kiki is certain that their neighbors are not missing a word of this. She carefully sets the brush back on Gen's vanity. "She's wonderful! She gave you everything!"

"No," says Fran, "she didn't."

Kiki is startled by the sound of Gen's stalking into the room. Her mother drops to the bed, sits with her arms tightly crossed, foot bouncing up and down. "Don't forget to put my brush back in the drawer where you found it."

Fran's voice wafts upward. "Her coldness, Mae, her . . ."

"I won't listen to this." Kiki hears the sound of someone trying, unsuccessfully, to open the sliding glass door.

With Gen sitting behind her Kiki cannot make out her mother's reaction to the scene outside. She wants to turn around but instead pretends to be looking at a bottle of pearlized nail polish. "It might just be better when she's gone," says Gen, seemingly to no one. Kiki thinks her mother means Mae, then considers the possibility that she is referring to the previous Mrs. O'Neill. Or is she talking about herself, as if she were supplying dialogue for the voices below?

"But she loved you," cries Mae.

"If she loved me—and she may have—she did not love me enough," says Fran.

All sounds from the yard have ceased. Gen waits, then whispers, "Kiki, see what they are doing." Kiki goes to the window and looks down to see Mae's hunched shoulders, sitting in the dirt, her long legs dangling over the edge of the unfinished swimming pool, face buried in her hands and she is sobbing as Fran strokes her hair.

"Kiki?" asks Gen.

"She's crying," answers Kiki. Then, "Don left me, Daddy. He has someone else," and Mae sounds so defeated that Kiki feels she cannot see this.

"What was that?" asks Gen. Kiki does not answer, which brings Gen to her side, there, behind the window screen.

"I'm a good wife," says Mae. "I am a good mother."

"Sure, sure you are, Mae," says Fran.

Gen puts her arm around Kiki.

"Believe me when I tell you everything works out," says Fran. "Look, you knew what he was like when you married him. You wouldn't listen to anyone. You had to have him."

"Christ," says Mae, "don't lecture me now."

"I'm sorry. You are right. But look, life is full of second chances. Trust me. You can't make someone want you; you can't force it. You'll be happy again."

Mae turns to him with an incredulous tear-stained expression, illuminated by the family room lights. Her mouth is slack until she spits out, "What the hell do *you* know?"

Kiki pulls back from the window, away from Gen's embrace. Leaving her mother looking down from above.

It is all addition and subtraction: the addition that comprised Mae's first marriage and motherhood; the addition of her married lover, Don, and, by extension, Don's wife and their children; then the deductions: deduct Mae's first husband, Don's first wife, his children; add Mae and Don's child; add Don's new woman; deduct Don; deduct Mae. Or similarly in Fran and Gen's marriage. The numbers are always the same—only two can be married to each other at one time; a third can rupture that marriage—the properties hold; the theorem proven.

During the last long hours of an afternoon on the day Mae left, having cut her visit unexpectedly short, Fran unhappy and a little lost ("She is truly gone from me this time, Gen, and will not return. Mae has vanished from my life"), is wrestling with some badly mounted shelves. He is frustrated, muttering, sad.

He sits back on his heels, Gen in the chair near his right. When he looks up she can see the thing he is fighting. He asks, "Was there another way?"

Work

Here is a question: Why do Collier, Gen, Nora and Les all crave some form of transformation? Kiki momentarily allows her concentration to relax.

Then, back to *Work.*

There are two basic parts to *Work: Job* and *Career.* Kiki writes: *A job is a task for which you have no passion. A career is often about personal fascination.*

One can have a great career that pays little; one can have a job that pays handsomely. The best of all possible worlds is the great career that pays handsomely. The worst of course is the low-paying dull job. Although a well-paying job is almost pointless because you may find yourself too overworked, pulling too much overtime to actually enjoy the money; a career for which you are passionate but not well paid can still be an end in itself. Clearly, a love of what you spend your time doing each day is preferable.

Nora, for example, has a dreary, not lucrative job. "It fills the refrigerator," she says, shrugging.

And worse than the unsatisfying job is the love affair or marriage that we are told requires "work" to stay alive. It seems mutually exclusive, this idea of excitement in another person being reduced to one more obligation. A culture, however, founded on the Puritan work ethic will readily accept the notion that everything—including love—exacts a certain amount of work.

So, when Nora senses her man is losing interest (to be fair, he would have to be very taken with himself to remain fascinated by a woman who quickly and willingly becomes his image and, if this is the case, then the woman he is with is immaterial and interchangeable with any other woman, ensuring that he will always be more important than she); or Collier tries to love the man who will not give himself over completely. Or Gen finds herself with husband trouble of one variety or another, and Les withdraws, unwillingly, from the man she wants and is then labeled cool and distant—they are only told, "Then you must try harder at making it all work."

Love and work, like love and birth and death, run side by side.

So is it any wonder that these women feel as they do? When told they must "work harder," they become accustomed to feeling unimportant, of reduced worth, which, in turn, engenders a variety of approaches to love.

Love

Collier: Collier first and only loved music. Her ears longed to be filled with tonal sounds; sweet strings, brass, woodwind pipes like a forest clearing, cool and floating; deep sounds, shining and heavy like mercury beads adrift in a child's palm. Kettledrums. She did not miss voices; Collier heard enough voices in the world and craved the wordlessness of music.

Her next impulse was to touch, talking in the wordless

words she was beginning to understand. The more she allowed music into her life, the less she listened to the pitch of another person's voice. Music would be her moral compass; she would live by its lights.

Then Collier fell in love with a musician, Gordon, and thought she could present him with the same simple application she exhibited toward her music. Until she learned that to love was to surrender herself to the image that Gordon saw when he looked at her. So, her feet left the ground and she began her existence as The Floating Woman.

And when Gordon had taken Collier's devotion for granted (she played piano with less frequency), she realized that she would prefer to be loved. It would allow her a measure of control (or so she thought) except that he refused to love her more than she loved him; the best he could manage was to match her affection and, in the end, she exhausted him by her demands. The more he gave, went the complaint, the more she wanted. She said, the more you give me, the less I seem to have, because being loved, as opposed to loving, is an arrangement essentially unbalanced and, as with music, she loved the balance of tempo, note and volume. Soon, her romance seemed to be dissolving into thin silent air. It no longer filled her, as music had; she no longer wanted to grab handfuls of it because it was handfuls of nothing.

In time, Collier mistakenly thought that this particular loneliness was due to not being loved enough, so instead of increasing the amount of love she gave, she began her quest to be loved in always greater amounts than she was loved and so increased her solitude. Her career in production was satisfying for the same reason that her love life was not (recall Collier's love vertigo and the attendant fall): She could orchestrate an entire video, yet remain powerless in romance.

Now, if she continually reinvented herself, she believed that she would awaken one day to being absolutely, completely, unabashedly loved. Collier would be a person worth loving, and not for leaving, worth slaying all dragons in her name, and berated the man who could not do this for her. In this way, she slowly forgot that the men she sought were as human as she was and humans can do, well, only what is humanly possible and not what is impossibly perfect.

For this reason, her pursuit of love was unreasonable, illusive, and impractical. It created within her a restless spirit who ended up with a career that locked together time and money, and with a man like Gordon; a man whom Collier wanted to "prove" himself over and over until she could no longer remember what she wanted him to prove.

Nora: The idea of being loved was, for Nora, lacking in a certain poetry.

In her jobs, she was the Perfect Employee. Selfless, punctual, cheerful, hard-working, tireless, efficient, placing her job first and herself second throughout forty hours of every week, leaving little time for the person she wanted to be. And because this feeling toward her job was intertwined with her personal notions of love—unlike Collier, whose approach to love was opposite from her approach to work—she began to act the same way in each sphere. She could not do less.

Nora and her journey to become other people so that she might garner their affection did not take into account the fact that not everyone is bound by self-love and that some men are not fond of who they are; some men require a complement and not a reflection in a mirror.

Gen: Gen began as one who loves, who gives, then was transformed into one who would prefer to be loved. With

Gen, like Collier, this reversal rose from disappointment in love, but unlike Collier's, Gen's reversal drove slightly deeper within her. To want to be adored was no longer a desire; it was a requirement of her company.

Gen's own interests became small and withered from lack of attention and care. No longer did she tend to her own life; instead, turned completely outward, said, "I want someone who has things [hobbies, friends, possessions] so he will share them with me."

And because she ceased all regard toward her own life, her spirit was starting to reduce to a trace. When this happened, she began to forget that what she wanted was companionship and soon she translated this to mean that she craved material things. She would proudly display a gift of clothing or jewelry or home furnishing as if it were a badge of admiration. *See,* she said, extending an arm that bore a diamond bracelet, *see how much he cares.*

Silly. Material things, of course, are the least gifts; the easiest of gifts; the most meaningless of items unless backed and bolstered by love. Too often they were not and when the man had gone (left, or, like Fran, passed on), Gen could not fathom why she felt as if she had been left with nothing. (Kiki writes: Answer: *Widow.* Question: *What is the Sanskrit word for "empty"*?) Except a box that sparkled with treasure; a home full of things; a car; and a confusion as to why she could not find comfort and, like Collier, experience only a vague and terrible restlessness.

Les: Les loves. Her husband, Gordon. Her children. Her parents. Sometimes she views her world of affection and knows its fullness and knows, too, that it could be further filled. If the love she gives is not returned in an identical amount, it is no less abundant. She, as with Nora, takes on the role of lover, having made up her mind, so many years ago, that she would take her chances and hope for the best. The greatest fear of the one who decides to love more than she is loved is that she will pursue someone who does not truly understand this arrangement and grasps it as an opportunity to rule.

Les is not long-suffering, nor unaware; rather, she has neatly divided her life into a series of expenditures and returns and as long as they remain separate she is fine. She watches her world with remarkable clarity and accepts it for what it is because she wants to; she would be diminished if she did not live this way. (Similarly, Nora is a good employee because she cannot be otherwise. Well, that is Les in love. She is the way she is because to be any other way is unthinkable.)

And she often thinks, If they all quit me tomorrow [husband, children, parents], I would love them still. Les is relieved that her life carries resolution.

Now Gen, Collier, Les, and Nora may ask the questions, Why isn't loving me enough? Why can't I remain as I am? Kiki recalls that *fin de siècle* artists saw in woman the moon, the vanity mirror, the completed circle that is full of self-love, wanting no one but herself. Women do not feel like unbroken circles. Here again is the difference between how you are seen and how you *are.* It seems that men understand that they must be taken for who they are; they are not to be tampered with. Common wisdom has always proclaimed, Do not marry him if you think you can change him. Again, the effort to change falls to you, not to him. On and on. As if we are never to be enlightened. As if we are never to fall for each other as we are, always desiring what we could be. These women can be no one else, of course.

. . .

So, it is not weakness or innate feelings of self-importance that prompt Gen to marry up, or Nora to assimilate her man's hobbies, or Collier to want a tabula rasa or Les to pitch herself into uncomplicated roles, but a world that tells them in a dozen quiet ways: You must work harder.

Gin #3

When Henry goes to Kiki's with a tinful of chocolate chip cookies, he finds her in the tiny garden behind her house, looking up at the sky, cigarette in hand. Sitting beside her, assuming her pose, he asks, "So what are we looking at?" He can note nothing of importance. The sky is inky black and barely illuminated by a miserly slice of moon; unremarkable sky, barely starred, no strange red glows or lunar eclipses or falling stars or comets in fevered races across the dome of night. No soft haloes surrounding the moon; no previously unseen planets.

"The stars," she says. "I'm looking at the stars."

"Let's see, I can pick out one or two. Definitely one." He is smiling. "Yes, some fine star opportunities tonight," he says.

"You think because we cannot see them they are not there," she says, still watching.

"No, I think it is too polluted and the city lights are too bright to see them. You should go to a place like Joshua Tree where they all cling together like damp sugar in an upended bowl."

Kiki shakes her head. "Now why," she asks, looking at

him, "should I have to leave my home to see the stars? If they are there—I mean, here—I should be able to make them out." She sighs. "Society has made their lives impossible."

One hand goes to the cookie tin—"Oh, what did you bring me?"—while the other reaches to her mouth to allow a puff on the ever smaller cigarette. Kiki noticing that the red ash appears to be free floating, as if moving toward her face of its own free will to meet her lips.

"Are you interested in astronomy?"

"No," she says, "only in the invisibility of the stars, and how they live."

Henry says over cards, "One day my girl and I hiked up on these cliffs somewhere out near Angel Ridge. Upon reaching the top, we sat down and began to talk until we were interrupted by the appearance of a knot of these tiny multicolored wild birds flying crazily around us. I'm not sure how many there were but it was quite a few and in constant motion, like Christmas lights that had all been strung together, then flung free of their wire, flashing color all around our heads. We could not speak; we could only sit in the very hot sun, open-mouthed, wondering at them. It was almost like I made them up." Henry's voice was so low that Kiki could barely hear him. "It was like a fiction. A dream. Then it was finished."

"What do you mean?" she asks. "Literally? Figuratively? What?"

"Does it matter?"

Kiki asks, "Did you grieve?"

"No," Henry tells her, "because it was as if I had this great dream. Then the story was over. It is not a good idea to grieve over an ending, if you see what I mean."

"When did it end?"

"I'll tell you another time," Henry says, gathering the cards, shuffling.

"Did you ever fight?" asks Kiki.

"Why would you want to know that?" Henry's voice sounds lost somewhere between irritation and genuine curiosity.

Kiki shrugs her shoulders, says, "I guess because you loved her so much, you've made it sound So Perfect that I find myself wondering many things. I think what I need to know, what I am asking is to hear the flaw."

He says, finally, softly, "I was the flaw."

Adventure

Nora sifts through the office mail. She is an assistant in a financial firm and her tasks include many things. Since her secretarial skills are not specific, she has been able to find work most anywhere: an accounting firm, a doctor's office, a brokerage house, a record company, an electronics company, an art gallery, an ad agency, a law firm, one or two life science labs; it does not matter; Nora is capable of adapting to many workplaces.

She is not crazy about her boss, despite the number of years they have spent together, nor about her job, since jobs always seem to be the same, finally. She is looking through the mail when she comes upon a flyer for a seminar to be held in the Caribbean. She laughs to herself; it is clear that this meeting could just as easily take place in the most out-of-the-way town in the United States. Yet she finds herself entranced by the still turquoise water and enormous striped umbrellas and tanned girls on sling-back chaises. Fancies herself one of their number, then tosses the flyer aside, thinks, Must be nice. She stops herself: Must be nice to just be able to pick up and go; to take a real vacation and call it "business," not her usual trip home to visit her family, which she actually enjoys, always thinking, This is all I can afford.

Nora is a frugal girl and has always saved faithfully. For what? The disaster that will devastate her? The rainy day that, thankfully, does not come? And suddenly she is overcome, sitting at her desk, in her office, which lies in proximity to her boss's, finds tears falling and spreading, caught on the papers before her. She is coming apart so slowly, so expertly that even her closest friends cannot detect the unraveling.

Her hand brushes aside the unexpected tears; silly, years ago she traveled through Australia and New Zealand all by herself with her backpack and limited funds. She dismisses the memory. I was so much younger then. I could do that sort of thing.

What has changed? she wonders. Shouldn't I be even more capable of taking a trip like that now that I am older? Aren't we supposed to grow and learn and become even more versed in life as we age? Traveling alone could be a proving ground of all we have accumulated in our thinking lives. When, she wonders, did aging turn into a reversing of adulthood? It seemed one day she was a child who could not manage such a vacation alone without a parent, and the next she was closing in on middle age, stumbling over these strange roadblocks that seemed to appear from nowhere. Why can't she travel unescorted?

Fear and rebellion have dug into her chest, holding fast. They tell her that people are entitled to that sort of vagabond freedom when they are young; that she must be a grown-up; that it is correct for her to work; that she should resist the impulse to look back. And if she chose not to marry or have children (which *still* makes her an anomaly, though she does not know why), then shouldn't she at least have a big career or freedom or *fun*?

Somehow, in between the time she took off on that jet bound for Sydney, making her way around Australia, on her own, no need or use for well-meaning "help," and today, at her desk, something had happened to her. It was as if her life had been reduced to a clear, sharp triangle: the movement up (traveling alone at the apex) and, almost without pause, the pull back downward.

This is what brought it all home:

"So," said Louisa, another woman working in Nora's office, "I heard the good news. Bet you're happy."

Nora smiled, nodded, got back to work. The good news was that her boss was receiving a nice promotion; up the ladder, taking Nora ("perfect, indispensable, cheerful Nora") along with him. She should be glad. She should be grateful.

Nora sometimes laughs to herself that so many people believe that things have changed so dramatically in the workplace. To a certain extent, they are correct: a few more women above, and there have been some adjustments on the lower levels where the majority of working women still reside: No one calls us "girls" as in the "girls in the typing pool." No one says, "She's a terrific gal," as in "What a secretary. A terrific gal." No one says "broad" or "skirt," something that might once have been said of a secretary with limited skills but, you know, a bit of vavavavoom going for her. Sexy broad.

Rarely is anyone asked to serve coffee except if an Important Client happens by, then two things are likely: One, Nora will be asked to get coffee or carbonated water or tea or soda for both the client and her boss, as in, We have guests so the regular rules are bent a little bit. This makes her feel most like a wife or hostess.

Or, two, she will most certainly *not* be asked to bring

anyone anything. Her boss will make an obvious show of getting his own refreshment, as well as fulfilling the wish of the client. This may, at first, seem like business as usual, except that it is usually accompanied by a small joke about never asking Nora "to get it." Still. The point has been made.

Nora can and does make coffee; she also serves the drinks. And she does not care; none of this matters or is important to her. There are other, far more important things to want, she knows.

And then there are the bosses in the building who are easygoing, benevolent, unless they feel their secretaries have "gone too far," in which case they must gently yet firmly remind them who is who and that the "rules can be relaxed" but the pecking order will be enforced if need be.

The worst are the bosses who think the best performances are the result of temper, sharp words, blame and, in general, rough riding. They say, I can't help it if I want the best, as if the only way they can get the best is through meanness. They think it also garners fear and respect. They are wrong.

In Nora's company the women hold the "support" positions, sustaining a commanding number of men. Men in higher positions are often brought in from outside; and the women dying to climb up, with so few women at the top, it is not lost on them that they will be allowed in one by one, like an exclusive club with limited space and strictly enforced fire laws.

Nora disliked the competitive spirit this engendered in the more ambitious women; this sense that one could be sold out quickly because it did not take much for women to understand that she who travels alone travels fastest. Nora saw only divide and conquer and, of course, one cannot have a united front if everyone will not join, and some people are not joiners. Some people do not care about The Top. Getting there. Staying there. These people often feel, male or female, a boss is a boss. There is an incentive to hold close to the boss as the Office Wife, the First Lieutenant, and watch one's power increase as his increases, which is currently Nora's situation. Except that the more entwined she becomes with her boss, the less there is of Nora. She "becomes" her boss yet he does not become her.

Nora is aware of an odd, uncomfortable gray area in the workplace; since she cannot reconcile herself to it, she wants to flee it. Her reasoning runs along this line: Someone kids you about some "woman thing," knowing you will not find it terribly amusing. You react seriously. They turn around and say, Geez, can't you take a joke? And if you don't react to something that, for you, is not a laughing matter, are you betraying some fundamental part of yourself; allowing yourself to be the butt of a joke you don't find funny? This is the old I'll-get-you-coming-and-going. Nora feels there is another version of this in her company.

If you oppose the men in charge, you are not a good sport. It is preferable that you be a good sport. You are, in fact, Too Serious, verging on Bitch Material.

Now, if you ride the crest, tell yourself that it is for the long-term reward; the greater good; that you are not "political"; that it really, really doesn't matter that much to you; that you *like* men; that you Can Take It and are as much of a man as they are (more so, really, what do they "take"?); that you won't be there forever; that you generally follow the path of least resistance; that if you take the heat it will probably make it easier for you, and won't matter to anyone else over a period of time; that your boss is as good as one can expect and who's to say a woman is a better choice?

You can dream up a million approaches; you can try to ignore that small, nagging, not-so-vague instinctual presence; you can tell yourself that now you will be accepted into the boys' club. After all, you stood steadfast against your natural impulses, laughed at yourself; and don't you deserve some kind of reward?

The answer, Nora discovered, having attempted this tack on her own, is no. You will never get into the club. Never.

Still, on this day Louisa congratulates her, Nora, for her boss's promotion. More pay for him; more pay for her. More power for him; more secondary power for her. As the moon reflects the sun.

He tells Nora, We're a team.

But she knows better. Or maybe it is different in other offices.

And perhaps women bosses were just more of the same; maybe it is the position that breeds the personality, not the gender. Of course, in all her numerous jobs, Nora has not yet had a female boss. Which, she likes to point out, says something right there.

Nora is made uncomfortable by her own conclusions. All this office power and the roles of men and women leave her on shaky ground. All the advances made, which cannot, will not be overlooked by her; all the distance still to cover; she exhorts herself to quit whining and get back to work.

Then she becomes confused, curious, and questions whether her boss ever felt such significant doubts.

She wants to succeed or fail on her own.

Love was showing itself to be elusive, difficult. As hard as finding happiness in her jobs. Nora thought a solid career might quell the longing for romance. Romance, it seemed, arrived on its own or it did not arrive at all; could be desired, longed for, but could not be pursued. It belonged to you or it didn't and, for now, it did not.

She was growing tired of waiting; so, so tired of her own life, and this seemed to her horrible; to be so overcome by one's own life. She would drag home, exhausted from her job, and awaken in the morning as if she had not slept at all, wondering if this was what her life was meant to be; not everyone, she reasoned, was lucky.

When she caught a cold or the flu, she suffered alone; when she was happy, she was happy alone; occasionally she gave in to the impulse to call out within her own apartment, waiting, as if straining to hear a voice in answer to her own. And the rash of self-help books were unappealing, and the women who gathered in groups to talk—Nora could not be a part of that, either. A life apart, she sometimes thought, was not much of a life at all.

Several weeks ago she had received a call from Kiki, who asked (and thank god she could not detect the tight emotion in Nora's voice), "Nora, just out of curiosity, what would you say you want from life?"

Nora had answered:

1. Love.
2. A dependable car.
3. More money.
4. Travel.
5. *Adventure.*

Books & Bookkeeping

There are, roughly, two kinds of books: the sort found in libraries and general ledger books that record figures belonging to a business. Recently, Nora Barrie had been keeping books as a part of her job and discovered that the thing she most wanted to do was to write a book.

"Write a book," she told Kiki, "not keep one."

"What do you want to write about?" asked Kiki, thinking, I may have a story for you.

"Traveling alone," she said.

"I'd read it," said Kiki and Nora was grateful that Kiki did not use this opportunity to tell her that one did not simply decide to write a book out of the blue and that there were scores of people who had been writing for years with nothing to come of their effort and that it was a nice thought—gee, maybe she should write one, too—but hang on to that job. Kiki neither discouraged nor disparaged her idea. She even added, "I definitely think you should do it."

So Nora asked her boss for a vacation. After reminding her that he just received a promotion, he said, "Look, how much time are you talking about?"

Nora, for all her efficiency, had not given much

thought to the duration of her trip. Nor had she planned an itinerary. Then it came to her that not only was she seeking a break from her workday life, but from her organized and punctual habits as well.

"A month," she said finally.

"A *month*?" he repeated.

She was about to negotiate by saying, I'm always here; I've hardly taken any vacation time at all; I'm rarely sick. Instead, she found herself replying, "I'd actually prefer two months, but I'd settle for one."

"Well," he said, "give me a day or so to think about it."

The next day, he stood by her desk and told her that one month was "workable" but could she wait a couple of weeks?

She agreed and was quite content at her desk during the interim. *It is only a vacation,* she told herself; *do not make more of it than it is.* Still, the thought of driving away from all this, and not toward family, was thrilling. She imagined her sadness receding as she drove away.

Nora bought a blue silk diary and wrote, in her measured, exact longhand:

San Francisco: I lived in San Francisco for ten years, coming from another part of the country that was open and rural and not as peaceful as city people think it is when they sit around after dinner (Irish coffees and port in hand) and imagine "escaping to the country." I could tell them stories that would equal any sort of city violence or hardship or disappointment. What I could say would fill a book.

Only I usually stay quiet because I have come to understand that they really do not intend to move—even if it were possible—and that this moving to the land is just a conceit; a way of saying, *If I were a little less brave, I'd leave.* Believing, as I think they do, that life outside the city must be so simple, so bucolic and effortless that anyone could do it; not for vital, complex people who need to tough it out in town.

Now, living in San Francisco was, for the most part, a life alone. Not lonely, because the streets were full of people and there were North Beach cafés and street fairs and Golden Gate Park on Sundays and restaurants so crowded that one was forced to share a table. And smoky little clubs that once were speakeasies. One can read at a table with an unintroduced couple sitting across the way and not be considered rude. When I was growing up my parents called me antisocial because I often preferred reading to conversation.

New Mexico: With its unusual light, almost like a trick or an illusion. And snow in the winter, this falling sugar, and summer desert heat and high bright altitudes where the air thins out, as if you were flying, only you do not have to leave the ground. The place makes you feel airborne because the air is so crisp and dry by turns. And the balloon parade in the spring when the sky fills with hundreds of perfectly graceful sailing balloons; you feel timeless. You could be part of the nineteenth century; your mouth parts at the blue of the clear sky, the air that lifts you and the colors of the balloons are just like so many floating flags.

Someone hands you a wooden cross encrusted with one hundred *milagros;* you feel you could wish for anything and receive it.

Texas: Low marshlands lie to the south, near Houston, and you can climb to the top of the San Jacinto Monument, higher than the Washington Monument, with its great Lone Star of Texas on top. A Texan tells you that it is taller because "everything is just a little bigger here, darlin'," and you can stand at the windows that surround the observation deck like the cap of a lighthouse. You see water and oil derricks, grasslands and ditches.

Dallas is the money place; Austin the music place.

A little farther south is Galveston, a big island with gorgeous antebellum homes once clawed at by a record-setting hurricane. When it was all over, the inhabitants raised the island nine feet up. Imagine, you think, lifting an island.

At the end of your day you will eat barbecue. People will talk to you. Of course, they will primarily want to talk to you about Texas and the ways in which it is superior to whatever state you hail from, but they are likable all the same. They do not understand why a "pretty little girl like you" is traveling alone, and you resist the urge to tell them that you are always alone and are currently writing a book called *Traveling Alone for Those Who Travel Alone.*

The Dakotas: The solitary traveler will be loneliest in the Dakotas. The people here are fair, decent. Many are farmers. Most of the ones you meet are natives, unlike on the coasts, which serve as destinations for a number of people; the Midwest is no one's destination. Dakota summers are too hot; the winters too difficult, cold, shining white and a trial. The people here do not like to be touched or handled by outsiders; they protect the heart of themselves here in the heartland and do not talk about money, ever, or the fear, every day, of crop failure, which can smash an entire family. They are protective of themselves and careful about their lives because they are at the mercy of the weather—the weather that controls their fortunes in wheat, corn, livestock—and their large families and this sense of always standing too close to the edge of nothing, which can suddenly swallow you right up.

Everything you love—dancing, reading in bed for three days straight without getting up or dressing, talking long distance for hours, eating out every night of the month—will not be welcomed here. They cannot afford, available as they are to the whim of the weather, to indulge in such activities. So they become confused and think they do not like these things, or the people who engage in them when, in fact, they like them as much as anyone else; it is just that the summers are too hot and the winters too hard.

Virginia: The upper South will take your breath away. Virginia is drop-dead beautiful, a knock-out, easy on the eyes. And West Virginia is more of the same. There are caverns, enormous, strange and frightening, hidden deep beneath the hills. There are grass fields like rocking oceans of green.

You will be told that people are friendlier, poorer, less tolerant in the Deep South; since I did not go there, I do not know if this is true or not. As for Virginia, some people will talk to you while others only smile. As they will say, It doesn't mean we don't want you around, just that we don't need you around.

Richmond has a nice warehouse area; a location in a state of flux. This is one of those areas where the person traveling alone can expect to find some company. The person alone may also be in flux. Do not miss the Edgar Allan Poe Museum. A recommended roadside attraction.

And when at Arlington National Cemetery do not miss the tour of Lee's house, where you can peer into the bedroom where, they say, Lee made his sorrowful decision to go with the South. You can almost picture this man who loved his country but, finally, loved his region more, sitting with his wife, her arms around him, as he told her of his thoughts. The person traveling alone will recognize the spirit of this unassuming room; that of a man taken with one notion but surrendering to another and though his wife's arms encircle him, he cannot feel her. So solitary is one in the midst of personal sadness.

New York, New York: The biggest city in the United States. Don't eat the food from the street vendors. Leave your handbag at home. Don't engage in games of chance. Avoid certain neighborhoods. No matter how friendly or eminently "fair" you think you are, you may not be welcome. Have respect. Every place I have traveled has held strong divisions between groups of people but not on the scale of New York.

What will strike you most strongly is that all the things you thought about New York are true; good and bad. The other thing that strikes you is that many different people can think many different things about New York and, you are sure, they will all be true.

This place does not disappoint.

You will not be lonely here; in fact, this place will make you rather happy. Not only because of the sheer numbers but because everyone is outside, on the streets, on public transportation, in cafés and stores. The cabbies often appear to be confused. This you must simply go with.

Los Angeles: The second largest city in the United States. The place where I have lived the last nine years; where I am both tourist and native. The place with one of the most beautiful names: The Angels, spoken in a romantic language. The invisible city.

You will need a guide. Definitely. This city does not reveal itself; it is a place like a secret. It appears to be friendlier and more welcoming than it is; you will not be welcomed. It will not be unusual for people to simply look through you even as they talk to you. You will experience the oddest sensation of being ghost and substance; you will feel alone. You will have days where you think, Thank god I have friends here or I would cease to exist.

You will want to be young, beautiful, moneyed. You will need to be young, beautiful or moneyed. Or you will not be seen. These things, it seems, are rumored to be indigenous to the landscape.

"What do you think so far?" Nora asks Kiki when she returns, one day before she is due back at her desk. "Please keep in mind that I have had very limited time and still have many places to visit."

"Is that part of your preface?" asks Kiki.

"Yeah, actually, it is, I mean, I thought I'd begin with a sort of large overview, then fine-tune it with notions of solitude."

"Those are pretty big generalizations," says Kiki.

"No, they aren't," says Nora; "they are merely my impressions. I did not have a lot of time, as I said. Besides, you know, one person's subjectivity is another person's reality."

Kiki, whose life is mired in the particular, says, "Shouldn't you stick a little to the facts?"

"I did, I mean, if that is how it appeared to me, then it was a *fact* for me. Now, if we were traveling together or I was with a tour group, or hooked up with a native of that location, I might write something entirely different. But I was not; I was by myself." She stops. "Of course, I still have some things to fix."

. . .

Kiki's favorite part was the invisible city of Los Angeles; the way in which it is there and not there. When Nora read this to her, Kiki laughed and said, "Ah, one of life's perfect moments," and did not explain to Nora.

Kiki long ago stopped wondering if her friends or mother noticed that she was disappearing; of course they did not notice. They were other women and women *see* women. Women watch women as they enter rooms, to see what they are wearing, how they carry themselves. Their eyes meet as they pass on the street. Magazine after magazine is published to enable women to look at women without being appraised in return. From youth, women are taught to scrutinize other women and, as Gen would say, learn. Hair, makeup, breasts, waist, hips, thighs, legs, ankles, facial lines, flesh. Details, details. Women watch women. Endlessly.

As with Victorian women who were literally shepherded into segregated social groups and so formed many strong attachments among themselves, the modern woman too knows that she is part of a larger crowd, only the boundaries are less apparent.

It is men who sometimes miss the details; who often note only that which clearly catches the eye. It is men who could miss you completely.

Nora found the main thing she needed to fix was that she was not simply writing a chronicle of a person traveling alone; she was a *woman* traveling alone and that made things slightly different. Nora did not trust certain places, nor did she freely venture out at night, which might have accounted for some of the generalizations; trying to get the picture without being able wholly to involve herself. Or, if she did, she hung close to populated places and indulged in the luxury of cabs. She accepted these limitations at the time, then, when she had returned home to begin her book, noticed what she called "my pattern of safety" and how it dictated much of her experience.

It was strange to some people in parts of the country that she had never been married (naturally she did not mention L.) at her age, past forty, and no children and no man to call her own and no significant career, a topic that cropped up more often in the urban areas, and always traveling on the cheap.

It was more than moving from place to place as an uninvolved observer; there were times when she felt invisible, nonexistent because of these, or lack of these, things: wife, mother, career. Since she was without a discernible role, and of a certain age, which made her life seem less full of possibility; that is, no one could say, "Oh, you'll have kids one day," for example; people seldom knew what to say to her. They found it odd (still!) that she would drive herself from place to place, occasionally sleeping in her car when she grew sleepy and could not make it to a motel, or could not budget a motel. It seemed understood that a *man may travel this way, but a woman? Was it safe? What was she thinking?*

Her loneliness sometimes intensified as she roamed from one shore to another, thinking, I have no place here, in this country, in this culture. Adrift, solitary, attempting to shake her own soul sickness, and no one really to send postcards to except Kiki. She could write to a couple more friends but do not forget that Nora was social, knowing many people, without being intimate; that is, Kiki knew about her ambitions but she had kept quiet with everyone else, including her family and Les.

One day, in a restaurant somewhere outside St. Louis, Nora almost wrote to her boss only to remember that he was not a friend ("We are a team"); rather, he was her office husband who only grudgingly allowed her this time to travel, grumpy, saying, What the hell am I supposed to do without you? All the while making her feel that she could easily be replaced with a halfway decent temporary employee.

She discovered pockets of this country that did not entirely find violent acts against women wicked and profane. There was some vague notion that occasionally the woman asked, not in so many words, to be punished, or ravaged. If the consequence of a woman's careless sexuality was pregnancy, then she should live with it. She should take care how she dresses, walks, talks and acts. All of which can draw her own bad luck.

For example, to be topless on a beach was to invite your own defilement and when all this came to light for Nora, she decided her next trip would be to Europe.

Language

(For $800) Silhouette: 1. A profile or image rendered in black or singular hue. The shadow was cast by candle or similar light onto a white sheet of paper. Sometimes they were freehand cutouts. Sometimes they were achieved with a contrivance called a physionotrace. They were then framed and displayed in the parlor.

Named for Étienne de Silhouette, an unpopular controller general of finance in 1759. It came to mean being shallow, empty-headed, without substance.

2. An outline of a person or a thing.

In love, the object of affection can become an outline filled in. Like the photograph of the two coats locked in an embrace, sent by Henry. Altered, idealized. To please ourselves. (Kiki makes a side note to herself: See *Romance.*)

In regard to M. de Silhouette, the line of his face and hair gives him form, sets a boundary, yet holds nothing.

A line sets a limit; it is easier to give Nora the boundary of Secretary; or Gen of Widow; or Les of Wife and Mother. These roles that can be defined; sometimes serving as a way of determining the person, without attempting to know the person.

A silhouette, then, is a person composed of shadow. If that shadow was placed upon a dark wall or set in a dark room, then, despite the care taken to render the subject's profile faithfully, that person could no longer be discerned.

With Gordon, Collier sometimes felt like an outline. Les has said that she often feels she has left the room even though she has clearly remained, talking to guests. Collier, on the other hand, has mentioned that when she leaves a room she can sometimes still envision herself back there, chatting happily to the people around her. Collier wonders if she is substantial to Gordon or if he thinks he can walk right through her; that she is some gentle, accommodating wraith who will allow him to pass straight through should he need to go to, say, Les. So maybe that is the meaning of mistress: someone whom someone else simply passes through. Collier closes her eyes and sees her feminine outline, her female silhouette; cordate.

In love, our memory bears the shape of a heart.

Gin #4

"I have to ask you something," says Kiki. "If you don't want to answer, you don't have to."

"Of course."

"Did you always love her? I mean, do you think that feeling for her was always present?" Kiki is slicing peaches onto a plate; expensive out-of-season peaches that Henry brought for their card game.

"Yes. She was meeting my friend and me for dinner. I thought she was only being kind to me because I was her lover's best friend; that is to say, she might not have given me the time of day in another context. Not that I will ever know since people can only meet, for the first time, once, so I have nothing else to compare it to."

"That isn't altogether true," says Kiki. "I have been introduced and reintroduced to the same people a number of times. Apparently, I made no impression at all because they handled each introduction as if it were the first." She wants to add, Let me tell you about the sort of impression I think I make these days.

"You always made an impression on me," he says. "Maybe they were having an off day. You know how the mind travels sometimes."

"I tried to tell myself that, except this has happened to me on more than one occasion, with more than one person. The worst was being introduced twice, at a party, to the same person in the space of two hours." Kiki is laughing. "The best part was that when we first met I told him that this double-introduction thing sometimes happens to me. So he was someone who *knew* about it and still did it. I'm not sure I want to think about the meaning of all this."

Henry is laughing too. "He must have been drunk."

"I don't think so. Still. You know, something strange has been happening to me"—then she breaks off, hesitates to go further, caught between wanting to confess her fears—to hear Henry say, No, you are all there. I don't know what you are worried about—and wanting to see what he notices on his own.

Henry says, "Gin," then, "Strange? How so?" But he is not paying attention to his cards, or rifling her hand for points; instead he is watching her with a serious, fairly direct expression.

"Um, nothing," she says, unnerved and ashamed at being such a coward. Someone not ready to hear any sort of truth. "My deal," and she takes the cards from him; begins shuffling so quickly that her fingers are flashing in and out of sight. This actually fascinates her and she is thinking, *He must see something—he is just being sweet. Just being Henry.* "When did you know you loved her? 'Your girl.' "

"From the beginning."

"Was it a look, a mannerism, a word? Was it a thought? I went to school with a couple who were friends, except the girl had a crush on him, which he could only echo back with friendship and not something more. She called him My Ethereal Thought. I mean, with him in the room."

"What did he say?"

"Nothing. Usually he just smiled. I think he was taking hallucinogens at the time. Or maybe his glassy eyes indicated happiness. Who could tell? It was an era of glassy eyes and random laughter—if you know what I mean. Nothing seemed connected to anything else. I used to think of it as the breakdown of cause and effect—that the two things were independent and unrelated. And how could any of us possibly recognize the real thing when so much time ended up being spent in unreal places?"

"Well," says Henry, "some may argue that notion." He finishes tallying up his score, looks across the table at Kiki.

"Would you?"

"No. Look. I simply loved her. She was a bit shy and so taken with my friend that I thought, I want someone to love me in that way. It was powerful, that undisguised fondness she felt."

"Were you being selfish? Wanting her because you saw that she could want someone else a certain way?"

"We're all a little selfish. And I suppose love is selfish until it eventually turns selfless; that is, I loved her more than I loved the way she loved." He looks at her. "Does that make sense?"

"You liked her spirit, then?" asks Kiki.

"You could say that. It seemed a very true spirit. It was a very true spirit." Henry picks up and discards.

"Did you think she was perfect?"

"Never. Thank god."

"What was she wearing?"

"Blue." He smiles.

"And what else?"

"Nothing. Just blue. Her shirt and trousers and vest and sandals were blue. Her lapis lazuli earrings and sapphire brooch were blue. I think even her makeup had blue, bruised overtones. It was all roughly the same shade of blue; a kind of French blue, I think she said."

"That is a little odd."

"When I knew her longer, I noticed that some days were like this night—she would wear only a single color. She said it was because she felt too 'cluttered' inside. Other days nothing matched properly."

"So, her colors correlated to her mood?" asks Kiki.

"Well, she appeared happier, more content, when wearing all one color; it did not seem to matter what shade. One day, I dressed all in one color and it upset her because she thought I was mocking her."

"Were you?" asks Kiki.

"No. I mean, I thought of myself as wooing her in doing this; I thought she would understand how much I liked her, with this sort of homage—to be a part of her."

"She might have thought you were trying to crowd her. Trying to erase her by blending with her. That is what I thought."

"My aim was so pure," insists Henry.

"Well," says Kiki, "a misunderstanding, then."

Timepieces & Calendars

The luxury that Collier does not possess is that of time: She does not have enough time with Gordon, nor can she choose the hour they will meet or its duration.

Her time is running short to marry and have a child. Of course, she can have a child without a husband but, as she tells other women who suggest it, "I do not want a child without a father." Oh, the other women say, as if Collier were not quite enlightened enough. Occasionally, they place a hand on her arm and reassure her, No, really, you'd be a marvelous parent. You just need a little self-confidence. Collier says nothing in reply.

It is not a moral qualm or a judgment or even a matter of doubling the effort it takes to raise the kid; she simply loved her own father so much that it is something she would want to give to her own baby. More love.

And still one more disquieting thing is taking place and Collier is not altogether certain what it all means: She thinks she is getting too old for her career. And she owns half the place! She is very good at what she does; efficient; creative, even. A fair and just employer. Between the two of them, she and her partner have made their video production company one of the best among those in California and New York. But they concentrate primarily on current music (rock, rap, soul), music that is singularly uncomfortable with aging; specifically, a woman's aging. Even if her job is behind the camera.

Recently, Collier went to a lunch meeting with a director who was little more than half her age. Collier is still quite attractive, her looks deepened by the years, actually, but found herself unable to concentrate on the business at hand because she could not help noticing the director's attention drifting, then circling back to her. Grudgingly circling back, she thought. And the more preoccupied he seemed to be the more she intensified her efforts to be charming. To no avail. Then she discovered he was watching young women in the restaurant.

It so surprised her, this obvious lack of interest; it so astonished her when she considered that, professionally speaking, he needed her far more than she needed him. As he was giving her his director's reel it struck her that this might be the way it is; or perhaps it will readjust and she will again hold a young man's focus when quite old and very powerful, her business having prospered considerably. For now, in these middle years, these strange doldrums, she may appeal only to a select group of men who like her face and figure, or who want her company's services.

Well, if that is how it is, that is how it is. She will adjust. She promises herself that she will not mourn the passing of her youth ("Face it," she said to Kiki, "young is enough to catch the eye. Of course, looks hold the eye. Still"). That her life will only improve; that she will not fade away. They cannot make her.

However, between now and then, it may be rough, what with the "Gordon thing" and any more terrible lunches like this, nasty reminders, she thought.

These musings fill Collier's mind as she walks into the

office to find a number of young women in the reception area, only one truly pretty enough to be a model; the rest not bad-looking but lacking that quality which compels one to look twice. As she settles herself behind her desk, her partner wanders in, says, "I just need a break. I've been interviewing all morning for an assistant and they are all starting to merge into one partially suitable person."

"Well, maybe if you did not have an age limit you'd have more luck," says Collier, joking.

Her partner smiled his broad, self-deprecating smile. "I like to look," he says.

"Nothing changes," says Collier. "I don't mean you personally. In general."

"Young has its advantages here. You know that," he says, then, "I better get back." He briefly takes Collier's fingers into his own, lightly kisses them. She laughs, pulls her hand back. Collier is not angry; she is resigned that theirs is a youthful business, dealing with young musicians, models, directors, record company women.

As she considers her earlier thoughts regarding her own middle age, she realizes that the world—her world—simply needs to change. Drops her head into her hands when she understands that she can barely change her own life and here she is thinking of taking on the world. As if it asked her; as if it cared. And she hopes that no one wanders into her office this minute to witness her damp eyes.

The science of timekeeping is called *horology,* Kiki tells Collier ("It was a three-hundred-dollar answer last week," she says). Collier laughs to herself, thinking, How appropriate, considering that her dealings with Gordon are all about time and that he is very married and she is certain that Les would call her a whore.

Astrology, on the other hand, says Kiki, maintains that the measurement of time is sacred. Our era lacks the ceremony or occult of ancient time; for us, time is money, politics, science. As with the transformation of the moon from a mystery to a real destination. Our sense of time is ruinous because it is treated as if it were limitless, in this country uncomfortable with limits.

Take work: What exactly is a forty-hour week? Who decided that was the amount needed to complete our daily tasks? Forgetting, of course, that we all have *different jobs* and that we do not all possess the same skills to perform each task yet we are allotted the same amount of time. Also arbitrary is the notion that "free time" (retirement) after the age of sixty-five is the same thing as free time at thirty-five or forty-five; that we are somehow unchanged as people. Our children are grown, our vigor altered, it would make sense that, at sixty-five, we are finally ready to settle down to a nice peaceful desk job, or to fall into the soothing routine of the workplace.

Instead, people are expected, during youth and active middle age, to be happy punching a time clock; that restlessness or resistance is cause for guilt. If one walks away from it all, he is called lazy by family and friends. Why is it that if a person does not wish to spend the young years of his life sealed in an office building, he is labeled lazy, undirected, without goals and who do you think is going to take care of you, Mr. I'm-too-good-to-work-for-a-living-like-my-father-before-me-and-his-father-before-him? Just who do you think you are?

Well. Maybe you *know* who you are and that was the thing that made it simple to walk away.

Kiki, a Pisces, understands only this about her sign: It is

ruled by Neptune, a farflung planet, out there in the dark, so far from sun. Water, a mutable force representing emotion, a female image, and the feet (to walk is to act). It is the final sign of the zodiac, embodying aspects of the other eleven signs; it is not pure and, since it includes everything, is reduced to nothing. Culmination and foundation.

Neither Collier nor Kiki regularly reads her horoscope; each afraid that she will somehow miss the good prediction, all the while ensuring the success of the "bad" prediction.

Not unrelated, Collier has a theory regarding two of the Ten Commandments. First, Thou shalt not commit adultery: It is a sin, she reasons, because of the heartbreak it leaves in its wake. Someone so hurt by it, so undone and sorrow-filled, forced to weep without end and made to discover, on the heels of love, the pulling away of affection. You thought you were adored. You thought you mattered. Having known love only makes it harder to live without it.

Second, if you ask Collier about coveting she will tell you that the problem there is that it makes us bitter. And bitterness, says Collier, is the true sin. It is a waste of life, and life is time. That which we are denied can turn us into dark-hearted strangers not fit to be around other people.

Henry, Kiki's friend, says, along a similar line: Why do people expect so much from God and so little from themselves?

Yet in times of confusion and unhappiness, Collier will indulge in the reading of astrology, turning as primitive as any unknowing human animal. Primal. Nonunderstanding, like those people thousands of years before her, of a sudden deluge that washed away millions of lives; or the violent convulsions of the earth, toppling and laying low all that was familiar and trusted; or a plague so sweeping and random and absolute and ugly that one's response can only be to face the stars, calling to heaven to the gods who reside there, for relief, and alternately shaking their fists and bowing their heads and wishing for a sign of any kind. Listening closely to the sky and hearing nothing. And in response begin to record the placement of celestial bodies, interpret them and try to understand the brokenness of this life.

Collier unconsciously thinks of her time with Gordon as sacred, full, magical, borne back to her across time. She quickens when she hears his voice; thrills to his presence and often wonders at what point lovers fall into complacency. Will there come a time when Gordon enters a room (restaurant, park, bedroom) and she will cease to register any bodily reaction? Does it happen after two years? Five years? Seven years? A diamond anniversary? How much time must pass before love is less sacred, more modern in relation to science?

It is a pheromone thing, a secretion, a musk, a heat, an odor, a chemistry that makes you respond to Gordon, Collier could be told. Nothing more.

Also, in regard to time, the phenomenon of older men leaving their wives for much younger women. It is easy to understand the draw of youth; to awaken one day knowing you have everything but youth, you think you will find it in someone else, love her and be loved in return; that you will not need to borrow it since it will freely be shared. It may even belong to you in some mystical manner. (Remember Walt desiring to own Gen's qualities.) Since this cannot happen, Collier thinks it would finally be a sad thing when the contrast between the lovers sharpens, making the man all the more aware that he is no longer young.

Gordon, on the other hand, belongs to a different group of faithless men who are "age blind." That is, youth does not particularly move him and his attraction to Collier is due to the fact that she is his age and because she reminds him of his own youth. He rather likes women of his own age; he does not have to lie next to a noticeable age difference and be made aware of the passage of time. Instead, with a contemporary, Gordon can almost convince himself that time has stood still.

Kiki is busy with a new category, *Timepieces & Calendars.* She begins:

Joss sticks, offshoots of the Chinese fire clocks of the sixth through ninth centuries, were used in geisha houses as late as the seventeenth century. They resembled large matches and calculated the interval of "entertainment" with a particular girl. Her name was placed on an ivory tablet, then hung in front of a lit joss stick. The girl exiting with her guest. A flower girl in Japan could earn several sticks a day and even today it is customary to ask, What is the price of a flower girl incense stick?

Collier at her desk is thankful that tears did not fall and has regained her grip. As she casually flips the pages of her calendar, looking at her schedule, she is shocked to discover that she has spent two years with Gordon without even realizing it. My god, two years! Where has the time gone? In one sense, those years were a continuation of their early years together, which means that it felt longer than two years, yet it all passed so quickly. All those separate, secret days together added up to months, years, but in a curious manner as they were not a solid mass of hours comprising days but something more inconstant, weightless, insubstantial. As if thinking about the time between when they did not see each other counted as a connection between the actual periods of time spent in one another's company.

What seemed incredible to Collier was her unawareness of the passage of time. She had owned her own business for ten years already, yet she had grown so casual about her personal life, she was on the verge of squandering it. Her youth had faded, and now, with her accumulated experiences, she waited for a sharper understanding of the world. (People laugh when Collier mentions age. They say, "Oooh, forty. Gee, that's so old. How can you still remember your name?" And she longs to reply, "It isn't young. I don't care what anyone tries to tell you; everyday life will tell you different. Youth carries its own attractiveness. Stand next to a twenty-four-year-old—one of my partner's assistants, for example—and know that while you were so much prettier at her age, it no longer matters because you are not twenty-four. And you don't *want* to be twenty-four most of the time. A beautiful woman of forty is an acquired taste, elite in its own way. While youth appeals to the masses; it is its own democracy. Youth is effortless.")

With age, Collier thought that her body would slow or significantly alter; that her intelligence would decrease or increase; that her musical tastes would undergo a rebellion, replacing what she had previously adored with something more "suitable"; that she would read a book she had not understood at twenty and admire its wisdom at forty. She thought a certain grace would be hers. A glow; an evenness.

But none of these things happened. It was as Kiki had said of thirty: She felt awkward and strange. Beginning to look backward at what had passed as often as she looked forward to what was to come. Collier thought aging would continue to carry the jolts and acceleration that it did when she was growing up; when she seemed to sneakily add inches, up and around, in the blink of an eye.

Surely there would come a day when she longed to be married or to have a child and this certainty would signify adulthood. Upon becoming an adult she would remain an adult; she had not counted on indecision, weird girlishness, which seemed to include occasional poor judgment in clothing, flirtations with someone a little too young, and an inarticulateness when expressing her views. Charming was fine but when did one cease to be charming and move, unknowingly, into "odd"?

No one told her it possible—no, likely—that she would hold a friend's baby and whisper to herself (as the small, newly made fingers wrapped around her own), "This is what I want"—only to awaken the following day, relieved, that she was without a child to raise.

No one told her that it was possible to lie beside a man, not legally hers, and be so in love that she felt a rise of a sob in her throat so just the littlest sound escapes so that he turns and says, "Honey?" and she would not be able to answer because she could not trust the stability of her own voice not to give away her emotional state. She did not want him to know the depth of what she felt; it was almost too much, too curiously private, and too miraculous to share with this man, not her husband, whom she had no intention of loving again, who marks the days of his own calendar and does not worry, she is sure, about the passing days.

Kiki writes and annotates:

This is the principle of the Shortt Free Pendulum Clock: You need two pendulums, the free pendulum and the slave pendulum. The free pendulum is enclosed in a vacuum cylinder fixed as immovably as possible on a large concrete base and not affected by vibration. (Gordon is seemingly immune to the vibrations within his own home.) There is an electrical linkage between the pendulums that keeps the free pendulum swinging and accepting the impulse when it is ready for it; the circuit keeping the slave pendulum in step with the free pendulum.

The slave pendulum does all the work and keeps count for the other; operating electrical currents and controlling dials and time. (Collier most comfortable with time and money.) The free pendulum, relieved of all work, swings with a minimum of interference. (Les is silent.)

The Egyptian shadow stick records time with a movable crossbar and horizontal scale. This is fine for daytime but what about nighttime? (Night being the time Collier seldom sees Gordon, unless there is a concert or Les is out of town; nights are spent with wives, and children are tucked into bed and read stories. Nights are not for apparitional mistresses who read themselves to sleep or listlessly watch TV programs or give themselves facials or hope they will not suffer from insomnia tonight because of too much thinking, too much darkness pressing on the outside of the window.) At night the Egyptians, who knew about the stars and loving the heavens, would peer upward to gauge the time, while commoners used water clocks called clepsydra, Greek for *stealer of water.*

Hourglasses, filled with sand, are still in use today. For timing eggs and phone calls and nothing as grand as

in the past like measuring the needed journey or awaiting one's wedding or coronation.

The Saxons used sinking bowls and had little interest in hours; instead, divided their days into "tides" of four equal periods.

Sundials are found in the garden. It is said that true love is defined as standing in the garden waiting to be betrayed with a kiss.

Monasteries broke their days into canonical hours.

The twelfth century had the mechanical clock, although the word "clock" did not show up until the fourteenth century, about the time public clocks arrived in an attempt to break the domination of the Church.

The clock spring made an appearance in the 1400s, which led to the watch; which gave way to private ownership of time.

Gordon gave Collier a beautiful old watch of rose gold, set with cabochon rubies, topaz and diamonds, for Christmas. Or maybe it was Valentine's Day. Or was it an apology gift because he had been neglecting her; had not been spending enough time with her; crazy to give a timepiece to someone with whom you cannot spend any time.

"I have to drive out to the desert this afternoon. Past Mojave. Come with me," says Gordon on the phone.

"Maybe I have to work," says Collier.

"Look, I have to drop by this college—"

" 'Drop by,' " laughs Collier, turning her chair toward the windows of her office. "How do you drop by someplace that is more than two hours away?"

"About two and a half hours, without traffic. We'll be out there another couple of hours, then home. All in all, we could spend almost an entire working day together. Come on, the weather is great. It will do you good to get out," says Gordon.

Collier looks down at her hands. This is the way of it: They have to take advantage of the bits of space in Gordon's life in order to see each other. It isn't always sex; sometimes it is a day like today, clean, clear blue winter sky; perfect, and the best they can manage is a long drive during which they discuss everything except his wife, "Crazy Les," as Collier sometimes thinks of her, and the future. Well, they cannot even safely talk about the present, most of the time. Love, thinks Collier, should carry with it a certain freedom, a release, but all this thing with Gordon does is lock her down.

Then again, when Gordon is driving with her, away from Los Angeles, she feels she has his undivided attention; she feels they move backward in time, then forward, then back again until they achieve an odd sort of timelessness. It is in this zone that they are at their best.

So she agrees to go, says, "Let me see what I can reschedule," as she flips through her green leather appointment book, asks to meet him in about thirty minutes, only to have him delay his answer due to his covering the receiver to talk to someone standing near him.

Once Gordon asked Collier what she thought she should do about his life with Les and his life with her. This took her by surprise: that he considered they shared a life. She almost had the sense that he wanted to hear her ask for a resolution. "Well," she said, "this really has nothing to do with me, now does it?"

"I suppose not," he agreed and fell silent.

Collier could not answer because she prefers to be the loved and not the lover; the loved would call for absolute allegiance. Curiously, her actions have always hidden this truth by always acting the part of the lover and not the loved; by never extracting promises; by her undemanding nature; by her easy laugh and willingness to forgive those little hurts that seem to pile up almost effortlessly.

None of this is correct; rather she simply has difficulty stating her desires. A shy, inarticulate quality. Collier professes to trust and free will but in reality she has very specific words and actions in mind that she requires from her lover, yet she will not tell him what they are. Instead, it is like uncharted territory that he (any man she loves, not limited to Gordon) must navigate and discover on his own, without her help, because to help him would mean, for Collier, the beginning of the end of love.

She wants to be known intuitively by her beloved.

So when Gordon asked her for advice, she could offer him none and still be willing to live with whatever he chose to do.

As Collier and Gordon drive out toward Lancaster, she is thinking that she truly enjoys the desert, with its joshua trees and scrub plants and vaguely lunar terrain. That a particularly flat valley surrounded by bare mountains can allow one the illusion of sailing along an ocean floor. Or the jagged shape of stone and rock recalls stalagmites.

Gordon pulls the car over to a dirt road. "Come on," he says.

She moves as if newly awakened, obeying him easily. "I want to take your picture," he says, grabbing his camera from the backseat.

"Oh, no," she says, "I look awful." She flips down the visor, tries to finger-comb her hair. Then takes a lipstick from her bag. She looks out the window as she throws her greatcoat over her shoulders, dipping her head to see the posted sign next to the car: Red Rock Canyon.

"Hey," she says, "these rocks are really red." They are; they look like carefully laid layers of colored sand, pushed and dipped into swirling formations of stone.

"What did you expect?" asks Gordon, "Agate Beach?" He is loading film in the camera.

Collier laughs. In all the years together, before and now, they would take frequent trips to the ocean and, no matter where they traveled there always seemed to be a place called Agate Beach, which, as Gordon pointed out, never seemed to contain a single agate. But these rocks are red.

The day before had seen rains so full that they washed out the highway they were driving on. Other side roads were still impassable. As they ascended a small embankment, Collier noticed that the earth felt strange, loamy, unstable. Her boot heels were sinking and caking up with a claylike mud. Very sticky and strong. Still, she followed Gordon.

"Aren't you going to be late?" she asks.

"No, we have some time." He stops walking, says, "Stay where you are," and begins to shoot. Collier gazing up at him, her eyes squinting in reaction to the sunlight. He directs her to recline on a rock; to stand above him, against the blue sky. He wants her smiling, not smiling, glancing to the side; walking away from him, back toward the road.

Collier did not care about the photographs or the hour of his appointment or her career or his life apart from her: She had suddenly, happily found herself in that place without clocks; here in the desert where nothing ever seems to change and the people who want to live here are already settled in and the people who do not want to live here will not ever move here, under any circumstances; and development will seem slow, if at all. *This is why I stay,* Collier says to herself with wonderment in her own voice. *This is what Gordon means to me: not time "standing still"; rather time becomes rare and sanctified.* With this thought she experiences the rush of attachment.

Gordon gathers her up in his arms and even though he tells her that it is time to go, he buries his face in her neck and does not move.

The people at the college assume that Collier is married to Gordon and he does not correct them. As she masquerades as Gordon's wife Collier is struck by the very disquieting sense of presence. An invisible presence. As she listens to Gordon's voice talking to a small knot of music teachers, she realizes that she has stopped listening to the immediate voices and is straining to hear something, someone else. At first she thinks it is Les whom she is sensing, then understands that, no, it is not Les but the phantoms of other women who may or may not be in Gordon's life currently, that is, in addition to her, or, who may enter his life as softly and invisibly as Collier has entered his life. Would a future with Gordon harbor more unseen women, loved by Gordon? Is she like the story of the woman who haunts her own home?

And the next thing she does, without thought or hesitation, is to turn to Gordon and hit him, hard, across his happy face.

Later that night, Collier finds herself wondering if time spent in love can be construed as lost or wasted time. Time transfigured into affection? Is that a waste? Is any small corner of love in the world useless?

The concept of "useless" time at first seems inconceivable to Collier. The affair's beginnings were not so much born out of intimacy as they were out of convenience and pragmatism. "I need a man to keep my edges off," Collier once told Kiki. "I'm not looking to be anyone's 'only,' if you know what I mean." Collier was not interested in permanence or tenderness, though Kiki was having the smallest bit of trouble understanding why anyone would enter something so clearly resembling a vacuum. Then it occurred to her that perhaps Collier had the correct approach to such things, not allowing herself to be torn by longing for "more."

Or maybe it was the disappointed heart that Collier sought to avoid, not true love. After all, a broken heart in your twenties is a bittersweet melancholy and singular thing. This can even extend a bit into your thirties. But past thirty, the fractured heart of a woman can become shattered and scattered into so many pieces that when reassembled one keeps noticing the missing pieces here and there and so gives up trying to re-create the original heart until those absent bits are almost forgotten. Until you reach into your pocket or accidentally step on a fragment on the floor and are reminded that there are still dangerous remains. Sharp. Cutting. Leaving little messes behind so you will not forget that they once belonged to the whole.

Marriage & Day Trips

If men and women grew up, as they did, in relatively homogeneous and segregated sexual groups, then marriage represented a major problem in adjustment. From this perspective we could interpret much of the emotional stiffness and distance that we associate with Victorian marriage. . . . With marriage, both men and women had to adjust to a life with a person who was a member of an alien group.

—*Carroll Smith-Rosenberg,* Disorderly Conduct

Kiki has marriage on her mind. Can it be translated into a useful category or are the possibilities too limited? Maybe she simply cannot stop musing on Collier and Gordon and his wife, and though she has met Les she cannot picture her with a life. She cannot see her; seldom thinks of her as Les and more often as Gordon's wife. She thinks it is because in a situation such as this, it is best to maintain a distance, to not mention names or daily habits; it would be too easy to begin speaking loudly about fairness and promises and ethics. Besides, it is not her business—unless she loses that sense of distance, then everything becomes everyone's business.

Victorian women had friendships that were highly colored and floridly romantic. Sometimes they became lovers, with marriage as a tolerated interruption to their true lives. They exchanged letters of love with powerful sexual overtones; the language a brilliant shade of purple; the emotion pure. But the thing that caught Kiki's eye was the lifelong loyalty. A sort of genuine, necessary sisterhood. No one looking to sell another out; no one lurking around to steal your man.

Then Kiki circles back to her meditation on Collier and Gordon and wonders if Collier is taking Gordon from his wife (the woman whom Kiki can scarcely attribute a life or a name to) or if Gordon's abrupt abandonment of Collier to marry Les meant that Les was the thief, leaving Collier as some sort of payback.

Or can people lay claim to people or spirit each other away?

That is why it is best to lock the moralist outside in times like these.

The day that Les happened upon Nora and Kiki at the Farmer's Market, she had already been out to the county arboretum and Asian Museum in Pasadena. The afternoon will be spent wandering the gardens of the Greystone mansion; then out to the harbor. Driven from her house and drawn to public places where she may or may not run into someone she recognizes.

But for now:

"Collier," Les says finally, that day at the Farmer's Market, as she sat with Kiki and Nora Barrie. It is raining harder; every sheltered table taken by the lunch crowd.

"Follow me," says Les, as they gather up purses, sweaters, half-eaten lunches. Les unlocks the door of her car and they all climb inside, the rain sliding down the surrounding windows. Music fills the car as Les switches on the ignition. "I think that's better, don't you?"

Nora reclines the front seat slightly. "I like this very much," she says, dipping potstickers in hot oil and vinegar. "Damn," she says as it drips onto the leather of the car seat.

"Oh god, don't even bother." Les waves her hand at the spot. "This car is such a mess from the kids that I don't even think twice about it anymore."

Kiki is eating quietly in the backseat, hoping to go unnoticed, wishing this invisible thing were like a magic trick she could conjure up at will. Instead, Les has turned herself sideways in the driver's seat, looking back at Kiki.

"That is your friend, isn't it? Collier?"

"They've known each other for years," adds Nora.

"Since college?" Les asks. "Before?"

"Before," says Kiki.

"Then you must know her as well," says Les to Nora, who replies, "I tend to meet everyone at some point."

Les opens the sandwich on her lap, tosses the bread aside, nibbling on the lettuce, tomato, and cheese separately. "That must be nice," muses Les, "to have such a long shared history with someone."

Kiki is not certain that she is the one being addressed but nods in any case, afraid to be asked about Collier's past since Gordon lives in that past just as surely as he is moving about in her friend's present.

Nora cuts in, "I don't think anybody knows everything about another person. Even after years together."

Les shakes her head, tears off a bit of lettuce, a sort of a smile crossing her face. "So true." She turns back to Kiki. "Which do you think is greater, after a long time, the known or the unknown?"

"Look," Kiki hesitates, "we might have seen each other before. At Navy's Café. Once. I think it was you."

"Were you with Collier?" Les waits, her face gives away nothing.

"Um, yes, actually."

"I remember her," says Les.

"From Navy's?" Kiki sounds surprised. *Or does she mean from college?*

"No. From my home. She came to my house. She knows Gordon." Now Les is watching Kiki again with an odd expression that Kiki would later describe as "unexcited curiosity." Almost a contradiction from this woman who asks questions without appearing as if she cares if she hears the answer or not. "How well do you think Collier knows Gordon?"

"Oh, I'm sure—"

"Do you know Gordon?"

And before Kiki can answer Les abruptly says, "I forgot the time. I've got to go—" tells Kiki it was good to meet her; kisses Nora on the cheek. Twice.

If Kiki's answer had been yes, I know Gordon, then Les would have known for certain that Gordon was romantically seeing Collier. Les, this woman who looks without looking, can only bring herself to the brink of knowledge, then pull away because *to know* means that one must elicit a response; take an action; change course. One cannot continue life as it was before—before knowing—because it is impossible. It simply cannot be done and that is why one must be so cautious when pursuing the truth. It is not enough to possess it; one must respond to it.

So Les, who cannot take her eyes off other women, travels around Los Angeles, searching for the truth, for evidence of Gordon and Collier; Gordon and someone else; wanting to find it and hoping that it eludes her.

It does not matter if Les dines out, walks Melrose, pays a

visit to the observatory, enters the zoo, crosses the Picture Bridge at the old Huntington Hotel, wanders the arboretum, tours Hancock Park, strolls the Watts Towers, moves past the La Brea Tar Pits toward the county museum, runs around Lake Hollywood. It does not matter. The fact is, she is spending her days in public places, searching for Gordon's woman.

After hearing that Collier was at Navy's Café, Les is divided by the urge to return in hopes that Collier will return, and to avoid the place altogether. Les wonders if Collier was there specifically for her; is Collier shadowing her? Les who follows without following; who covers so much ground in Los Angeles that it is possible and unlikely that she will stumble upon Collier with Gordon.

And what if she did? Find them?

Les tugs gently on her ear, absentmindedly, thinking how funny it is to be shadowed even as she is looking for her reflection in other women. Maybe another configuration of yin and yang is not the feminine and masculine; maybe it is Les and Collier, only she is not certain that they are opposites; they could be complements, they could be twins, with like coloring and size and the link consisting of Gordon. For now, it is difficult to discern the pursuer from the pursued. Les from Collier.

The drive north on Pacific Coast Highway is full of cars, not very scenic, but leads the way to the Getty Museum, skipping the Greystone mansion. Inside, among the gardens and galleries, which are reproductions of a structure buried beneath Vesuvian mud, is a tiny box containing lead fishes, very old, the purpose of which is to ask, or thank, the gods for a fine catch.

She pauses, remembers in school when the girls tied knotted leather bracelets to their wrists, each knot a wish, waiting for them to break, wear out, fall off to grant their desire. Les's bracelet held two knots, one about school and the other regarding a boy. So afraid to add to her bracelet of wishes, not wanting to appear greedy. And she, all of thirteen.

Her hand reaches toward the fishes, then pulls back. Turning quickly, she heads for her car to her final destination for the day.

There is a lighthouse in San Pedro, above the Los Angeles harbor, called the Point Fermin Lighthouse. It was designed in the summery, decorative Eastlake style and dates back to 1874, when it was one of many wooden lighthouses that lit the California coast. Two sisters once lived there, driven off by loneliness for the positioning of the place is solitary, the landscape desolate, despite its proximity to the busy shipyard and its placement on the outer edges of Los Angeles.

The sun is warm on this end of winter day, as Les sits on a bench near the now closed lighthouse. She understands isolation amid the crowd; solitude in union, considers it an equal combination of blessing and trial. It is here that she sits and thinks.

Marriage between men and women really is like a shake of a stranger's hand; a meeting of different species. Why is it that for some the connection is tight and immediate while for others it is a shower of lights? Les is tired of looking for the mark on other women, exhausted by her day trips and her marriage. She longs to step close to the water's edge, grasp the shining, sleek body of a passing fish, fashion its image in lead and drop it into the Getty box of fish wishes and gratitude.

Just this morning, Les sat up to glance over at sleeping Gordon and wondered what he would do without her.

Gordon moved in his sleep, pulled the comforter closer

but did not, Les noticed, reach out for her. In the early years of their marriage, if she awakened before him, in the morning or during the night, she would quietly, softly ease away from his grasp to see if he would follow her across the bed. In the beginning, he did. When she was pregnant, he did. But in between times, Gordon stretched out, assumed more of the available space in the bed, as if suddenly, dreamily happy to find that he had so much more room than he had previously recalled. Leaving Les untouched and huddled on her side of the mattress.

Now she felt huddled on her side of the marriage; as if he had somehow assumed all the open area; space she vacated, not that he conquered. And then, Les thought, instead of pulling toward her and drawing her back into the circle of their marriage, he proceeded to fill the vacancy with other things. All of which caused her to ask what sort of woman allows such encroachment? Who does not give the pretense of a fight and is not happy to be so easily cornered and forgotten.

Well. Well. I was busy. I had a household to run and children to raise and dinners to give and presents to buy and all the rest. Someone had to keep our lives running smoothly and I thought it made Gordon happy—she catches herself, realizes that she has never known if it made him happy or not. It had not been a discussion of theirs.

She loved aspects of her life: her husband, her children, her friends, but could she be content being so many people and no one at the same time? Ah, the great irony of her life is that she can be wife, mother, friend, daughter and that the sum of her parts could equal zero. That so many roles did not appear to add up to one significant role. At least, it seemed so for Les.

She laughs to consider that by inhabiting all these roles, Les was becoming less. She was less Les.

Decisions needed to be made; for example, tomorrow morning she will shake Gordon awake and before he has time to think about it will ask him if he loves her and wants her. And if he does then they will both have to stop looking at other women. But she must hurry before the facts are upon her.

When Gordon arrives home that night, Les has to retrieve some receipts from his glove compartment (Les is responsible for the household bills). As she slides into the passenger side of the car, her bare foot crushes the mud that is stuck to the carpet, in a nearly perfect silhouette of a pair of shoes. As if the person with the dirty soles had sat very still, primly almost, with feet together, long enough to make a dusty, brown impression.

Les stares, almost stupidly, her eyes looking at the bits and dust of the dried mud, her mind reeling over what she was seeing and not seeing. It was as if inner and outer vision could not quite line up, creating a weird double vision.

Inching her body back into the seat, a passenger about to be taken somewhere, she fitted her own feet into the outlines on the carpet. The shoe size was roughly the same, which did not surprise Les somehow. These prints that could've been, but were not, made by Les herself. Her eyes are drawn to Gordon's camera, which is lodged between the dashboard and the deeply slanted windshield and she suddenly understands that the undeveloped film will contain pictures of another woman. She suspects it will be Collier's smile rising up through the developer and water.

Les runs her hand across her forehead, down the side of her face and across her mouth. She remembers a day when Gordon and she were newly married and he held both her hands in his and said, Sometimes I think the whole world shrank in size for the two minutes it took me to meet you. I cannot imagine otherwise how it is we are to find each other.

Her love for him was still constant; it is only in movies that people walk out with strength and resolve. It is only in books that love is like a flow stanched by the failures of devotion. When Nora asks her about Gordon, Les wants to answer, Don't you think if I could cease to care for him I would?

Here is what she knows: that she is tracking a woman who keeps company with Gordon; that the footprints in the car are hers; that the pictures in the camera are of her; that Les very likely spent time today in a parked car battered by rain in Farmer's Market parking lot with this woman's friend. That Les was so crazy as to think that a woman who walked into her house would not be a woman to mistrust. And it occurred to her further that perhaps Collier was the reflection in the glass.

That she guesses and could *know,* if she was so inclined, is troubling. Because knowledge always presents the problem of a subsequent action; that to know and not use that knowledge was to be the ground beneath another's feet, so the only way she could hold her pride was not to know.

When Gordon comes looking for her in the garage, calling "Honey," he finds Les emptying the partially shot film from his camera. The door opens, light falls in. They hold each other's collusive gaze, and Les is certain she sees the smallest dark mark on his face (so accustomed to searching out scars similar to her own on other women), near the corner of his eye and tells herself it is a shadow.

But they both know it is a lie.

Language

(For $1,000) Ephemeral: Evanescent, fugitive, fleeting, impermanent, transitory. The distance of the day. Something not meant to be kept. Say, for example, tin foil, hotel stationery, childhood, Collier in the case of Gordon.

Is love ephemeral? Is it defined by the words *something not meant to be kept?* Love, it seems, should always be for keeps. Maybe it is considered transitory because, some say, it cannot last; as if it somehow wears itself out with use. Who could possibly be interested in love that is not put to use?

Recall that there is a "vocabulary of love" and the words can only be spoken and heard, given and received, by involving the body. Tangible, solid, material. It carries the message of love, by voice, by touch. Felt in spirit; expressed in fact. Certainly, the length of time allotted the body on earth is, ultimately, ephemeral. A return to dust. [Kiki once read that human life, in its earliest and least complicated form, derived from the dust of stars.] So love, that wondrous abstraction, can best be expressed by the tangible—arms, hands, mouth, tongue, genitalia, eyes, ears (sound, sight, smell, touch,

taste)—arrived from the heavens, connecting the spiritual to the physical.

But if love lasts and the body fades, then is the physical of little importance, bowing before love? But if the carrier of this passion, the connection between two people is clearly the body, then does it become as important as love itself?

The intangible is paramount to Nora, who longs for a life of travel; an act that provides memories, experiences, friendships, love, exposure to art and culture; but does not provide, generally speaking, tangibles.

Gen wants to be married; Collier is drawn to music; Les seeks harmony within her own home. Ultimately, Gen, Collier, Les, Nora, and I would like to locate love. But in the meantime, we pursue other things that cannot be touched or balanced in the fingers of the hand.

Kiki thinks to herself, I am being made ephemeral, a ghost, a spirit. She is turning into shadow through the telling of her friends' lives, not her own; she is vanishing slowly from a society that has little use for one's growing older, little interest. And, according to one definition of the word, Kiki will soon pass from ephemeral to fugitive in rather natural and undisturbed order.

Food

ITALIAN STUFFED ARTICHOKES

Gen writes in her diary: *When Luke makes stuffed artichokes I can almost pretend that I am back home in that tiny New York apartment and my mother is in the kitchen—when was she ever* out *of the kitchen—the Good Italian Wife in her housedress with her stockings rolled above the knees, laying out fried eggplant on torn paper sacks to soak the oil. A cigarette held in her pretty mouth. Laundry hung from the window on a pulley line. Only I know she was the perfect wife because she wanted something more from her life, though she would not say such a thing out loud. She said to me, I think I could've been someone else. Instead, she fulfilled the expectations of her time in history.*

What a mistake. To try to live up to an expectation; still, I hate my widowhood and miss being married. Women from my generation are supposed to be married; that is how I see life.

Gen has been seeing a man named Luke Rafael for the better part of two years; fifteen since Fran had gone, leaving Gen hungry for the sound of his big voice calling her *Sweetheart.* During the immediate years of his absence,

Gen would still listen for him: for his car pulling up the driveway, hoping to gaze out the window to watch him, on his knees, planting bulbs the following spring. Under his hand, their garden was almost beautiful. Since he could not manage a house, the outdoors took all his attention. It was never quite organized enough to be spectacular, the sort of garden that caused people to stop on their evening walks past the house to marvel at the complexity of design and color. Every year Fran sat down with Gen and said, "I know what I am going to do next year. I have figured out how to get everything to come up at once, the different colors and flowers; the correct height of stalks and hedges."

Instead, plants seemed to appear before schedule or a little late and something always failed completely. Or the cosmos would overtake their own corner, edging out the roses or dahlias. And weeds, more than he could pay Kiki or Robert to pull. Kiki and Robert only marginally interested in Fran's garden.

When Fran died, Gen allowed the gardens in front and back to follow their natural patterns of wildness, turning into the eyesore of the street, which upset the neighbors, who would not say anything because, well, Gen O'Neill was a widow with enough to think about without adding landscaping chores to her list.

Still, they discussed her yard without ever offering to help. Forgot about the evenings spent in the O'Neills' home. Or Fran and Gen always waving or chatting with the other people on the block. And the sad appearance of the place made them resist inviting her to their own tidy homes and yards for barbecues or luncheons. She was, after all, a single woman and it would upset the balance of their dinner parties to have that extra woman around. Which is often the way of it, couples pulling together as if their own marriages depended on it. Naturally, the single man is welcome because he is so helpless, would enjoy a home-cooked meal and there is always a stream of single women with which to pair him, you see. Or maybe this is only true for Gen's time, in her very late middle age.

One day, Gen ordered a truckload of green gravel, covering all the dirt and weeds and silly patches of obstinate grass, as well as hardy stray flowers. She made sure there was nothing outside her home to care for.

Even so, it came too late for by this time those couples had more or less forgotten about her and when she passed by in her car or ventured outside to pick up her newspaper, were relieved of guilt by saying, Oh, I'm sure she's doing fine now. It has been almost a year and she seems to be holding together.

Occasionally, during her bereavement, a man would ask Gen out; men she had known previously but not well; sometimes men who had wives and believed the Myth of the Grateful Widow. Surprised when she turned them down. They shrugged their shoulders, said, Your loss.

She smiled back, That's right. My loss.

And it came to her with such clarity—the reason for her exclusion from couple events—these untrustworthy men needed protection from a single woman like her.

CHICKEN RICE AND PEA SOUP

Luke makes this dish for Gen every Thursday night. Not Friday; on Friday he always cooks fish because he is still, more or less, a practicing Catholic of the old school. Not that he wants to impose his beliefs on Gen; he just adheres to his own ways and, besides, he enjoys sharing a meal with her. She can be good company.

They met at a restaurant where she would eat dinner almost every night. Never much of a cook when she married, she no longer cooks at all, despite a kitchen that is equipped with all manner of specialized items: an asparagus pot; a glazed steamer with a hole in the center; *two* food processors; scales; a pasta maker; an automatic bread maker; a yogurt machine; an ice cream machine; a pizza stone. All she ever really uses is the microwave oven. She writes: *Unless all these gadgets can actually* cook *what good are they?* So, she goes out, night after night, accustomed to dining alone. She writes: *Initially, I hated, truly hated, sitting by myself at a table. Until it dawned on me that no one noticed me at all.* But prior to that entry, she had written, on the subject of eating alone, *I look pathetic.*

To this restaurant, at least twice a week, came Luke Rafael. He went on those evenings when it was too hot in the kitchen or the loneliness of his own life pushed him from the house. He once told Gen, "My wife was the only woman for me, from the moment I saw her. I sometimes wish it were not so." Then whispers a quick prayer of apology, causing Gen to say, "Excuse me" (at the whispering), only he does not answer and she pretends to have said nothing.

Luke was on his way out the door the night he first talked to Gen, though he had seen her before. He tripped over her purse. Gen has always carried extremely large handbags; in fact, this latest bag was not a purse at all but a small piece of luggage. Friends used to kid her about the size of her purses, speculating on what they held and why it was so necessary to haul around so much stuff. Gen said, joking, "In case I decide to run away from home."

So Luke lost his balance when his toe caught on her bag, which was situated on the floor, dropping him to the carpet, unhurt, with Gen only barely aware of him, but apologizing anyway. She noticed this man, older than she, who said he was sorry in return, then mentioned he had seen her here before and would she like to go out sometime?

"That isn't necessary," she said.

He looked baffled by her reply. Puzzled, and it occurred to her that he might not have understood what she meant, which was, You do not owe me anything. Not even a date. She could see that he was a gentleman of a time past, sweet, and he wore this sweetness as naturally as his nicely pressed clothing. He gave her a small nod, turned to leave, when Gen, who finally noticed his niceness said, "Oh, here's my phone number."

RISOTTO AI FUNGHI

A Wednesday night supper with Gen waiting patiently at the table and Luke cooking in the kitchen.

"This is wonderful," she tells him. "You make it all seem so effortless." Gen can see that he is pleased, which only increases his cooking habits. They rarely went out anymore; he brought breakfast to her house; stocked the fridge with sandwich meats for lunch; grilled peppers of all colors and heat; purchased Sicilian cracked olives, cheeses and Italian sausage, beef roasts, whole chickens, stuffed pork chops. He fed her and fed her. He talked about what he would make for the next meal and the way in which he would prepare it as they were eating what would soon be the previous meal.

Gen devoured every morsel he offered. Her waistline thickened, her hips widened, her bosom grew heavier. Friends noted the weight gain in her face and said nothing since Gen remarked on her own weight before they could speak.

"I've got to tell him to stop," she told Liz Beth, her old friend from many years ago, who lived near her in the first little house where she lived with Walt. And privately she wondered, in her diary, if food was all they shared. They did not sleep in the same bed, nor did they travel much except for the occasional weekend out to the desert or up to Santa Barbara. They did not have a great deal in common except their Italian heritage, both from back east; Gen thinking how similar he was to some of the men she grew up knowing, not the loud kind, but the gentle kind, which got her to remembering the neighborhood boys and fathers and brothers and how she had left all that behind, run out west, when still in her twenties, eventually marrying Walt (not Italian) and Fran (not Italian). And now, here she was, completing the circle with Luke, My Roman Catholic Cook, she called him at home. My gentleman friend, as she said to other people.

"I want to write you a letter," Luke told Gen one day. "I want to tell you something."

Gen called Kiki, excited (she was not sure why) that she was about to receive, she thought, a love letter. What would he say? How would he word it? They had not yet exchanged any sort of talk of affection and he did not seem a man who carried on much correspondence, in any case.

Almost a month passed before Gen began to wonder if she'd misunderstood him since no letter had materialized; she found herself anxious with each mail delivery. Their conversations continued as always: food-related. The matinees they attended in the afternoons went unabated. Their desert drives went on and still no letter. No talk of love or permanence or a shared life. Gen told Kiki, "It is as if Luke and I exist side by side."

"Do you love him?" asked Kiki.

"I love Fran," said Gen.

But Luke was a man and Gen a woman who could not

properly define her life without a man; either having one, looking for one or losing one. It seemed to allow her days a certain structure and direction. In this way, the letter gained in importance. It made her almost girlish with its possibility of romantic attention.

Gen found herself acting flirtatious with him, calling him Lucca instead of Luke. For his part, he seemed shy and pleased. Kiki could tell that he liked her mother very much, was devoted to her and appeared to want nothing more than to care for her, nourish her, connect his life to hers. He once mentioned something to Kiki about "your glamorous mother," making Gen happy, always, to be considered glamorous. Gen never left the house for any reason—to gather her mail, pick up the newspaper, venture to the drugstore—unless she was in full makeup: heavy, dramatic with false eyelashes, blue eye shadow, deep blush, bright lipstick. Still the red reds of her youth.

She did not wear flats, but the same spike heels she had worn for years; for so long, in fact, they went out and came back in style more than once without Gen's taking so much as a breather in between. Her natural hair color was a distant memory; currently she alternated between reds, blonds and silvers. And she wore turquoise, or green, or purple or gold contact lenses. "I like to coordinate my outfit," she said. Kiki was certain that if Gen ever passed out at home and had to be removed by strangers, she would still find a way to will her appearance into order.

Her mother's hands were graceful and patrician, though they carried long, manicured nails ("Not acrylics," she told other women who marveled at the length; a little too long, thought Kiki, but then she was unadorned as Gen was gilded). In regard to housework, typing, gardening, cooking, anything really that Gen was not interested in doing, she would smile and say, "I would love to but I've got nails." Kiki once imagined Gen's car with a handicapped plaque in the window: a drawing of a hand with the words "I've got nails" written below.

And jewelry so loaded and sparkling and exaggerated that children were almost overcome with its glitter, like found treasure. When Gen first saw the cursed treasure on the Pirates of the Caribbean ride at Disneyland she commented, "Now here's a place I could live." She loved to show it off to anyone interested and so could be found, with anyone's children, letting them turn over the rings and bracelets in their small palms as Gen explained carats and weights. Gen kept it all at home in three separate tool and tackle boxes.

Before Luke, Gen's life had begun to unnerve Kiki. Even Gen's eating habits changed. Kiki said, "You eat like a wolf."

"What is that supposed to mean?" demanded Gen, who only liked compliments and did not think this wolf remark was one.

"With your head down, quickly, no conversation. Before anyone else is served. When you are done often you just drift up from the table and you do not return."

"I think you are making this up," accused Gen.

"No," said Kiki, "I'm not." So these days Kiki is very happy that her mother is keeping company with Luke. Perhaps he would tame her mother before she turned completely feral.

There were two aspects to this singular life of Gen's, when she behaves with the absence of manners of one who believes herself physically alone.

First, she would put on her lipstick and touch up her makeup at the table in a restaurant when she finished her meal. Or remove her bridge, or clean her contact lenses. If a dressing room is crowded in a department store, she simply tries on a blouse while standing in a corner of the store. For a split second, any shopper passing by can turn to see her in skirt and bra. Or she burps in front of Kiki and Robert and does not excuse herself.

In the second, Gen will drive with Kiki (or any passenger, for that matter), setting the automatic lock on her windows—as if she were still the young mother of small, unpredictable children—keeping the car sealed with cold air circulating around. Kiki demanding that she release the lock in order to open her window. Gen ignoring her and cranking up the air.

"That is not the point, Gen," says Kiki. "The point is I can't breathe. I am a living being and if you want me to ride with you, then you are going to have to crack a window."

But Gen just changes the subject, begins searching for a parking space. She will only park close to the entrance (of the mall, movie theater, restaurant) and when Kiki points out that there are no vacant spots near the door, Gen keeps circling until she finds one.

"See," says Gen, "it is always like this. As if it were waiting for me."

"How so?" asks Kiki.

"I simply ask God."

"You ask God to find you parking in shopping malls?"

"Well, not just malls. Wherever I am, you know."

"Don't you feel guilty?" asks Kiki. "Don't you feel that there are other, more important things that He should be attending to?"

Her mother gathers up her jacket and pocketbook, says, "*I'm* not important?"

At first, Kiki thought of Gen as inconsiderate, with her recent lapse in table manners, her airless prison of a car, her partial undress in public, only to realize that Gen was unaware that her actions affected other people. So Kiki asked, "Gen, when do you feel most alone?"

"All the time," she answered.

Kiki's breath caught up short with the discovery that Gen, unknowingly, acts as if she were no longer there.

A few other Genisms: One cannot criticize Gen; it is not allowed. She will often answer, "At least I don't have a martini in my hand and a needle in my arm." As if that covered it; as if that negated everything.

Along this same line, Kiki, after a number of nights spent with her mother, said, "I cannot sleep in your room. You have too many lights and recording and video equipment and phones and timed radios and clocks. Besides, you snore."

"I do not snore," sniffed Gen.

"I am only surprised that you do not wake yourself up," said Kiki. "I just might record you some night on one of your *five* tape machines since, of course, I won't be sleeping."

There is a photograph of Albert Einstein on her shelf amid the pictures of family. Since she never showed any sort of interest in the man, Kiki asks why the framed picture of the scientist. "Because he has such nice eyes and since I am currently without a man, I thought he would do just fine. For someone to look at, you know." Gen smiled fondly.

This is what scares Gen: that she will be sent and forgotten in an old-age home and frequently tries to extract promises, to the contrary, from Kiki, who says, "I promise I will not put you in a home. If you become wheelchair-bound and a burden, I'll simply toss you down the stairway. Like an evil, dutiful child. Not to worry."

When Kiki was very young she and Gen used to stay up late at night watching old movies, eating ice cream. Occasionally, there was a wheelchair scene, or a variation of it. Usually the beautiful daughter wanted to be rid of her invalid mother; or she is out dallying with her insincere lover as her mother rings for the medication that can save her life. Something of that nature.

Once, Kiki met with Gen only to see her mother dressed very unlike herself and more like Kiki. "I call this my Kiki Outfit," she said happily.

"No," said Kiki, "this isn't going to work. You can't be me. I'm already me. You have to be someone else. Besides, I thought you didn't like the way I dress."

"I don't," said Gen. Then, "I'm thinking about changing my name. I never liked it anyway." Gen already had so many names: first name, middle name, adopted name, married names; at one point in her life she wanted to be Sean Dean because she liked the way it looked written down. "I'm considering Kiki."

Kiki's voice climbed an octave. "Oh, no. I'm too old to be a junior. You should have thought of this before."

"Look," said Gen, "*I* chose your name because *I* liked it. It had meaning for *me*." She paused. "You could say it was mine first."

"But it is mine now," insisted Kiki. Disliking to defend the name she would not have chosen for herself. But, unlike Gen, the name that was given to her is the name she claims.

"It's so—"

"No," says Kiki again. "No, no, no, no, and no." She

crosses her arms and refuses to continue this line of conversation. Ever since Fran died Gen has gradually been turning into "someone else," someone Kiki does not always know. There are days she misses her mother, then stops to wonder if Gen is as she always was, only more so now that her life has stretched longer, or if Kiki has become so adult, or is it all lost somewhere in between? Much of the time she seems to want to be Kiki's best friend; cannot understand that Kiki has friends, does not require more friends and really would like to keep Gen as a parent. None of this draws her closer to Gen.

And if Kiki tries to tell Gen to stop all this, just stop, Gen turns to Kiki and says, "If this is going to turn into one of those things where you blame me for the way you were raised, don't bother. I happen to know *you picked me.*" That is Gen's final word. She claims this notion is compatible with her metaphysical beliefs: that the spirit of the child seeks out its parents prior to its birth. Whereas Kiki thinks it is one more way of Gen's shutting out words she does not want to hear, like a child jamming her fingers in her ears, saying, loudly, "I can't hear you." Kiki tried to argue this point with Gen once or twice but finally gave up.

Mother and daughter are sitting in the enormous kitchen at Gen's house. In the corner, once the eye has scanned all the myriad and unused appliances, is a high-quality xylophone shrouded in heavy plastic, the hammers crossed and resting across the wooden bars, midscale. Though it has belonged to Gen since before Kiki's birth, Kiki has never heard her play it. It just keeps being moved along with all her other possessions every time she changes residences. Kiki has seen it placed in bedrooms, family rooms, dining rooms, living rooms—everywhere but a bathroom—and now it is taking up room in the spacious kitchen that Gen seldom uses.

Right now there is two days' worth of mail sitting on it, which Gen keeps eyeing without approaching.

"So," begins Gen to Kiki, "do you ever think about marrying?"

"Of course I do," says Kiki, knowing this conversation ranks right up there on Gen's Topic List with The Nursing Home and Grandchildren.

"Wouldn't you like a big wedding?"

Kiki knows that Gen would like a big wedding; for whom she could not be sure. "Not really," says Kiki with a shrug.

Gen walks over to the xylophone, toys with the unopened letters and bills. Today she is wearing a blue metallic jumpsuit. It looks to Kiki like some sort of futuristic flight suit. She briefly imagines Gen at the controls of a high-tech rocket, one stilettoed foot bearing down on the pedals, right hand cranking up the air-conditioning. "I suppose you'd want your father to give you away." She takes a sip from her can of soda, pursing her lips as if for a kiss, so as not to smear her lipstick. "Not that he was around to raise you."

"Don't start," says Kiki.

"He could have shown more interest in you kids," Gen says as if Walt neglected to pick them up for weekends and holidays; or reneged on his support payments; or simply disappeared and was never heard from again.

"He was fine," says Kiki, who does not want to involve herself in the discussion of What He Could Have Done. It bores her.

"I always extended my friendship to him. He's the cold one," says Gen.

"Well," says Kiki, "maybe you shouldn't have left him."

Gen sniffs. "I hardly think that's relevant." She drops all the mail down on the plastic. "I think that is why you have not married."

Kiki laughs. She has spent much of her life trying to remain neutral in regard to her parents; bears neither any ill will.

"I do," insists Gen. "I've thought a lot about it. I think it's because you came from a broken home, even though there was no way *I* could continue living in that marriage—oh, your father was a good man, a good husband in his way, but he wasn't any fun (at least with Fran I had fun). I simply couldn't stay."

"I'm not blaming you, Gen."

"And well you shouldn't. I'm not the one at fault."

Gen and Kiki do not discuss the fact that Gen left Walt for Francis O'Neill without so much as a breath in between; that Walt was heartsick at the loss of his little family. That it was not easy to get over.

"Look," says Kiki, her voice edgy, "I'm not blaming you and that is not the reason I'm not married in any case. That is not the reason."

"Whatever," says Gen.

Kiki carries too many versions of what a life can look like: the unmarried artist; the couple who carry on secretly for years; the long, happy marriage; many children; no children; a life of travel; a remote house in a field; perpetual travel with no permanent address; life in a foreign country as an expatriate; many lovers; a single love. "Have you been playing lately?" asks Kiki. She knows the answer: Gen never plays.

"No," answers Gen.

"Thinking about it?" Kiki is watching her mother's face.

"No," says Gen emphatically, finally. "I never played that thing. It was strictly your father's idea."

Both children had grown up hearing that Gen was an excellent 'phonist, as Walt called it, before she had Kiki and Robert. She would play at the parties they gave in that first house in Pasadena. The neighbors, said Walt, were entranced. When the marriage fell apart and Gen found someone else, she screamed at him, "And take that goddamn thing with you," meaning the xylophone. This after years together and their first boy and Kiki and Robert and their mutual friends and Walt's career and new cars and house and everything seemed only to be moving up and up.

"Who," asked Gen later, "needs to cart around something as cumbersome as a xylophone?" Yet here it is.

Gen thinks and talks and wishes to date. She wants to be married, occasionally waxing nostalgic at her marriage to Walt, sometimes wanes on her marriage to Fran and is, mostly, bored. Kiki says, It is because you are a woman without hobbies. "Why don't you get a hobby?"

"What do you mean?" asks Gen. "What should I do?"

"Well," says Kiki, "what are your interests?"

"I want to get married."

"I'm sorry," says Kiki. "A husband isn't a hobby."

"It is for me," says Gen.

Imagine, thinks Kiki, sixty-two and no interests. Then, as if reading her mind, Gen says, "I do have interests. I just don't feel I can explore them."

"Such as?"

"I like to dance, play golf, entertain, travel."

"Can't you do it with a group?"

"Please," says Gen, "all those little old ladies arguing about restaurant checks? I don't want more women in my life," she says. "I want a man."

Maybe this has something to do with Kiki's retiring

life, which is now fading into nothing: She does not want to hear herself, a woman in her sixties, saying, I want a man. And though she knows one must work around it, the words that Gen has recorded in her diary, more than once, do ring true. Gen writes: *It's a couples' world.*

Gen awaits the arrival of Luke's letter. Maybe it contains a marriage proposal? Maybe he wants to live with her. Would she marry him? He lacks the formal education she would like in a man, something Liz Beth finds amusing. "At your respective ages," she says, "what difference can it possibly make?" But it does matter to Gen, who has not quite understood the notion that being older is supposed to affect the emotions and cause us to not care about the things we cared about when younger. When I look in the mirror, Gen thinks, I see my mother but I feel eighteen. And when does a person's outside fit with the inside? So afraid it will happen; so afraid it will not. (This is the secret that age knows and youth ignores: that we all will feel, more or less, the same all our lives.)

Maybe it is a declaration of love. Even if she does not return his ardor (Gen, who is given over to being loved more than loving), she would like to hear the words; to fall asleep at night knowing she affects a man in such a way. That Luke may glimpse the eighteen-year-old inside her makes the prospect of his letter breathtaking.

One night, after dinner, as they are strolling past the houses on her Pasadena street, Gen slides her arm through Luke's, smiles and asks, "So where's my letter, sweetie?"

Luke looks ahead. He is so quiet that Gen is suddenly quite embarrassed, having, she is sure, asked the wrong question. Or maybe he did not hear her. In any case, she allows the silence until Luke answers, "I am working on it."

Gen looks away. Working on it? How does one work on a love letter? Then it dawns on her, she only assumed it is a *love* letter; perhaps she misjudged and it is a letter saying he no longer wants to see her. Gen has grown heavier on the meals he makes; is she now too fat to be loved? Or has this man of whom she is fond found someone else? Tears push behind her eyes and she is mute so as not to allow the unsteady timbre of her voice to carry, uncertain, not wanting tears to fall. What sort of life is it, she wonders, where she cannot bear the thought of a very nice man giving her the brush when she is not even sure she wants him? How did she arrive at such a place?

Now Gen observes Luke for signs that he is leaving her because she thinks he is too nice a man to tell her outright, may have trouble putting it into words.

Gen is tossed backward within her own memories to the final years with Walt Shaw, when she was seeing Fran on the sly and was having a difficult, truly tough time of figuring out the best time to say, I want someone else. I am leaving you. Then she watched summertime come and go; she told herself that she should wait until Thanksgiving was past (being just around the corner); soon, Christmas was upon them; in time for New Year's to be gotten through. A year passed in a moment and Gen was still trying to decide what to say and when to say it to Walt. She was facing another summer with Kiki and Robert at home and Walt making plans for their summer vacation.

So, thinks Gen, I know what Luke is going through.

There. She admitted it. Luke was leaving her. Having recently been part of a couple, she does not want to be alone, socially. Gen has always treated her unattached years as a temporary condition soon to be put right. Kiki, impatiently saying, Why can't you simply have a life alone?

Because, my darling daughter, Gen says, the world is unkind to the aging single woman and you are still too young to know it.

Kiki shakes her head, says something like, Your generation joined, mine remains unconnected.

Gen getting sadder daily at Luke's imminent departure and tired of spending her life longing for something (being married) that she does not know if she even wants anymore except that she thinks life is too hard without it and she is too old to try to fight it. She did not forget her exile from the world of couples after Fran had gone. Having her Own Life surely means fighting off everything she was taught as a young woman about her increased value as a wife. It is difficult to live in a world that is kinder to couples and punishes you in tiny ways for being alone. Gen wishes to live outside it all, but she cannot, crazy to think that she would have to "be outside it all" to manage, and if she cannot change the world, then she must change herself and she is not certain she can.

Gen laughs at having so little in common with Luke previously except food and, now, since she senses the silence and procrastination of abandoning someone; why, she muses, we have finally come to common ground. Some similar thing that we can discuss. Great.

On Saturday, Kiki and Gen go to see the Man Rays. Gen pausing approximately the same length of time in front of each piece, then wordlessly moving on. When she has completed her sweep, she turns to Kiki, says it's time to go. Abruptly, without asking Kiki if she is ready to leave, or what she thinks about what they have just seen; Kiki, who was by this time used to her mother's Man Ray trips and had looked at these pictures and sculptures for so many years that she almost did not see them at all. It was strange, really, to find herself before them in her twenties actually "seeing" Man Ray for the "first" time. To look at a thing repeatedly and never know it at all.

Gen wants to eat at the mall where a large food court is located. "This way," she says, "you can have what you want and I can have what I want and maybe we'll shop a little after."

It was past noon and the crowd was considerable. "You locate a table and I'll go get the food, okay?" says Kiki to Gen, who then tries to press some cash into her hand, but Kiki shakes her head, says, "My treat."

Her mother looks distressed for a moment, says Honey, with Kiki insisting and knowing that Gen gets the smallest kick out of being taken to lunch by her child who has not been a child for many years.

TIRAMISU

Watching for signs of Luke's estrangement is wearing Gen right out. Each morning she is twice as careful with her makeup; spends more time choosing an outfit that flatters her full figure; listens to Kiki telling her that perhaps she ought to involve herself in a class or group activity. Maybe perform "good works." Buy a gym membership.

None of this is acceptable to Gen, who, instead of concentrating on saving herself, works like mad to become someone to love and not leave.

"But," insists Kiki, "what you get for yourself you have always. What you do to please someone else belongs to him, because it is tailored to his likes and dislikes; it leaves you with nothing."

"I have nothing now," snaps Gen.

"Whatever," sighs Kiki. What Gen does not know is that Kiki's own words have startled her as well as setting into motion a linking of thoughts regarding the body and the self and vanishings, in particular.

Even in the matter of losing weight, Gen stalls, not because she likes dragging around the extra pounds but because they suddenly seem like a gift from Luke to her by way of his fabulous, affectionate meals. Still, she begins distancing herself as a way of holding on without holding on and thus enters a period of misery; that is, she dislikes behaving in such a guarded fashion, constantly watching herself.

Luke creates more and more elaborate desserts until she scarcely seems to be eating real food anymore. He makes: luscious, rich, fattening pastries, custards, zabaglione, semifreddo, gelato and tiramisù. She leaves nothing behind, devours each bite as if it were her last. See, she appears to be saying, how much I care for you? Caring without caring; holding on without holding on. Certain that if her weight keeps climbing, Luke will surely go, ashamed of his once pretty lady friend.

When she is resigned that it is over between them, Luke's letter arrives. For three days Gen cannot open it; moving it from the top of the xylophone to her desk to the stack of books near her bed. Luke has not called since it arrived. A sign! she knows; wanting, she tells herself, his written words to speak as his voice, to say his good-bye.

"If you don't open it, I will," says Kiki.

"No," says Gen, "it is my letter," and she wonders if it is the last such letter she will ever receive from a man.

"Suit yourself," says Kiki, then notices the plastic has

been removed from the xylophone and the placement of the sticks changed.

"Something spilled on it," says Gen. "I had to clean the cover."

"Oh," says Kiki. And, later, getting into her car, Kiki can hear the rolling bell tones of Gen's playing.

Dearest Gen,
I'm no good at this—how can I say about you—you're my good friend and it has made my life better knowing such a friend like yourself. I always hope to be together with you and not away.

I'm sorry it has taken me so long to write this but I wanted to tell you what I hold in my heart. You mean it to someone like myself.

Yours truly,
Luke

Gen finished reading it to Kiki. "What will I tell him? What can I say?" Her voice is cracking and she is not sure if it is relief (he is not abandoning her) or sadness (he is not abandoning her).

"Why do you have to say anything?" asks Kiki. "Can't you just say thank you?"

Gen is quiet. Gen, who always dreams of marrying up, is not sure how to overlook this letter. Walt and Fran would not have written the simple note that took so long to write. The women of her time made so much of the sort of man one married. She could, of course, tell herself that not *all* women cared; that it was only society that accorded the wife of a successful man the same attention; that love, that intangible, mattered more than anything the hand could grasp. It had, she knew, to do with visibility. Drawing on her own strength may make it easier to live, but it would not, she knew, make her conspicuous.

Kiki breaks the silence. "You've been alone too long."

Gen seems distracted. "I don't think you understand the way I see things—" And before Gen can explain her misgivings, Kiki blurts out, "Gen, I'm disappearing."

"Oh, honey," says Gen, "we are all disappearing."

The day that Kiki and Gen had lunch in the mall at the food court, Kiki was carrying a tray of food, moving along the periphery of the crowd, scanning for Gen. She cannot find her, circles again, is jostled by shoppers, saying Excuse me to those she knocks into, concentrating on the whereabouts of Gen. She does not see her anywhere and somewhere, buried deep inside the woman that Kiki has become, is her kidself, panicking because her mother is nowhere to be found. Kiki reminds herself that this is ridiculous, she is an adult, and that Gen would not simply wander off. Gen is not a wanderer.

Suddenly, Kiki spots Gen speaking animatedly to a man of about forty. They are sitting opposite each other at a small round table; Gen is in what Kiki calls her Talking to a Man Pose. Gen leans toward him, chin resting on the back of one finely manicured hand, head slightly tilted back. Smiling her large smile, bringing her facial lines into full, happy, bright-eyed relief. Kiki can hear her mother's social laugh (though she is still a short distance away); it is different from her natural laugh in that it is a little too earnest, a shade too loud.

"Oh, I can't say that I agree with you," Gen is saying to the man. Kiki cannot make out what he replies. Then Gen's voice comes up, commenting that "my daughter is about your age" and, mortified, Kiki hears her ask if he is married. Arrives at their table just in time to hear her mother say, "And what do you do?"

As Kiki clears the food off the tray to set it on the table, Gen explains that this man was "kind enough to share his table" and that he is an accountant. Kiki smiles, nods, can see he is uncomfortable and looks around to note that there were other tables with a single person eating lunch. Larger tables. Oh Gen.

None of this is the reason that Kiki hesitated to catch her breath before she reached the table, nor the thing that forced her to compose herself before sitting down. No, it was not Gen's singling out of the accountant; rather it was the realization that, as Kiki was searching for Gen in the crowd, her mother had been in view all along, only Kiki did not recognize her. Kiki had, actually, seen this woman in her sixties but not as her own parent. Instead, she had been looking for the slim, dark-haired mother of her youth and, in this otherwise unimportant moment in both their lives, understands that Gen has grown old.

Transportation & Hovercraft

There are three ways England is linked to the Continent: ferry, jet and Hovercraft. Soon, there will be a fourth, though it is of very small interest to Nora Barrie. When Nora found herself in London, she took the train out of Charing Cross Station to Dover, where she boarded a vehicle that resembled a propeller plane, life raft and train, yet a Hovercraft is none of these things. Nora was rather attracted by something so efficient—why, it is like me!—that has a likeness to a number of different things not easy to define; it is a transportation hybrid. Nora loved watching it glide across the hard sand of the beach, then deflate to allow passengers on and off. She liked the constant raining effect outside the windows from the ocean spray.

She had begged, pleaded and received a leave of absence amounting to six weeks. Dipping into her savings, she bought an economy fare to London, crossed the Channel, then traveled by train and car, alone and happy to be by herself. She had changed the title of her travel book from *Traveling Alone for Those Who Travel Alone* to *A Moving Woman: Travel Notes for the Solitary Female Traveler.*

She writes:

Prague: Too beautiful, haunted and lonely. You can almost convince yourself that you have stepped into another time, the buildings are so untouched by this century. Standing in the middle of a square said to be of the exact dimensions as Red Square, you'll be told that the most recent building is from the 1500s. There is a Gothic-type archway and a clock, very old, with a golden rooster, Jesus and the disciples, and the Grim Reaper setting it all into motion.

There is a Renaissance building with etched walls that fool the eye into thinking each block is either jutting outward or receding.

There are houses near the president's office on a street of gold that look far too small for adult human habitation.

There are convents, and crammed cemeteries with the most recent grave from the 1700s, and wine bars, and sandwich bars, and an island lush with chestnut trees and swans.

The people do not seem very happy and there is the language difference, so even when you are wandering around no one really talks to or looks at you. And some of the restaurants can stand empty and you will only be given a seat if you pay something extra. Or locate decent accommodations if you pay with foreign currency. So, for the woman traveling alone, it is lonely. All that beauty only makes it more so.

They say that in the nineties, Prague will be like the Paris of the twenties. And Budapest is said to be the Paris of Eastern Europe. Buenos Aires is the Paris of South America. Why is that? Why is Paris, particularly of the twenties, the measuring stick for other cities? As if time and place can be retrieved and re-created.

Not much bustle except for the Charles Bridge. Public places feel awkward. The young vendors on the bridge with their handcrafted wares remind you of San Francisco in the sixties and, at this point in your life, you are not seeking out nostalgia, or Paris of the twenties, so this does not particularly interest you.

Barcelona: Everyone eats dinner at midnight and the men will follow you down narrow streets. You like the nighttime activity of the place, although you often see couples sitting in underground cafés or wedged in intimate alcoves, the man's mouth so close to the woman's ear and, for a moment, you want nothing more than to be wooed in that way; so a young man may ask you in broken English to dine with him, only it is not so appealing since it lacks all pretense concerning the quality of your company. What could you possibly discuss, when neither speaks the other's language?

You each understand what is desired and if you are a woman traveling alone, you might be tempted and still feel utterly alone.

Austria: Clean & green. Gorgeous, truly. Mozart and chocolate, not to mention Mozart brand chocolates. Efficient. Civilized. Polite. Clean. Because of all this you do not care if you are traveling unaccompanied or not and you should *always* care about such things.

Venice: You need a lover. Period.

Rome: See the Sistine Chapel as early in the day as possible. Know that you are a ladder's climb from heaven. Sit inside the Pantheon, which is obscured by scaffolding; walk the Circus Maximus; call to the cats of the Colosseum.

Stroll about the Forum until you meet a photographer, who will ask you back to his studio and because you have spent a great deal of time on your own, were exposed to the romantic possibilities of Barcelona and, worse, Venice, you will accept. He will simultaneously offer you wine and to photograph you partially disrobed. The wine makes you brave and when he asks you to lie down on a beat-up old sofa draped in worn amber velvet, you are willing. With a black felt-tip pen he draws pictures on your naked back, apologizes for not having more colors, says, "I did not know that I would meet you today," as if he could have prepared for this lazy afternoon.

In the evening he cooks a fine risotto, plies you with more wine—not that you are in need of persuasion of any sort—and there are sweets for dessert. He takes you walking past the Trevi Fountain, also under scaffolding, and sits with you on the Spanish Steps as he points out the apartment where Keats died; says it is immaterial to him that you are a secretary and unmarried and past forty. He actually finds it a bit wonderful that you are all those things.

Later, after you have taken a shower, it will be possible for you to raise the back of your T-shirt to someone who will still be able to make out the sketch of a naked woman on your back. And, just above that, the remains of a singing cowboy and his guitar ("I have a love affair with things American," he tells you), but he is blurred, half washed away. The photographer will sign his work, MERCE, pale and near the nude woman. Abruptly, you will drop your shirt, taking away the image of a naked back drawn upon a naked back and the person, not Merce, to whom you have been showing these figures will later recall seeing, near your shoulder, a faded bruise, roughly shaped like a set of human teeth.

If this should happen to you, you will find yourself wishing to return to Rome if only you had the time.

London: A very good place to start. The English are friendly enough to make you feel welcome and aloof enough to make you feel safe. They will allow you your privacy since they are finally too distant to bother with you in any fashion. You like them quite a bit. A woman traveling alone will find this a pleasure. And the roll of the green landscape outside the city regenerates you.

Poets' Corner; Hyde Park; the lions of Trafalgar Square; Knightsbridge; Tower of London; the maze at Hampton Court; British Museum; etc., etc., etc., will pull you around this way and that. There is a great deal to see and the tourist walks—in my opinion the most entertaining—like the Ghost Walk or the Jack the Ripper Walk. Theater, of course, more museums, of course.

Unfortunately, you must leave because your funds are too limited.

South of France: Specifically, the Riviera, where you can wear a bathing suit rolled down to your waist, exposing your breasts, and *nobody cares.* Elderly people do it and women of all shapes and ages and sizes and even me. This is such a small thing—this bit of personal freedom—but when you come from a country that suggests a correlation between apparel and an invitation to sexual violence, then you love the little thrill of lying topless (and ignored) on a public beach. That is, you do not feel titillating, nor judged. With the warm, balmy air encircling your body, and the water so blue.

Did I mention great food?

Paris: The greatest place for the woman traveling alone. You can sit, undisturbed, for hours in a café, just watching the world. You can wander through gardens and museums and you are never lonely. If you are in the mood for company, you can find that as well. And the women are amazing, angular, beautifully dressed and cared for and everyone seems ageless. As if these women of a "certain age" understand that they matter. Such a minor thing, and natural to us, but here there is a leisure to it all.

Scarves abound! Jackets abound! Even as the temperature tops eighty degrees. It is as if everyone looked at her calendar and saw it was autumn and dressed for autumn, all unseasonable heat to the contrary. I like this approach. It is senseless and hopeful.

Books and movies and food and art and history and one of the most unusually beautiful cemeteries ever: In this place, for example, I saw thin arms of stone rising from two separate graves with interlocked fingers, a connecting arch. You needn't speak the language, though it goes without saying that it would be nice if you did; a certain politeness will help you get by. But I must say, I keep returning to the women. They are compelling and seem confident in a way that I do not think I have seen elsewhere. Almost as if someone has decided to let them all be.

Terra Firma

Two days before her birthday Kiki has been receiving calls from friends and family to wish her a happy, happy birthday. When she explained to each that she would be spending it at home, they told her she must take a few hours to see them. So, in the end, she agreed to what amounted to a small tour of greater Los Angeles.

And when the two days had passed, Kiki, at work, noticed that her body was in sync now. No longer did she find limbs and torso appearing and disappearing according to the quickness of movement, or absolute stillness. Kiki was all one faint outline; so much so that she overheard a couple of people at work asking each other when she was due back from vacation. Her old colleague Bill thought she had quit her job because he had stopped seeing her some time ago. "It's a shame," he said shaking his head. "I thought her work was quite good." His favorite recent category, he went on to say to his co-worker, was the one she tried to assemble on *Landscapes.* He liked the fact that *Homo sapiens'* love of expansive suburban lawns is entirely derived from a primal need for great savannas on which to forage and, naturally, survive. Atavism, not vanity, he chuckled. "Yes," he said, "she was a good egg."

To return to those two days prior to her birthday:

Gen arrived to take Kiki to lunch at the Smoke House for their salad and garlic bread—a favorite of Kiki's since she was a child. No one went to the Smoke House anymore, not really; it was a dinner house of an earlier time and had remained largely unchanged over the years; neither elegant nor shabby. Kiki discovered that she was rather happy to be sitting across a moodily lit table from Gen.

Her mother smiled, laced her fingers together and began what Kiki called the Litany of Your Birth. Every year, without exception, Gen launched into the play-by-play of her labor with Kiki; how she was "put out" at the Great Moment, which was normal for the time, Gen said; Walt saw Kiki first; and how her name was not to be a diminutive of Katherine, but to be forever and completely "Kiki," named for the famous model and mistress of Man Ray.

Kiki does not mention to her mother that Walt had called to wish her a happy birthday, reminding her that "I saw you first," then referred to her as "My girl of forty." He had moved far away and so could not see her.

Kiki excused herself to call Henry, to tell him that she might be a little late tonight and when she returned to their booth, there was Gen, taking in the room wearing a perfectly round red clown nose. "You know," said Gen as Kiki sat down, without commenting, "birthdays should really be a celebration for the mother. After all, she went through all the pain and trouble."

"You are probably right," said Kiki, silent in regard to the nose.

"Okay," said Gen, "I know you know I am wearing this thing." She tapped the front of the red nose.

"I'm waiting for your lead, Gen." Which prompted her mother to sing the birthday song very softly to Kiki. "I wish I had a picture," said Kiki, smiling, at the end of the song.

"How is Luke?" asked Kiki.

"Luke is Luke. He is a doll."

Kiki's gaze drifted across the room, focused on nothing in particular.

"You think you are so old," said Gen, pulling off the red nose, "and I wish I could make you understand how young forty is."

"It's just—well—I guess I thought my life would be different. That by forty—and"—she sighs—"there is this *problem*—"

Gen dismissively waved her hand. "Problems are for when you are my age. You girls have it so much better than we did. So many things you can do. No one even thinks about a 'woman of a certain age' around here; I may as well be wandering around with my dress over my head."

"That could be a good look for you," said Kiki.

"I have been losing weight. Anyway. I've been getting tired of it. I almost believe them when they say I should act my age. Forget about it. So here's my plan: I'm going to buy some time on public access TV and talk about whatever I want. I think this might be something I can do. Who knows, I may even interview you someday."

Collier is at the wheel as she and Kiki drive up to Angeles Crest National Forest. They wanted to spend less time on the road and more time hiking around, so they went to the closest place. Besides, Kiki liked the idea of walking around in a forest with the name of angels.

"So, what are you doing for your birthday tomorrow?" asked Collier.

"I think Henry is coming over," replied Kiki.

"Really."

Kiki laughed. "It's not like that."

"Why isn't it like that?" asked Collier as she pulled into a dirt lot with a redwood and glass sign that contained a map of walking trails.

Kiki got out and locked the car door. "You know why." They studied the sign, decided on a path. "Speaking of which, what is going on with Gordon?"

Collier was quiet for a moment, then, "He called me after that day, said, 'I think she knows,' which made me feel, well, strange. Not happy, not sad and I could not ask him anything because all I could think about was his wife and that awful second, you know, when someone 'confesses.' That moment when your entire world shifts and turns unstable. So, I hate that. And I could not help but think that she must hate that as well."

Kiki nods. Thinks to herself that, yes, the tangible world is susceptible to all sorts of abrupt movement: earthquake and volcano; gigantic plates colliding; and that the intangible world is equal parts faith, trust, forgiveness, betrayal, infidelity; and a life is the line that divides it all.

"Anyway, he said, 'I don't know the right words to say to her,' as if it were true that we are all foreigners to each other. So I said, 'I could explain it to you but I won't.'

" 'Why not?' he asked.

" 'Because,' I said, 'she will know that another woman is in your life, interpreting for you, so to speak.'

" 'What if I get it wrong?' he said.

" 'Then get it wrong. In the end, she will hate you a little less for it.' "

"Do you think that is true?" asked Kiki.

Collier shrugged her shoulders. "Maybe it is only true for me."

They walked on, kicking up fine dust, careful not to venture off the trail. The day was sunny, not too hot, with high clouds. "So now what?" asked Kiki.

Collier smiled. "I am back at the piano, taking lessons, going to school as well, just started last week, as a matter of fact. I decided, what the hell, so I'm forty—old enough to be the mother of just about every classmate of mine—and by the time I'm done I'll be forty-three, but I'll be forty-three anyway. I'd like to end up teaching or working in a club."

"What about your company?"

"I like it but I do not love it. I'm easing out, trying to put in a lot less time. I want to do something else. My dream, it must be told, is to play in the Redwood Room in San Francisco—I'll never be a concert pianist—I'll never be"—and here she laughs—"*Gordon*. So, maybe I'll be good enough for the Redwood Room.

"If not, I'll find a few pupils—enough to make a little money—or maybe I'll try to get work at a school or conservatory or play backup on records or meet someone rich and untalented who simply wants keyboard accompaniment while he sings to his guests after dinner. I could do that, you know, turn a deaf ear to an untalented rich person. Because, other nights, I'll dress in a very expensive, very well-made and flattering black dress and discreet jewelry and play in a beautiful place like the Redwood Room.

"Once a week, though, I'll perform in a dive with a brandy snifter to my left. On those nights, I'll tease my hair up high and bring a thick notebook of terrible popular songs, which I'll place in front of me, openly reading the words and no one will really notice or care.

"On the piano I will be polymorphously perverse.

"Once a year, however, I'll finance a trip to Europe and have a love affair. Very passionate, rich, and full of unrealized possibility because we'll both understand that it is of limited duration. Oh, we'll make the pretense of sorrow at being parted and, yes, of course we'll meet again—in his country or mine—only we'll never do it. We won't even write to each other. And, at the end of my life, if I do not ever fall in love again forever and for real, I'll think back on those once-a-year loves and know that they all add up to a sum of passion and sweetness."

Kiki and Collier are laughing. "When you go to Europe don't forget to button your sweater up to your neck, old maid–style. For the complete effect," said Kiki.

They continue their walk, chatting about this and that and soon they are back to the car.

Les, on her own tour of Los Angeles, took a drive out to Joshua Tree. She climbed on the huge rocks (many of which were festooned with amateur rock climbers, strung together with rope and calling out to each other with loud voices). She wished the terrain allowed for less echo from the climbers; provided a little peace. Grasping the large boulders she pulled herself upward, then hopped across, from rock to rock, then found a place to her liking and sat down to eat her lunch.

The other day she'd said to Gordon that he needed to come to a decision.

He said nothing, then, Well, can't we work things out?

Now that is really up to you, she said, but think about

this: I can only be one woman. I can no longer try to be many women and remain myself. You better be certain that it is me you desire.

Earlier today he'd come to her, said with great sadness, I'm not sure one woman is enough. Les stroked his hair, said, That is what I thought, and kissed him deeply and lovingly as a reward for telling her the truth.

This caused Gordon to pull away, saying, Wait, maybe you could be enough, but Les tells him, No. She understands that he was taken in by the kiss; said, We are better, I think, as friends, and is astonished to feel relief. Also fear at the unknown, though it is as if they had been moving toward this moment forever; she is sad and sorry but she thinks that as every viable thing possesses a specific nature, the nature of their marriage may be to be apart.

The calmness of this morning belies the fact that in the ensuing years they will participate in many bitter fights, more vicious and wounding than when they were married (they scarcely ever fought when married), causing them to wonder how they were ever married and how did they avoid all this going for the throat? These times will be punctuated with time spent companionably together, as the intimate friends they finally are.

But in the beginning, when they were courting, Les sometimes thought the sun rose and set on him while Gordon adored her in fits and starts but knew inside he would always find it difficult to love only her.

Nora and Kiki are sitting on the sea wall at Big Corona. The waves lap and throw themselves against the smooth rocks as the women drink beer from bottles. Nora had bought six different imported brands, as well as bread, cheese and, for Kiki, a small chocolate birthday cake. "Though you do realize," says Nora to her friend, "that chocolate and alcohol are not a pleasant combination." Nora is the more serious drinker of the two. She also brought four cigarettes. "I bummed them off Louisa at work. It's your birthday. For old times."

Nora says, "I'm off to the South Pacific. Not on vacation this time."

"Really?" says Kiki. "What will you do for work?"

"I sold my travel book, *A Moving Woman: Travel Notes for the Solitary Female Traveler.*"

"That is wonderful!" says Kiki, hugging her friend and clinking their beer bottles as a toast. They share one of the cigarettes.

"You know, my boss wasn't even fazed when I told him, I worried for nothing. He was even a bit cold so I thought, well, maybe he just doesn't care; then I thought maybe he realizes that he will miss me more than he cares to admit. But no. I think I was correct the first time and that I was truly nothing more than a shadow who made things run so smoothly he forgot I was making them run at all.

"It's funny, once I'd decided to go I realized that I could do without a great many things: I will not miss my boss or my job; my living needs are rather small; I am not in love with anyone. Of course, I'll miss my friends." She smiles at Kiki, who briefly wonders about Les.

"I am so happy, Kiki, and my only regret—the usual one—is that I did not do this sooner. Getting past forty has been a good thing, I think. It is so crazy the way in which I allowed myself to become less important in my own world—what can I say about an arrangement in which one is both hanged and hangman? Silly, human beings, what we tell ourselves; what we believe without proof.

"The only thing I do know"—she turns to Kiki—"is that a woman traveling alone in America is a target and an outcast and a rebel and a topic of concern and conversation and never forget that you are a 'threat' to another woman's man and aging is going to be hard on you."

Kiki dropped the cigarette butt into one of the empty beer bottles. "I'm not traveling in America, Nora."

"Traveling alone, living alone, you know what I mean." She put her arm around Kiki's shoulders. "Remember," she says, "you can bathe topless in France."

Gin #5

"Happy Birthday! Happy Birthday!" exclaims Henry as Kiki opens the door to her house, his arms full of wildflowers; Kiki's favorite despite their brief display of life. "You look great. And—" He produced an angel food cake with whipped chocolate frosting. "You love this combination—the only one I know who does—but it is your birthday, so here it is." He kisses each cheek, then her mouth.

Kiki smiles back, accepts the flowers. She'd dressed for the evening in gold, yellow, ocher, saffron, titian and apricot. In velvet and silk, topaz and amber jewelry.

"You look regal," says Henry.

"Thank you so much," says Kiki.

"No cards tonight. Here," says Henry, holding up a photograph without revealing the image. "I have a picture of her."

"God," says Kiki, "do we have to do this?"

"I want you to see my girl."

"If it makes you happy," she says.

"Didn't I mention that I often illustrate my stories? I will show it to you later, after I finish my roman à clef."

"Actually," she says, "I am interested to see which one

you chose." She curls up on the sofa, drawing her legs beneath her, adds, "You know, you really don't have to say anything if you don't want to. It is up to you."

Henry runs his fingers along the back of her hand. "I should finish it, I think."

Kiki is slightly reluctant to listen to Henry's words; however, she wants to hear what he has to say; she thinks it may shed some light on her recent ghost life. Before the evening is over she may even ask him if he has noticed her fading away.

He gathers her hands in his, holds them for a moment to his face. His eyes close, then open, catching her gaze within his own, an odd expression crossing his face, something halfway between relief and regret. "Are you worried?" she asks him.

He releases her hands. Gently. "I'll just begin. It ended with her because I could not be true. I was faithful in my own way; fidelity, I guess, can be open to interpretation." He shakes his head. "Actually, that's not true."

"Did you both have the same definition of fidelity?" asks Kiki.

"Yes. If not, then the question would have to be how did you stay together, not why did you break up. All of which makes it worse, if you know what I mean."

"Well, if you loved her—"

"I did."

"—if you shared things—um, how does this happen?" Kiki is drinking a glass of wine and absentmindedly picking at the cake frosting. She feels lost without a gin hand in progress.

"You mean, if we once were so careful with each other because we could not bear any sort of harm. If we were once so certain that no one else ever felt Quite This Way? If we are both in a crowded room only we are 'alone' and your heart behaves exactly like a wild thing caught in your chest? Maybe you see her cry for the first time and it just kills you. If she has some sort of awful habit which could drive you nuts but you decide, instead, that it is the thing you love best about her? And since you cannot imagine a week without her company, a lifetime without it seems unthinkable. That is what you are talking about, roughly, I mean? This connectedness of love? And you laugh a lot because that is half of it anyway."

Kiki nods.

"And you want to know what happens to change all that?" Henry pours himself another glass of wine, sinks deep into his chair.

Kiki whispers, Yes.

"It is simple. *People forget.*" He stops. "That is it." His glass is full of wine but he does not move to drink it.

She considers this. "Do you think it is that way for everyone?"

He hesitates and she is not sure that he will answer her. "Yes. Well, more or less." Henry takes a swallow of wine. Continues slowly, "People like to think they are all so different; we are not so different. Oh, maybe it becomes more complex when you examine the particulars of a situation, or that people like what they like and want what they want at that moment, or that some of them are horribly afraid of dying. Add one or two more tailored items—shove it all into some sort of crucible of thought and emotion and something primal and there you have it: broken trust and betrayal. Of all kinds"—Kiki is looking at him—"of course, we are talking about the lover kind.

"I don't know if it is worse to feel something for that Other Person or not. It is bad enough that you love the one you're with, so to speak, when, uh, memory fails.

("Wait," says Kiki, "isn't it worse to fall in love with that Other Person?")

"Look, the best that can be said is that what you are

doing has some sort of *meaning* behind it. But I am not at all sure about this."

("Oh," says Kiki. "I see.")

"But if you don't care, you will hear yourself uttering the stupidest thing you can say—which is also the truest—'it meant nothing.'

"Now your loved one has picked up on this line of reasoning immediately, follows the logic of your statement and says, Then I meant nothing? And the worst thing you can do to another person—whether you care for them or not—is to make them vanish."

Kiki takes a sharp intake of breath as Henry continues.

" 'It meant nothing' comes perilously close to erasing them, rendering them invisible, and all because it was a little too messy for you to think of them at all, if you see what I mean, so you had to, momentarily, rid yourself of them. Your loved one invisible, exorcised from heart and mind.

"It is that people forget that finally cracks the heart, moves us to cover our faces and weep copious tears. To grieve. Have you ever been to Florence or Paris or Budapest, oh, almost anywhere in the Western world, inside any old cathedral with tombs, or in cemeteries hundreds of years old? What you will see are crowds, gatherings of statues in varying postures of sorrow; with bowed heads, sitting or draped over a grave, appearing to wander to and fro as if they were stunned into indecision and no longer understand what direction to follow. Faces are hidden in open palms or crooks of arms, defeated by loss. And the ones that look as if they were walking may have a shawl pulled across their faces, or hands over their eyes—either because they cannot bear to be seen (this sort of sadness is very intimate) or because it does not matter where they are walking and so prefer to step blindly. Tears can and do impair our vision anyway. Do you know what compels them to sadness? The absence of the loved one; those who are no longer visible. Whose memory they can feel but who cannot be touched."

Kiki is silent; Henry leans toward her from his chair, his voice low and soft. "Kiki, you don't know how much I wish the story ended differently. I thought if I said it out loud and took you with me, step by step, something new would be revealed."

Kiki has moved off the sofa to sit on Henry's lap. Her arms are around his neck, her cheek resting against his shirt. "Let's see what musty old photograph of us you brought."

In the picture, Kiki and Henry are sitting at the edge of the pond at the Gamble House. Some of the many geese, brave and tame due to their extended contact with tourists, are swarming around them. One has his beak dangerously close to Henry's pants pocket, so, in the picture, they are laughing with parts of their bodies blurred in motion. And since the camera had been on a timer, the framing is slightly askew.

"This one," says Kiki. "The vicious goose attack."

"You look brave," says Henry.

Kiki knows that Henry believes what Barthes says but only the first part about the camera reproducing many times what has occurred only once. The telling of the story is a reproduction of sorts while she understands that nothing in life can be repeated at all.

"Ah," says Kiki, "I don't think about these things. Even as I needed to hear these things."

"Kiki!" calls Henry, leaping up with a jolt from the chair, dropping Kiki rudely on the floor.

"Henry, what the—" she begins, then stops.

"Kiki!?" he calls again, rubs the heels of his hands quickly in his eyes, blinks, begins to walk quickly around the room. More of a pacing than a searching.

She stands up, goes after him, close on his heels. "I'm right here, Henry, here," she says over and over even though she understands that it is useless since she now is truly gone.

So, Henry kept the photograph at the Gamble House because he loved that day, which is the exact reason Kiki is not comfortable having it in her house. And further, she realizes that one can be erased by the world (America does not know quite what to do with the aging single woman); one can also be disappeared by love ("people forget"). With that in mind and nothing to keep her, she decides to leave this place. Just quit her job, finished with categories and trivia and truth in tiny doses (half the staff thinks she has already gone anyway), lock up her house and go.

Transportation & Flight

Georgia O'Keeffe was inspired to paint an enormous painting consisting of blue sky and fields of white clouds because of a plane flight she took in her sixties. Having never before seen the world from this angle, she was compelled to record her vision.

Kiki was terrified of flying. Once, on a cross-country flight, she asked the stranger next to her if she would mind talking to her during takeoff and landing, only to end up crushing the sleeve of her silk shirt into a damp ball in her fist. "I'm so sorry," she apologized to the woman, this comforting stranger.

The flight attendant who sat across from Kiki watched silently as Kiki's fears grew to huge and embarrassing proportions, asked, "Excuse me, but is there something about this flight that I don't know?"

Kiki was amazed at the calm of the attendant, as if she were working in some dull, safe job. As if, thinks Kiki, she doesn't recognize the potential danger involved.

But these days Kiki feels challenged by the prospect of flying; now that she herself has become lighter than air. She thinks her disappearing self might enjoy the experience of being airborne, gazing downward, like a star.

Paris

Kiki Shaw flew to Paris on the cheap; she stowed away on the Concorde because she thought she might as well travel well and quickly. Being unseen could have its advantages. She needn't dress in the morning, could lounge around in her T-shirt and ratty old bathrobe; she might not need to dress at all for that matter, except she was not entirely invisible. The occasional woman sighted her; still this did not pose a problem in terms of travel. The disturbances in the air were a little difficult to manage—without a seat or seat belt, although if someone got up to go to the restroom she would sometimes assume the vacant seat—but fortunately the ride was fairly smooth, the turbulence tame. She told herself she was adrift on the open sea, riding the waves.

Kiki chose France as her destination, because of Nora's words. Because James Baldwin went to France and Josephine Baker and Sylvia Beach and Isadora Duncan and Gertrude Stein and Alice B. Toklas. Exiles all from an intolerant homeland, one which thinks nothing of forcing one into the crowded margins.

Kiki traveled south and swam topless in the clear water of the Riviera, all the while thinking that she would not show herself in a bathing suit back home (recall Henry's description of Kiki's springing from the palms of his hands in the tropical moonlight) and no one approached or stared at her or made her feel in any way ashamed of her figure. And it was not the same sort of indifference she had become accustomed to at home; she was not always invisible and remembered how self-conscious she felt, how judged she felt to be in public with an imperfect body.

Now eventually Kiki became happy and whole and seen, but before that time:

When Kiki arrived in Paris she took a room at the Hôtel Roches et Fleurs, where she had her own bathroom and the entire place smelled of fresh paint. It was run by a friendly Frenchwoman who spoke no English, so when Kiki had to ask for something, the woman would call her daughter to interpret; this college-age girl, as kind as her mother, who acted as a relay between stations. Kiki was surprised at first that the woman could see her at all and could only attribute it to 1) women *see* other women, 2) her kindness toward people, 3) perhaps her fading process had slightly reverted; that is, she was very pale in France as she had been initially in the United States, 4) a time change. The hotel was located off the Boulevard Raspail, a block from Le Dôme in Montparnasse, the old haunt of that famous local girl Kiki de Montparnasse, of whom Kiki Shaw was her namesake.

One day, sitting in an overpriced café near the Seine, Kiki sighs, wishing for a little company and conversation. The only other person in the café is a dark-haired woman, sitting close by, with her back to her. Kiki notices that many people smile, lift a chin, flutter fingertips in greeting as they pass her table. I wonder if she is some sort of celebrity, or popular local, thinks Kiki, and tries to get a better look at her without drawing attention to herself, never trusting her recent invisibility to consistently hold. Suddenly, the dark-haired woman turns toward Kiki and says, "I am well known locally and I am a celebrity. To answer your question."

Kiki Shaw says nothing; her impulse is to apologize for being rudely inquisitive until it occurs to her that she has not spoken aloud. This stranger read her mind, unless, oh god, Kiki is a transposition of body and mind; that is, her body cannot be seen while her thoughts exist in remarkable clarity, noticed by all. And the woman talks to her in heavily accented English, not French. Looking at the woman's face, Kiki realizes that she is quite familiar and when Kiki finally speaks she says, "Why, you're young!"

"Oh, no," says Kiki de Montparnasse, smiling, "I am not young, Kiki, I am an illusion. A ghost."

"I'm a ghost, too," cries Kiki Shaw, astonished.

"That, you see, is why we are talking." Kiki de Montparnasse signals for the waiter and asks him, sweetly, to bring her another coffee, then motions to Kiki Shaw's table. Throwing her bag over one shoulder and gathering up her cape, she sits down at Kiki Shaw's table.

"Well," says Kiki Shaw, "if you are a phantom, then how is it everyone can see you? I mean, you aren't supposed to be *around* anymore, either." Kiki feels strange to remind someone of her own demise; it seems a breach of good manners.

"The people who pass wave at me because I smile at them. I catch their attention. Oh, some of them think they recognize me but they do not consider that I am Kiki de Montparnasse because, as you pointed out, I'm not 'around' anymore." She thanks the waiter, drinks her coffee.

"I don't understand," says Kiki Shaw.

"They see me because I make them see me. Do you understand now?"

"Can they see me?" asks Kiki Shaw.

"I don't think so."

"Can they see you, here, with me?"

"Oh, no," says Kiki de Montparnasse. "You are quite invisible."

"Then why can't they see you? I mean, if I'm the invisible one?" Kiki crosses her arms.

"I am a ghost. Always. But the difference between us—which I see you have not guessed—is that I am seen or not seen at will. Whereas you are out of control." Kiki de Montparnasse lights a cigarette and hums a song under her breath. "I used to sing around the corner from here. I was astonishing, even though Man Ray never saw me. Clubs were one of the things he avoided. He was a man of absolutes, in his way."

Kiki de Montparnasse's memoirs, published in 1930, were known by various titles: *Kiki's Memoirs* (English translation); *Souvenirs Kiki* (French language), and, finally, *The Education of a French Model* (all translations) in 1950. Now, they could have been called *My Life with Man Ray* (one of the most famous of her lovers) or *My Life in Montparnasse* (as if she were a possession of the district), or *Man Ray Was Not My First.* Calling them, in 1930, *Kiki's Memoirs* attached them to Kiki without featuring someone other than the author.

Another way to think about this is: There was something intrinsically appealing in Kiki herself, as famous artists' model and mistress, beyond her associations. She sang, she wrote, she painted. She had a life independent of other lives.

Her given name was Alice Prin but by the time she was seventeen and had been out on her own a bit, she took to calling herself Kiki de Montparnasse. As if she belonged to a section of Paris; as if she were a feature of some timely and artistic landscape. "There are Le Dôme, the Luxembourg Gardens, the Boulevard Raspail and Kiki de Montparnasse." It is a matter of identity. Alice Prin of Burgundy identified strongly and was identified with Montparnasse. A place, not a person.

In her very early years in Paris, when she was thirteen she met a boy named Dede, nineteen, who became her lover, despite his living with an older woman. Dede left bruised, strawberry-colored kisses on Kiki's neck, observed by her mother, with Kiki amazed to know that kisses could leave marks like a pinch or a slap. She said, All flesh is brightly colored from passion, and, after the marks made themselves known, I'll know better after this.

Les, too, in another time and country, will experience and understand the mark of love.

Kiki Shaw accepts the invitation to walk beside the river with Kiki de Montparnasse. Anyone passing by would notice, if they could be noticed, two women, roughly the same age, with similar eyes and dark hair, very nearly of identical height. It is possible for them to be taken as sisters. Remember Gen's attraction to *Le Violon d'Ingres* because of the silhouette of the former Alice Prin of Burgundy's figure, the resemblance of her own body shape and, by genetic inheritance, the similar figure of her daughter, Kiki Shaw. Three women, three graces, arranged as a pleasing trio of strings.

Kiki de Montparnasse was saying, "Hemingway was correct when he said that I have seldom had a room of my own." She laughs. "I usually shared the room of the man I was with, or with a couple. Without my own lodgings I ended up with many couples. Some married, some not. This was as I was making my way, bit by bit, into 'artistic circles.' You could say, unlike the other one with the room of her own, I became my own room. In this way, I carried many things with me at all times. But the men . . . I loved the men." Her eyes shone. "And I was loved back."

Kiki Shaw walks next to her in silence, still trying to understand how she came to be speaking with the spirit of the famous Kiki; wondering if it was just one more illusion in the life of hers that could no longer be believed to present fact as fact and fiction as fiction. One of the attractions to her job with the TV show had been the opportunity to ferret out snippets of truth and stash them in various categories; no one, reasons Kiki, should be asked to embrace the absolute truth in its entirety. Maybe with the instability between What Is True and what is real, fact and fantasy, her job was easier to abandon than she first thought. So, here she is, walking along the Seine with a phantom companion who does not elicit a single smile or nod of greeting since she is hidden to all save Kiki Shaw.

"Tell me about yourself, then I will tell you about myself," says Kiki de Montparnasse. "You know, one of the men who wrote an introduction to my memoirs said they never could have been done by an American or English Kiki. Those were his exact words. He said it was because the English language is too crude—but I think it is because it would not be allowed. Now, talk to me."

"My life will bore you," says Kiki Shaw.

"Tell me anyway."

So Kiki began by saying that she'd recently turned forty—

"Good for you," interrupted the other Kiki.

"But it is middle age," she laments.

To which the other Kiki replies, "What of it?"

—found herself turning ethereal, came to Paris. She explains her job, and friends Collier and Nora; her mother, Gen, and all their lives.

When she finishes, Kiki de Montparnasse suggests aperitifs and oysters for dinner, says, "Then you can tell me your life." She says this happily and Kiki Shaw is confused because she had done nothing but talk for the past few hours, as the sky above the water darkened to steel and dusk settled upon them.

"Weren't you listening?" asks Kiki Shaw.

"Oh, I always listen. It is one of my finest traits. Ask anyone."

"Then—"

"I heard all about the people at your office, your parents, your friends, their lovers and husbands and bosses, but I did not hear about you, except to say that you are 'disappearing'—something which frankly does not much surprise me." Kiki Shaw obediently follows Kiki de Montparnasse into what looked to be an expensive restaurant. Kiki Shaw wondered if she is expected to pay for dinner.

"Of course not," says Kiki de Montparnasse, responding again to Kiki Shaw's unspoken question. "I have been very poor in my life and I will take care of this. I know how to get around things. I used to know the man who ran the place but he is gone now." She smiled. "Or, as you would say, 'not around.' " She chose the best available table, ordered for both of them. "Now," she says, elbows on the round table, "continue."

But Kiki Shaw is dumbstruck, wondering if perhaps friends and family and work did not constitute a life. Her life. Then she sees that it goes beyond her friends and family and work and into theirs; she sees that it is possible that the genesis of her absence within her life is not entirely cultural—that is, she was a citizen of a country that maintained a passion for youth—but personal as well. If women are to be the keepers of the home and office; to track what everyone is doing, to be concerned for the well-being of others and able to perform many tasks at once; to be the "perfect hostess"; then maybe she fulfilled her woman's life a little too well. She would have to think about this.

"Yes," says Kiki de Montparnasse. "Then we will talk about my life and you will see how it is done."

Kiki de Montparnasse begins with certain facts of her own story, with Kiki Shaw reflexively listening for trivia, truth, and categories. And this is what she heard:

("I shall begin with Man Ray, my friend.") Kiki and Man Ray met at a Paris café. He, new to Paris and unknown; she with her limited popularity, was sitting with a girlfriend. Man Ray later told Kiki he recalled the dark curls that fell about her face in a fashionable haircut of 1922 and, it must be said, he took in the girlfriend as well. He noted that the girlfriend's hair was straight with brief little bangs above very made-up eyes.

Kiki's eyes bore a line of kohl that traced the upper and lower lids, extending beyond the corners like thin animal tails creating a popular, vaguely Chinese effect. Very romantic. Kiki wore it well. This smart Asian exoticism on an extremely white French girl of the twenties. Her small face powdered pale and dusty; her lips painted red red red and limned in a perfect Cupid's bow, like a permanent kiss, crimson like Dede's kisses to the throat, her young lover who knew her before Man Ray ever spied her in that café, all of which made a man like Man want to preserve and smudge.

Hemingway said, "It was very pleasant after working to see Kiki. She was wonderful to look at. Having a fine face to start with she made it a work of art: painted eyes, painted mouth, matte-finished cheek. All before anyone thought to paint it on canvas. She had a wonderfully beautiful body and a fine voice, talking voice, not singing voice, though she later became a chanteuse, and she certainly dominated that era of Montparnasse more than Queen Victoria ever dominated the Victorian Era."

When Kiki met Man Ray she thought him an American who makes the nicest photographs and decided to pose for him. She was pleased by his accent; thought him mysterious. She recalled stretching out on a bed and watching him work in the dark with a "little red light illuminating his face" and the excitement, "pins and needles," of waiting for him to finish. They hung out with Dadaists and Surrealists though she claimed she could not tell the difference between the two; was not bored by their conversations, surprising since, by her own admission, she did not know what they were talking about.

She admired Man Ray's art; his art being the path to her heart. She said Man Ray was "driven to despair with her flashy tastes," and it is true that when Kiki Shaw met Kiki de Montparnasse, she was, now as then, dressed in the manner of the quarter; "glad rags," she called them: a man's hat, an old cape, three-toed shoes that upset her balance.

When Kiki Shaw asks her about the men in her life, after Dede and prior to Man Ray, she says, "I posed once for Utrillo and was knocked off my pins to discover that he had been drawing a little country house." Kiki de Montparnasse laughs and orders a dozen more oysters. Kiki Shaw is in awe of her appetite, only to have the other Kiki remind her that when one has been poor one never feels full.

Kiki de Montparnasse continues, her curiosity regarding life is inherited; that her grandmother was just like her: full of wonder, and Kiki Shaw did not correct her saying, Doesn't the granddaughter follow the grandmother, not vice versa?

Another artist asked Kiki de Montparnasse why she lacked hair and her feet were always dirty. "Actually," says Kiki, "I was not wild about posing because I lacked development in a certain spot and needed to dab myself with black chalk—I can give a swell imitation of hair!"

She spent what little money she had getting all dolled up and to see if she could spot any artists at Le Dôme or Rotonde.

Another asked her to sing "Louise."

More than once she was asked by men, not artists, to expose her breasts to them for ten sous.

"What did you do?" asks Kiki Shaw.

"I complied."

Still another artist asked the manager of a club, when he first laid eyes on Kiki, "Who's the new whore?" then went on to call her a slut and a "syphilitic old bitch"—but in the friendliest way, insisted Kiki. "Then," she says, "I acted insulted and made up my mind not to talk to him. But it was too bad because I liked him!"

Kiki Shaw swallows more wine and thinks, *Was there ever anyone you said no to?*

"Naturally," answered Kiki de Montparnasse, reminding Kiki Shaw to be more careful about her thoughts when around this other Kiki, "but not very often. I had to eat, don't you know. I always had fish to fry."

More oysters are ordered and Kiki Shaw lights a cigarette, done eating but fascinated watching Kiki de Montparnasse putting them away, chatting happily between each mollusk, punctuated with sips of wine. Now Kiki de Montparnasse is saying how at thirteen she would swipe a petal from her mother's artificial geranium each day to rouge her cheeks and mouth. That she loved to read. That she had a passion for yellow socks. This makes Kiki Shaw laugh, that and the wine and the possibility that she has left the phenomenal world for a pleasurable evening spent in the company of this funny spirit.

"Now," says Kiki de Montparnasse, "there are some café singers, the kind who think they are just too Spanish for words, don't you know?" She also mentions that from time to time, she had heart trouble, palpitations, with nothing to be done. And, once, she traveled to the hospital in only a coat and nothing underneath.

After requesting cheese and mousse, Kiki de Montparnasse says to Kiki Shaw that all Man Ray's women had the most beautiful names: Kiki—she bats her eyes—Adrienne, Lee, and his wife, Juliet. "And we were all committed to paper and sculpture; almost as if he made us up altogether."

"Listening to you," says Kiki Shaw, "I feel as though I have had no life."

"That is it in part. Let me finish now," says Kiki de Montparnasse, selecting the cheese she likes best, allowing the many little slices to be arranged on a platter between them. Soup bowls of chocolate mousse arriving in close order.

Kiki Shaw is organizing, categorizing, filing the story that the other Kiki relates. Paying such close attention because, as Kiki Shaw is well aware, the truth lies in the details.

As a point of fact, Kiki Shaw knew that Man Ray's painting titled *A l'heure de l'observatoire—les amoureux (1932–1933)* was said to have been inspired by Mademoiselle Kiki de Montparnasse's marvelous mouth. The words, *Observatory Time—The Lovers,* are written on the canvas, by Man Ray, to head off other interpretations, he said. The central image is a pair of giant lips floating above the landscape. Basically. The story is as follows: Man Ray had a few "rules," which included not seeing Kiki sing in the club, not belonging to a single clique or group and not inviting Kiki to accompany him when he had a "straight" photography job to do, such as visually recording a social event.

One evening, he was dressing in his tuxedo to attend one such dinner. The host and guests had, as they say, "money," so Kiki, all sweetness and yield, helped him arrange his dinner clothes, pushing cuff links through his cuffs, brushing his hair, admiring the fineness of his appearance. Embracing him with terrific tenderness, she whispered, Don't come home too late.

Later, at the party, Man Ray asked the wife of the host if she would care to dance. She accepted with the stipulation that he retire to the washroom to adjust his clothes. En route, Man Ray ran a quick, tactile check of his person—jacket, shirt, trousers—finding nothing amiss he stepped into the men's room and gazed in the mirror to see "the perfect imprint of red lips on my collar."

Perfect red lips.

And Man Ray said of the painting that followed this incident that if he could have discovered a process to enlarge the mouth photographically, placing it over the landscape, he would not have painted *A l'heure de l'observatoire—les amoureux (1932–1933),* he would have shot it.

The other thing he said was "Your mouth itself becomes two bodies separated by a long, undulating horizon. Like the earth and the sky, like you and me."

Who, exactly, is he addressing and who is he referring to when he says "you" of "you and me"?

. . .

Perfect red lips. Flawless. The impulse to inscribe a loved one may be primal. It was not necessary that Man Ray see the mark; let everyone else be witness. Respond to it as the wife of the host had done. This one act makes Kiki de Montparnasse someone worth talking to in a café. Clever girl. Jealous girl. So different from Les, who bore an inscription, the pale crescent on her ankle, and did no imprinting herself.

Then again, there are those who claim that the lips in the painting belong to Lee Miller, Man Ray's student and inamorata during the period that opened the thirties. American girl. Post-Kiki.

And that Miss Miller gave Man Ray more than a run for his money with her free love and independent ways and intelligence and her own observant eye, that always seemed to include a measure of hurt and sorrow for one who misjudged and was unfortunate in giving over his heart. Foolish man. Careless man.

This painting that functioned as talisman, charm, amulet and valentine also seemed an indication of obsession playing itself out in oil and canvas. Whose obsession? Kiki's for Man Ray? Man Ray's for Kiki's mouth? Man Ray's for Lee Miller?

Kiki's tale of the white collar and scarlet lips is whimsy edged in suspicious love. In a sense, then, Kiki de Montparnasse was the original creator of the lip painting with Man Ray's starched white shirt as canvas; only it took Man Ray to transfer it to a much grander, more enduring form. The lasting scale. This collaboration of sorts.

Now if the mouth in the picture is Lee's, then the story loses its charm and carries the echo of confusion in love and washed by loneliness. Because in any obsession one is always by himself.

Man Ray resided in Hollywood for a time, not too far from Collier's apartment and Kiki Shaw's modest bungalow. Between 1940 and 1946. He said he had a beautiful studio with palm trees, courtyard, flowers and birds. So intoxicating were his surroundings, so fortunate and pleasing, that he says, "I forgot I was in America." Later, he will say the same thing of France. He said, "I live within my own four walls."

As Kiki de Montparnasse told Kiki Shaw that she is her "own room."

So, now and then, the impression of the floating lips above the horizon could very well be Lee Miller's.

Because in any obsession one is always by himself.

What does it mean to "forget you are in America"? Does it hold greater significance if it is uttered by an American? More to the point, why would it be desirable to lose this memory of place?

Kiki Shaw flying from America to France asks herself the same questions. Why, she wonders, has my homeland seemed increasingly dangerous, or is it that I, in my ghost state, have only felt more vulnerable? Then again, isn't being invisible only a moment and a couple of consonants away from being invincible?

It must be a matter of harm, she decided: physical since America can certainly claim that toward women and it is on the rise; personal: How many times can the heart be mishandled before it hides itself?; economic, surprising in a country where so many live on the streets, roaming the cities without shelter.

Kiki de Montparnasse is talking about her trip to America (the complement to Kiki Shaw's trip to France), how she booked passage on a ship, sharing a cabin with two other women who "liked to show each other their teeth." The ocean gave her the creeps and when her mind wandered back to Montparnasse, Kiki became dispirited and blue.

Once in California, Kiki de Montparnasse auditioned for the movies; well, she never actually made it to the audition, having forgotten her comb back at the hotel. She needed to return to retrieve it. So, she told Kiki Shaw, over a cheap plastic comb, she lost her chance.

She tried acting in France and came close to being torn apart by monkeys. Of a picture called *Galerie des Montres,* she said, "The bear wanted to lay a leg with me, and the lights blinded me. But, as they say, that is another story!" And when pinched while in the studio, she said, "I've got a behind that's proof against anything."

"You gave up a possible movie career over a comb?" asks Kiki Shaw, spooning mousse into her mouth. "This is very good, by the way."

"Here, let me explain it to you better: For me, Montparnasse is the land of liberty; I can cut up all I want to here, without having to be afraid to eat beans again. There are so many people here, like Man Ray, who always seemed to be looking into little pieces of glass or dreaming up a new photographic apparatus. And the people who make a mistake and end up here unintentionally, because they followed the wrong directions, they stay in the district all their lives.

"As for the middle-class citizens who happen to pass through, they do not know what it's all about and are frightened out of their wits and do not stay any longer than they have to. Because Montparnasse is a village like a circus—I really need to learn Chinese, she says aside—and sometimes you can go into the Djiguites, where you are waited on by what are supposed to be Russian princesses.

"America is middle class, I think, that great scared group who do not like Montparnasse because they do not know how to like it. What would someone like me do in a place like that? I ask you."

When Kiki de Montparnasse returned to Paris, a man in a bar called her a whore. She was sitting with her girlfriend, enjoying herself when he said this. Her response was to clock him, which shortly landed her in prison, then to trial. Her lawyer appealed to the court, saying his client was "a little bit cracked and had nervous trouble." This fabrication naturally infuriated Kiki, who maintained that the man had begun this thing when he called her a whore and that she was only defending her honor and right to be in the bar, drinking with a girlfriend.

The court agreed to set her free, after she had spent time in jail, if she would cover all damages and admit her guilt. "I could not bear another hour in a cell," she says to Kiki Shaw, "so I agreed, though I did not *feel* guilt." She thought it was all behind her until her lawyer demanded one more thing: that she "thank these gentlemen for their kindness." Kiki de Montparnasse said to Kiki Shaw, "My life has been difficult and I have had some very low times, spent the night with men to have a place to stay and something to eat. I know what I do and I know who I am, but having to express gratitude to men who had attacked me first was the lowest time. Ever."

"Cocteau was a great friend of mine, with eyes like a pair of diamonds," said Kiki de Montparnasse. "I ran into him once in Villefranche and we would meet each evening and watch the sailors and the whores from the hotel bar. Years later he came to hear me sing at the Boeuf, rue de Penthièvre. It made me confident and he gave me a necklace fit for a queen."

Man Ray photographed ("I paint what I cannot photograph and I photograph what I cannot paint") a woman named Nusch, wife of his friend Paul. They were vacationing in the South of France, along with Dora Maar, Picasso, and Ady, Man Ray's friend. It was around this time that Picasso painted *Night Fishing At Antibes,* as well as pictures of Dora Maar, with sorrow so large and overflowing that her eyes, under Picasso's exact hand, were transformed into teacups, spilling out tears.

Some say this sadness was due to political unrest in Europe. Others believe only personal, not political unhappiness can turn one's eyes into teacups of tears.

Answer (in a category called *Film*): *Emak Bakia,* which is a Basque expression for "Give it a rest."

Question: What was the name of Man Ray's experimental film that ended with a shot of Kiki's eyes, closing, looking directly at the camera?

This film was projected onto dancing couples dressed in white at a costume ball given by the Count and Countess Pecci-Blunt. The guests a pale screen in motion.

When Kiki closed her eyes at the finish, painted on the lids was another pair of eyes; so, the viewer had the illusion of Kiki's eyes closing only to reveal Kiki's painted eyes open. Eyes on eyes. A woman with eyes continually open, watching.

No sadness. No teacups dropping tears, quickly.

For Kiki was not a woman to be undone by anyone; this was a woman who could see that it is a good idea to mark your man when he attends fancy dinners without you, asking other women to dance.

Man Ray placed a photograph of Lee Miller's eyes on the arm of a metronome. No chance of this inspiration springing from Kiki de Montparnasse, because he was unsure and troubled by Lee, the clicking of the metronome fell in sync with the beating of his heart and the ticking of a time bomb with a serious blast.

Larmes, 1930. Not to be outdone by the portrayal of tears, Man Ray photographed a pair of eyes not belonging to Kiki or Lee or Juliet, artificially made up with glass tears resting on the cheeks.

What, exactly, is the value of a glass tear? Kiki's friend Cocteau ("his eyes like a pair of diamonds") had Beauty cry diamond tears on the inanimate broken Beast. Madame Yevonde, an English photographer, took *Larmes* as a blueprint when she shot her own model, close-up on the eyes, and crying. The difference between Picasso's painted tears of Dora Maar; of Man Ray's glass tears of the unnamed woman; of Cocteau's diamond tears falling from Beauty is that Madame Yevonde's model bore genuine tears, so heavy and profuse that they almost seemed fake; less real than the other tears in the other depictions—painting, photograph, movie, respectively. Something had irritated the model's eyes, causing actual pain and discomfort, making them less "artistic," less graceful than those of the other sobbing women; this photo taken by a woman of a woman.

Still, wasn't Dora Maar in actual pain and discomfort? Or are we given to understand the difference being that hers originated from the heart and were not the body's response to soothe and protect itself against intrusion?

Among Man Ray's ten favorite photographs are these:

1. Close-up of an eye with lashes, a glass tear resting on the cheek.
2. Frozen fireworks on the night of July 14 in Paris.
3. Photograph of a painting called *The Rope Dancer Accompanies Herself with Her Shadows. 1916.*

Kiki de Montparnasse tells Kiki Shaw, "There is a Rayograph of my beads. Of my kiss." Kiki's mouth. Kiki's kiss. The floating lips. "Of me drinking from a glass, which is actually a *shadow* of me drinking from a glass."

"Yes!" cries Kiki Shaw excitedly. "That is what I am like: a shadow drinking from a glass, walking down the street, driving in a car. I am like the Rope Dancer and her shadows."

Everyone wanted to be solarized by Man Ray, says Kiki de Montparnasse. Solarizations were made in the light and not the dark (recall the masculine sun and the feminine moon) and had the effect of rendering the subject singular, isolated, apart. Beautiful. A sort of personal aurora borealis. This had nothing to do with Kiki and much to do with Lee Miller. Maybe specific people, like the photographer, are susceptible when in contact with other people, say Miss Miller, to feelings of isolation, singularity and apartness. It is not the subject who is separate at all.

"But that is how I feel," says Kiki, following the meal and walking back to Montparnasse with the other Kiki. "Very apart and like a shadow."

"Do you feel old?" asks Kiki de Montparnasse, answering before Kiki Shaw has a chance, "No, you do not. The trouble is not how you see yourself, but how you are seen. Like the man who called me a whore. I had to beat him so he could see that *I am not one.* At the restaurant tonight, we were visible when we wanted something and grew transparent when we had run out of requests and it was time to leave."

"I still think we should have paid," says Kiki Shaw.

"I am a ghost. I do not carry cash. And tonight was more than you could spend, right? Well then." A couple nearly walks into them. Kiki de Montparnasse caresses the man's face as they pass. "In your day, today, they try to tell you that the inside is more powerful than the outside around you. They lie. The inside soon listens to the outside and the next thing you know—you are a ghost! You must tell the outside what you want; that is one way to force yourself to be seen."

Kiki de Montparnasse approaches a lone man, asks for a cigarette, and Kiki Shaw can see that he is smiling, as she shakes her head and walks away from him. Kiki Shaw notices the man still admiring the other Kiki.

"Now I am with you again and hidden," says Kiki de Montparnasse, passing the cigarette to Kiki Shaw. "Okay, think about this: I was immortalized by Man Ray as I immortalized him. I was quite good at deciding for whom I would and would not sit. It was not 'dumb luck.' I must go. I will meet you tomorrow."

And Kiki Shaw is left alone. She is turning over in her mind the two things—this Kiki who pays attention to minutiae—Kiki de Montparnasse deemed crucial: 1) Ask and be seen and 2) Kiki and Man Ray immortalized each other.

She looks around to see the lone man who had given the other Kiki the cigarette she is smoking. Hesitant at first, she shyly starts toward him. *Ask and be seen.* He crushes his cigarette beneath his foot and walks briskly past her, without seeming to notice her. Maybe Kiki means "Demand and be seen," thinks Kiki Shaw. Tired, a little drunk and much too full, she strolls back in the Paris night to the hotel she calls "roaches and flies" for much-needed sleep.

So Kiki de Montparnasse followed Man Ray home and stayed for four years. Or maybe it was nine years.

Kiki and Man Ray fought loudly, vociferously; though he will say he is not combative, some claim he harbors a cruel streak with regard to the opposite sex. The two of them claim to despise discord but, as with many lovers, this is false. They like the sensation of anger in their throats and the bass of thunder in their voices. He likes the high color in her normally pale cheeks; she thrills to the violence of his raised hand, which may or may not come down. Or perhaps it is she who strikes; opposite; so joined, so inseparable, this artist and model.

They scream and make up; they can be seen walking down the boulevard, or in the Luxembourg Gardens, wrapped up in one another, cut off from the Big World. They entwine their arms—he, slight; she, much more full-bodied—too involved to notice the sailboats in the fountain, or men playing chess, or people licking ice cream cones or dogs running wild. The world is not their concern right now, any more than it is their concern when they argue. They are surprised when a neighbor complains about the noise; they think they are as hidden in their anger as they are in their affection.

They discuss children.

He tells her many things. He loves her. They are friends most of the time; comrades in art. And she loves him back. They form a circle of completeness, unlike the *fin de siècle* painters who juxtaposed women and circles and the moon and mirrors; wanting and needing no one but themselves. They have some awareness of this.

In making Kiki a violin, Man Ray addresses the notion of hobbies as pastimes; of women as hobbies; of Ingres and women.

He encourages her in her own endeavors: writing, painting, singing. He, according to his rules, will not enter the club to listen to her voice. Either that, or, as Hemingway said, she should avoid music and Man Ray was too polite to say anything.

Kiki allows him to make her image over and over; he does it justice and never, as with some artists of his time, there in the first half of the twentieth century, pairs her with stone.

Kiki Shaw sleeps late the next morning, certain she would awaken with a headache from all the wine and food that she did not normally eat, briny oysters, buttery cheeses, and a three-serving bowl of chocolate mousse. Instead, she feels better than she has felt in a long, long time. The day is bright and mild; after breakfast she will go to the Musée d'Orsay, maybe climb to the top of the Eiffel Tower, just to have Paris at her feet.

During breakfast, she suddenly remembered Kiki de Montparnasse's promise to meet with her today. Did she mean at yesterday's café? My hotel? thinks Kiki Shaw. Did I even give her the name? Kiki Shaw no longer questioned the other Kiki's existence because she liked her and had given up seeking the logical and predictable in this life. Then it slowly dawned on her that maybe this signaled the beginning of forty: Life would move unexpectedly, happily, and that instead of closing up, one should practice flexibility. And perhaps Nora was correct when she told Kiki that the further she got past forty, the more relaxed she felt. Maybe not. Maybe forty was just forty.

As Kiki Shaw stands in line outside this museum, which is a wonderfully renovated old train station, she thinks fleetingly of Gen and her museum love. She knows that her mother would be overwhelmed to spend time with one of the subjects of her favorite, Man Ray. As she wondered about the possibility of this occurring, she noticed that the person in front of her in line looked quite familiar; so happy was she when Kiki de Montparnasse, in response to Kiki Shaw's tapping her shoulder, turned around, that she embraced her new friend wildly.

"You're *here.*" Kiki Shaw breathing into the other Kiki's hair.

"I'm always close to art. It is my life's blood, as you can imagine. I am soft for it."

"I did not know if I'd see you today. I mean, sometimes you are here and sometimes you are not," says Kiki Shaw.

"Here is a clue: As long as you are vanishing, you will always find me. Two old ghosts that we are."

They walk together into the museum for free, of course. With Kiki Shaw rather liking this "gratis" thing, and Kiki de Montparnasse spinning a running commentary on everything, until some of her "information" began to sound suspiciously made up: That Gauguin never really left France, often asking people traveling to the South Pacific to send his correspondence to friends. That Seurat had an entire crew of apprentices who placed each dot of paint in his pointillist pictures. That Modigliani was a woman passing as a man. And so on. But then there were the good things, like Monet's lilies being experiments in light and shadow.

As for the *fin de siècle* painters, men mostly, Kiki has little nice to say. With Cabanel, Kiki de Montparnasse stands with Kiki Shaw before his *La Naissance de Vénus,* says, disgustedly, "Look how she reclines on the waves. As if it would be impossible for her to stand on her own. And the tilt of the hip looks like an invitation. Weakness."

They view von Stuck and his snaky women; Leda and the Swan pictures; at women gazing in adoration at the mirror; women whose feet do not touch the ground; and

Victorian wives, fading on their deathbeds, too young to die, too moral to live. Kiki Shaw does not want to tell Kiki de Montparnasse that she rather likes some of the paintings, but Kiki de Montparnasse knows what she is thinking anyway, says, "It is the execution that attracts you, not the content."

Kiki Shaw was not sure, just that they made her want to look again.

At lunch in another expensive restaurant, Kiki Shaw experiencing less guilt, more enjoyment as Kiki de Montparnasse says, "On the matter of being seen, I will say this"—and as Kiki Shaw listened closely, the other Kiki gestured for the waiter to come and take their order; please bring more wine—"I will tell you again you must learn to make clear what you want." She took a gulp of wine. "Let me say the other this way, two examples:

"Man Ray and I talked about marriage—though I was philosophically opposed to it. We liked the idea of vagabonding. Sometimes, I dressed him up in my clothes and made up his face to resemble my face; almond-shaped eyes with tails of kohl, white face, red mouth. He said, I like it! He also once said of the public, They have accused me of being a joker.

"I rarely dressed as Man Ray. Men's clothing did not interest me much; I liked my girlish things. I liked flash. Besides, his suits were not built for a woman's figure.

"When you got down to it, we disliked the symmetry of cross-dressing. It lacked imbalance, surprise, imagination, spark. What I am trying to say is that, man, woman, we are not the same and that is a strength. The other way, all that sameness is killingly dull."

"What is the other thing?" asks Kiki Shaw.

"I introduced Man Ray to Montparnasse. I was more established; and he immortalized me in *Le Violon d'Ingres.* You ask anyone about the girl in the turban, transformed into a musical instrument, with sound holes at her back. It is sometimes called Kiki as a Violin. Man Ray's picture of me lasted through time. We are connected, and connected to Gen, and so I am to you." Kiki de Montparnasse smiled.

Kiki Shaw says, "You said something like this last night, about being immortalized. I need more—" her voice faded.

"Listen. People know Man Ray and they know me. I do not think anyone recalls the names of the models in many of those paintings we saw today, like that lazy Venus on the waves.

"Do you follow? No? Men and women are not the same. I did not want to be exactly like my lover, so I did not dress like him. He wanted to be me for a minute, for a joke, you know how lovers play these games all the time. We did not exchange identities exactly; I remained me and he became me. We were not the same, not even in our desire to be other people. Wait. I told you about the middle class—they want everyone the same. Some of these women say there is no difference. They are wrong. We will never understand each other. Men and women are complementary. This is a good thing to keep in mind if you are going to let anyone force you to vanish."

Kiki de Montparnasse devours a mountain of food, with Kiki Shaw still trying to sort out what she has been told by this ghost. Kiki de Montparnasse stops eating for a moment, takes Kiki Shaw's hand into her own. "You want it even plainer?" Kiki de Montparnasse rolls her kohl-lined eyes, "The secret is love. Man Ray is not forgotten and I am not forgotten because we did not forget each other." Kiki Shaw flinches at the memory of Henry's summation, *People forget,* and its link to disappearance.

"Say it is art; say it is love. It is art and love and rebellion and fighting and making up and kissing and longing and absence and adoration, don't you know? It is friendship. It is the sum of all our parts; finally, this lock on each other is about *seeing."* She takes an enormous bite of veal.

"I have to think about this," says Kiki Shaw while Kiki de Montparnasse shrugs her shoulders and washes down a hunk of bread with red wine, which leaves a brief, faint stain on her mouth. Then, "Do you always eat like this?"

"Always," says Kiki de Montparnasse. Her fork full of fresh, steamed green beans.

Kiki Shaw did not run across Kiki de Montparnasse again. She searched but could not find her and missed her less and less since she replaced her with other, new, "substantial" friends. As she became happier and more peaceful, she grew more solid and soon her inside was in line with her outside. No longer was she overlooked, or looked past or through.

She did not go home ("I am home," she would say of France). Men smiled at her and her eyes met other passing eyes and no one asked her why she wasn't married or a mother or what she did for a living. Not like in Los Angeles, or anywhere in America where this particular conversational shorthand is freely employed, wanting to know the tangibles about her: profession, love life, children, before they wasted any more time on her. In America, one must fall into these categories, a way of indexing that Kiki understands. If not, then the questioner's eyes would glaze over and he would find someone else to talk to. So, to try to know someone beyond the easy avenues was work; it meant you must show interest and be interesting. No one here cared about her profession or her age, instead wanted to talk *to* her, or about her ideas. Which was rough in the beginning because she did not know the language of her own story.

ABOUT THE AUTHOR

WHITNEY OTTO is the author of *How to Make an American Quilt.* She currently lives in Portland, Oregon, with her husband, John, and their son, Sam.